Christmas Cockta

Dedication

To snowy, cold, and inspiring December nights. To red, green, blue, and yellow Christmas lights. To candles that smell as if they are fresh-cut Christmas trees, and most of all, to the Three King Guys.

Christmas Cocktails

Paul John Hausleben

Paul John Hausleben

Contents

Dedication . . . Pg. 4

Acknowledgement . . . Pg. 7

Preface from the Author . . . Pg. 9

Prologue . . . Pg. 12

Mistletoe and Mayhem . . . Pg. 15

Waltzing at Christmastime . . . Pg. 120

In the Window . . . Pg. 168

Mr. Keating's Christmas . . . Pg. 201

The Magic Fox . . . Pg. 221

On Christmas Day . . . Pg. 278

Epilogue . . . Pg. 281

About the Author . . . Pg. 286

Acknowledgements

Thank you to Mr. Harry M. Rogers Junior, and to my friends and family. Thank you to Ms. Lydia A. LaGalla for the advice with this book and for the assistance with the book title, story titles and other various aspects of this book. Thank you to Mr. Mark Knopfler OBE, for the inspirational music.

"They found the greatest gift of all. The gift that saved all of us. They found love."

Paul John Hausleben

04 November 2018

Preface from the Author

I guess when it comes to PJH composing another volume of assorted, Christmas-related-poppycock . . . the written phrase composed so long ago of, "Never say never" is very relevant. The dreaded Grammar Police always preach, never to use two negatives in one sentence.

Oh well, it works here.

In my futile defense of previously swearing off another Christmas composition, I did leave a disclaimer and as the old man would have said, "Ya left the back door open," when I wrote the preface for *Reflections, The Christmas Collection*. At the time that I wrote that particular collection of Christmas stories, I was quite confident that there would be no further dabbles into the world of Christmas. No more sappy Christmas season emotions, no more holly, ivy, and holidays wrapped around mangers, and certainly, no Three King Guys and goblin-like, bearded, red-suited chaps, who rather eerily creep into people's houses on Christmas Eve. However, it appears that with the publication of this book, I have failed rather miserably on my previous vow and intentions.

Please, dear reader let me try to explain my motivation here. Many years earlier than the publication date for this book, during a Christmas season, I wrote the Christmas fantasy story contained herein, titled, "The Magic Fox." The original intention was to write a collection of fantasy stories mixed with holiday and Christmas themes. We included, "The Number Fourteen," which was another Christmas fantasy story that I wrote during that time, into my book, *Reflections, The Christmas Collection* and because, we purposely decided to keep the page count and cost down on *Reflections, The Christmas Collection,* we decided to leave out, "The Magic Fox" and we placed it into the PJH story vault. The conundrum resurrected a few years later, when after rereading the story, I found that the story had some merit. The story stuck in my mind and the question remained therein, as to what to do with it. I even considered releasing it with a hand-drawn cover by our cover artist and making it an E-book single version.

Around the same time in September 2017, we began to receive emails and inquiries from readers asking if there were more PJH Christmas stories or books coming out for the upcoming holiday. Disappointment arose whenever we reported that there were no plans for any Christmas compositions now or even in the future.

My close friend and "behind the scene consultant" and business partner suggested to me that I should really consider the reader's desires before shutting down any Christmas possibilities, but I folded my arms across my chest and stood firm.

"I am done with Christmas!" PJH spouted off like a big, obstinate blowhard.

Ah, okay, well, you big dope, never say never.

Then, as so often occurs in my life, some weird and uncategorized type of fate intervened. Shortly thereafter all of this drama, I picked up a solo music recording by the great, and amazing, Mr. Mark Knopfler OBE, the front man for one of my all-time, favorite musical bands, "Dire Straits." A song on that recording, "The Secondary Waltz," reminded me of an adventure of Harry and Paul (the "actual" Harry and Paul) from a long, long, time ago.

BANG!

Inspiration hit, and it hit me hard.

Christmas of 2017 was bearing down, and I knew this collection would be for publication for the following year, but regardless, I charged into the project. When the project was still in the outline stage, and during one long and inspirational evening, after indulging in a few pints, I texted my close friend and collaborator with a very cool title that popped into my head. "Christmas Cocktails" was what floated around inside of my mind for the title of a Christmas book and almost immediately, the answer came back that it was a winner. I agreed. The title was very cool, and it purposely invoked an eclectic mixture of stories.

Off we went, from start to finish, in a mad writing fever pitch, with many directions of inspiration flooding my mind. I wrote the first words of the new stories right before Thanksgiving of 2017. Henceforth, I pulled, "The Magic Fox" out of the PJH vault, dusted it off, and dumped it into the manuscript. In a rush of inspirational fervor, I finished a drafted copy of the entire manuscript on Boxing Day of 2017.

Now, I am going to leave this preface off with no further words, insinuations, or mention of Christmas, no further expounding on future writing plans with Christmas themes or any blowhard proclamations.

"Never say never" will be my only statement.

As far as using two negatives in one sentence is concerned . . . well . . . it worked for Mr. Dickens, so it certainly works for PJH.

I will also finish this preface as I usually do, by saying that I hope you enjoy reading this collection of stories as much as I enjoyed the experience of writing them. If you are reading these stories at Christmastime, it is my wish that these tales enhance your Christmas experience; however, if you are reading these at another time of the year, then it is my wish that they enhance your spirit.

Thank you for reading them.

Paul John Hausleben

04 November 2018

Prologue

Fred Kelleher was not exactly sure why he was so nervous. He patted the pocket of his suit jacket to make sure it was still there.

It was.

Just as it was, the fifty or so previous times that he patted the same pocket. Fred had planned this evening out ahead of time, and he felt as if he had not missed a single detail. In fact, he was sure of it.

It was Christmas Eve and the love of his life, Miss Marlene White, sat opposite of him, at their favorite table, in the quiet corner of their favorite restaurant. A restaurant where they went on their first date, shared their first kiss, and a restaurant where Fred was sure they fell in love.

Everyone was in on the plan. Gregory, who was their usual server, Hal the bartender and Gladys, the night manager. The plan was perfect. The setting was immaculate. Hal perfectly dimmed the lights in the nook where they sat. From their table they could look out the windows and see the snow gently falling upon the streets of the city. The Christmas candle in the holly and berry Christmas centerpiece in the center of their table flickered, danced, illuminated their faces, and added to the already glorious ambience.

Marlene, as usual, looked stunning. Her hair was perfect, the black dress that she wore enhanced her amazing figure and the white pearl earrings in her ears matched the white pearl necklace around her neck. Gregory stood on the sideline, just far enough away to watch the scene unfold and still attend to his other two tables. Gregory was carefully watching from afar, and he knew the plan and carried it out to perfection. First, a round of cocktails, a bourbon Manhattan in a cocktail glass with ice for Fred and a rye whiskey sour for Marlene. When he dropped off the first cocktails, he would also drop some bread, the menus, and then leave the two lovers alone for about ten minutes. The first cocktails usually go quickly and when they finished the first round of cocktails, Gregory would drop two more without Fred requesting the refilled drinks. Gregory would disappear without taking their meal order, and Hal and Gladys would team up to make sure there were no interruptions. Fred wanted two rounds of drinks to soften his nerves. . ..

Gregory dropped the second round of cocktails on the table and Marlene laughed and nervously giggled while commenting, "My dear, Fred. My goodness, I barely finished my first drink. I might get a bit tipsy too soon here and look a bit foolish!"

Fred knew that it was the perfect time and with a gentle shake of his head, Fred said, "You could never look foolish. You are the most gorgeous woman in the world." Marlene blushed while taking another sip of the drink and she giggled again, this time at Fred's comment of praise and adulation. "I think there is something uniquely special about Christmas cocktails. Don't you agree, Marlene?"

"I do. It might just be the glorious atmosphere here, but I have to say that they taste extra marvelous tonight. Hal is always wonderful at mixing cocktails, but tonight, I think that he added some extra Christmas magic to the Christmas cocktails."

"He might have and I brought some magic along too." with those words, Fred moved quickly as Marlene's eyes danced in the candlelight and she searched for the meaning of Fred's words. Without hesitation, Fred reached for the box in his pocket, took it out, jumped out of his seat and dropped to one knee in front of Marlene. Marlene gasped as Fred slowly took the box in his hand and opened the lid, revealing the stunning diamond engagement ring inside.

"Will you marry me, Marlene? Will you be my wife? I love you with all of my heart and soul and want to be with you for all of eternity. Every Christmas Eve, every Christmas, every birthday, and every day in between. Good days and bad days. I want to be with you forever." Fred remained on his knee and his eyes searched Marlene's face for her answer. For a few seconds, Fred thought about how he might have made a major mistake because it seemed to be taking a long time for Marlene's answer to arrive. In reality it was not, it was just the shock of the situation, which stalled Marlene's words.

"Yes! Yes! Yes, of course. I will marry you, my beloved, Fred. I too, love you with all of my heart and soul and I will love you now and forever."

Upon hearing her words, Fred breathed a sigh of relief, took the ring, and gently slipped it on Marlene's finger. While they kissed, the entire restaurant erupted in joyous applause and heartfelt congratulations.

For sure, it seemed as if Marlene was correct, because there might have been a little extra magic in those Christmas cocktails.

Then again, at Christmastime, there always seems as if there is magic in the air and love in our hearts.

Christmas love and magic in the air, seems to make quite a Christmas cocktail.

Mistletoe and Mayhem

Christmastime in downtown Newark, New Jersey was a wonderful time of the year. The city was sparkling once more. It was vibrant, and it was exciting. It was busy too! It was the day after Thanksgiving, the retailer's dream day known as Black Friday. I scratched my beard and thought that everyone down there, in the city, underneath the window that I stared out from my lofty perch, was pursuing his or her own dreams. In some manner. Creating memories, getting the job done, plowing through life. Purchasing a dream gift for a dream person. My eyes glanced to the middle of the main drag and the elite jewelry store, "Bergman's Jewelers" and thought how right now, some nervous chap might be picking out an engagement ring. Taking the plunge. This was so glorious. In my writer's heart, I could imagine a hundred different stories evolving fifteen stories right below my feet.

Urban renewal of this great city was fully underway, the Christmas decorations and lights gaily twinkled in full display in the late afternoon, and they blinked a cornucopia of glorious colors at me from their holiday posts along the streets below my window. Formerly vacant storefronts along the main drag were now bustling with activities; city buses chugged merrily along, carrying full loads of passengers, rather than empty seats. The nearby office buildings, including the one where I currently stood, now filled previously vacant offices with starry-eyed young people who were beginning their careers and staking out high-tech start-ups, and giving capitalism a whirl. I met them in the hallways, on the streets, in the lobby of the building and in my favorite pub on the corner. They stared at my long hair, my facial hair, then studying the black suit and clerical collar, and after determining that I was not a wayward hippie ejected from a time machine, they told me their dreams and aspirations with breathless deliveries. It made my soul sing praise to God for this roundabout revival of the city and its indomitable spirit.

So much has changed now. More than I could ever recall or even imagine. I had witnessed the cycle. The circle of life and change here in Newark. From a sad, almost crying city of despair, it had burst back into life. The circle of life. I, too, had experienced the circle of my own life in my time here. The many years. The sadness, the glory, the despair and then a rise out of the ashes to begin anew.

I rubbed at the window glass. The heat in the office clicked on and the vent above my head broadcasted warmth. A bit of condensation from my breathing had formed on the glass. My eyes caught the activity once again, far down there, on the streets of the city. Workers, shoppers, and businesspersons all hustled about on the streets, and it was a welcome change to see. Certainly, it all had changed for the better from when I first arrived at this office. An office, towering some fifteen or so stories over the heart of the city. Arrived so many years and so long ago. If I put my mind to it, I think it is over twenty-five years or thereabouts, since I first sat in this chair, in the bishop's office. Sat, as a confused and uncertain replacement for my mentor and dear friend, the late, great Bishop Werner Beck Clodhopper Von Houten, as the Lutheran Bishop of the Northeast District of our Lutheran synod.

Sat, and wondered, 'Okay, this is great. I am the bishop. Wonderful. Exactly, what is it that I do now?'

Yet, with Bishop Von Houten's mentoring and his assistance, the love and support of my glorious wife, Binky, and the love of family and friends and with a touch of the Grace of God, I did the job. And here we are, all these years later, still chugging onward. The loss of my beloved wife, Binky, was still a huge hole in my heart. I picked my sorry ass off the canvas of life, but even all of these years later, I still felt her tragic death and loss to this world in every step that I took. Then, two years ago or thereabouts, we lost the great Harry M. Redmond Junior to this world. My brother, my lifelong friend, went to his reward and another piece of me broke off and floated into Heaven. Now, it was the holiday season once again, and the memories floated in on great waves of holiday emotions. Happy times, glorious times, uproarious times and, of course, despair. Yet, Harry's widow and my greatest and dearest friend in this world, Rose, and Pastor Paul John Henson, held hands and hearts and went on with our lives.

Acceptance of God's plan is not easy, but faith guides you through the holes in your heart.

The circle of life is often painful, yet the journey has grand rewards and, in the end, it is glorious.

The office was quiet and a glance at my watch told me that it was two in the afternoon and I planned to plow through endless and frankly stupid and mindless emails today.

Email is a modern-day plague invented by humankind to fiddle our lives away under the pretense of efficient communication and modern-day business. No one actually speaks anymore. We chat, text, and email, all while we sit on our impersonal asses. In my opinion, not all change is for the good.

Yesterday was a fabulous Thanksgiving Day.

All of our family visited my townhouse along with my

faithful and longtime office assistant and friend, Martha Wiggins and her husband, Bradley and their three sons. Another great friend, and now retired from both professional hockey and his clerical career, Pastor James T. O'Malley, visited with his stunning wife, Kate. My sister Dottie and her family arrived, and we shared so much love together. Of course, Rose Redmond cooked an incredible traditional Thanksgiving meal of turkey and all the trimmings, while assisted by our daughter, Heather Sarah. Before the meal, and afterwards, we sat in front of the fireplace, enjoyed wine, beer, and snacks, watched football, and told stories.

Actually, I told stories. . ..

After the dinner crush and a total decimation of a twenty-five-pound turkey, while the rest of the gang snoozed and relaxed, Jim and I performed the kitchen clean up duties. Jim asked me to scrub the turkey pan, and I agreed after some haggling and upon working out a trade with Jim. We exchanged the turkey pan for the stuffing pan. It was a draw for the worst one. Two old hockey players and "men of the cloth" on kitchen clean up duties! Heather Sarah fretted about her kitchen. But after an intense inspection, our daughter proclaimed number eleven and number twenty-seven, masters of clean up!

What a wonderful holiday!

Ever since my wife, Binky, passed many years ago and then Harry passed too, the dynamic between Rose and I changed. Our relationship was always very close; actually, it was beyond close. A bond. She was Binky's best friend, almost a sister to Binky, as Harry was a brother to me, but as of late, something was shifting. The way we looked at each other, the way we touched, the manner in which we hugged. The way she gently kissed my cheek. I know that we were both feeling the same emotions, mutually struggling with all of them; yet I waited for God to reveal the plan in full to us. I was sure that Rose was doing the same.

Today, the women of the family, along with Martha and Kate, were all out with the rest of the world. They were all traipsing through the madness of the holiday shopping in search of bargains. No doubt, they were stopping along the way for lunch and fine wine.

Since Martha was off from work today, I was alone in the office. Heather Sarah wanted me to stay home and relax, but I wanted to come into the office and, for some reason, be alone for the day. Lose some memories while staying busy. As glorious as my family and friends are, and my love for them all has no boundaries or description, I needed to be alone today. The ghosts that continually haunt me arrive in full-force during the holiday season and yesterday. They turned it up a few notches. All of them, floating around all day and all night, reminding me of too many stories to tell, flipping my mind, through the seemingly eternal adventures of Harry and Paul, my parents, my former life within professional hockey and of course, of my life and love with Binky. As wonderful as the Christmas season is and the celebrations of the holidays are glorious, they have a habit of stirring up the ghosts.

The trick is to ensure that the happy ghosts outweigh the sad ones and you somehow manage to plug the holes in your heart with joy.

I walked away from the window and from enjoying the scenes and sights of the city below and looked around my office. It was obvious that Pastor Paul John Henson was not being very productive today. My computer screen sat on the desk and stared back at me. Emails lined up in tall columns and they begged me to read them all.

My eyes caught the table radio on a nearby counter and I thought, 'Okay, yes, music. That is what I need. Some soft background music. Christmas music will drown out the ghosts.'

I walked over to the radio, flipped the "ON" switch, and

the radio dial glowed with life. Long since gone was the classic "easy listening" radio station WPAT broadcasting out of the nearby city of Paterson, New Jersey. The format long since went out of vogue and faded into radio oblivion. Too bad, because you could always count on the station for some seasonal Christmas music and it was a particular favorite of my parents. Dear Mum would play the station continually on an old tube-type table radio with an array of vacuum tubes inside of the radio that helped to heat the kitchen, while the radio sat proudly on a shelf in our kitchen, at 182 Belmont Avenue in the Borough of Haledon, New Jersey.

Spinning the radio dial, I settled upon a "soft rock" format from a station across the river in the big city that you could see from the opposite side of the office building. I figured that might be the best bet to hear some seasonal music. It was not WPAT but it was the best bet. After adjusting the volume knob, I glided back to the chair at my desk, sighed a bit, and settled into the chair to battle email monsters with a mouse as my only defense.

No sooner had I attacked the first email, when the radio station announcer (disc jockeys were also a long-gone-tradition) proudly blabbed, "This holiday season, as we have in the past here at WLUV, we are proud to sponsor our holiday contest giveaway! Yes, indeed, our famous contest, where each day, for twenty-eight straight days, until Christmas Day, we give away one-hundred-dollar gift cards to lucky listeners! Then, at noon on Christmas Eve, we giveaway the grand prize of a brand-new Zippymobile to a super-lucky listener, courtesy of Fast-Talking Joe's Zippymobile dealership in Crooksville, New Jersey. Where Joe always makes sure you get a good deal and a good deal more while emptying your bank account. . .."

Suddenly, I felt my heart pound in my chest, and a huge smile immediately formed across my face. The sad ghosts all fell in a great heap on the floor of my office, as if I had shot them all out of the air with a bullet of happiness and my smile. The happy ghosts took over, and they stared into my soul. The happy ghosts were floating everywhere, laughing and celebrating, and my previous melancholy mood dove out of my soul and fell into a heap with the now defeated, sad ghosts. A memory of an amazing Christmas of so long ago emerged in my mind and it arrived through my soul. The website of emails of the Lutheran District faded from my computer screen and instead, the screen turned into a movie screen. Magically, before my eyes, the scenes played and in full-color and layers of emotions, and magically, once more, I was with Mum in the kitchen of 182 Belmont Avenue. The ghosts floated in the air and all around me, and then they, too, settled in behind me to watch as the scenes played on the screen full of joy. Joy, because it was displaying a Christmas adventure from my youth and a joyous memory of a time when my old man shared his love of Christmas with not only us, but many other people too.

"Hey there, Mum! What smells so good?" I asked, as I burst rather enthusiastically through the back door of our family home at 182 Belmont Avenue in Haledon, New Jersey.

I dropped my books from the trade school that I attended on the kitchen table and Mum with her back turned to me, waved her one free hand in the air and said, "Beef stew, and take your school books off my table and put them in your room. It sounds like one of the books is the electric shop book. That one is so thick and heavy. The coursework is extensive for that class. Oh dear, I hope the stew is done and not under-cooked. I have had it on a low simmer since around ten this morning."

I picked my books up and marveled at how Mum seemed to have eyes in the back of her head. Yes, indeed, my Basic *Electricity* textbook was on the top of the pile. Mum hovered over a deep pot perched over a low flame on the cooker and she stirred the contents while trying hard to breathe while enveloped in a cloud of steam billowing up from the pot. Mum always fretted that food was under-cooked. From the amount of steam billowing out of the stew pot, there was no way that bacteria stood a prayer of survival. I was amazed that Mum's ladle did not vaporize.

"I am sure it is fine, Mum. It smells great and I am starving."

I was a typical teenage boy of the age of sixteen. I was always starving.

Christmas Cocktails

It was mid-November and unusually cold for this time of the year in New Jersey and bowls and bowls of my English-born mother's hearty beef stew was just the ticket that I was looking for, in order to stem off "starvation."

"I hope so . . . I always worry that someone will get sick if the food is not cooked enough. Paulie, you are late today. I hope that Harry and you did not get into some type of mischief. You are not bleeding all over my kitchen floor, so my assumption is that you did not stop to shoot those ridiculous and dangerous hockey pucks around. Anyway, I have been waiting for you to come home. Please leave your coat on and grab that pile of mail on the shelf next to the radio. Please take it to the mailbox and drop it for the postman. You have a few minutes before the pickup time. There are some bills and a postcard. It has to make it into the mail today."

"Sure, Mum. I have it."

I glanced over at Mum and she stopped stirring the stew, placed her fortified and defiant ladle on the cooker's spoon rest, and wiped her hands on her apron. I nodded and picked up my books, and turned to my room.

"Here, please give me your books and give me a kiss, Paulie. Always remember that you are never too old to give your mum a kiss."

Of course, Mum was correct about the kiss. You can never hug and kiss your mother enough. All too soon, time escapes us and we look back and wish for more time, more hugs, more kisses, and more precious moments.

I handed Mum my books, and since I already towered over her; I leaned in to kiss her cheek and explained, "No hockey today. I stayed after school to work on some projects in the electric shop. Mr. Grossi asked for help from a few of us. We are building light controls and wiring up all the lights for this year's Christmas show and display at school and for the Christmas pageant. Harry had to stay after school again, cuz, he ended up in Mr. Nazzaro's office. Something about wandering over to the business side of the school and flirting with some gals in the typing class." I cleaned that statement up for my mother. A more factual description of Harry's behavior as reported by the typing teacher, Miss Steinmetz, to the Vice Principal, Mr. Nazzaro, would use the word, "ogling" rather than the word, "flirting."

Mum suppressed a smile at Harry's antics and reserved comment on them too. After all, this was the legendary Harry M. Redmond Junior, and by now, Mum was used to these types of reports. Instead, Mum jumped to the electrical class subject.

"Oh, okay, well, that sounds like a nice project. You have many talents, Paulie, and I am sure Mr. Grossi is happy for the assistance."

I picked up the mail and glanced at it. An electric bill, the telephone bill and a postcard to the radio station WPAT with, "Holiday Contest Entry from Mr. Paul William Henson" and our address and telephone number jotted down on the back of it.

Hmmm. . ..

'Interesting,' was my thought, and I was about to ask Mum about the postcard, when the soft padding sound of four paws on the kitchen floor, a wagging tail, and a set of sad eyes greeted me. The mailbox was on a nearby street corner, only a short walk from our home to the corner of Belmont and Burhans Avenue and I stopped in my tracks as my faithful fox terrier, Skippy suddenly appeared on the scene, looking up at me and begging for a walk. I surmised that Skippy must have awoken from a nap, and when he heard the conversation, Skippy must have decided to see if he could come along for the mail run.

"Hey, Skippy. I wondered where you were off to this afternoon. Yes, c'mon along." I grabbed Skippy's leash and hitched him up, and as I did so, I asked, "A postcard for a contest entry to the radio station, WPAT? What is that all about, Mum?"

With a chuckle and a warm smile, dear Mum answered, "Oh, who knows, Paulie. Just a dream of mine. I never paid much attention to the Christmas contest before this year. It seems as if no one ever wins the grand prize, just the smaller prizes. Nevertheless, it is only the price of a postcard. I guess that I might as well give it a bit of a whirl. Most likely, it is just an unrealistic dream. Who knows who really wins those silly contests? The radio station has that ridiculous contest every Christmas season and this year, it caught my ear, because they are giving away free cases of Big Bob's Famous Pickled Onions and other crazy prizes. You know, how your father loves those stupid pickled onions. In addition, the grand prize is quite remarkable this year! It is a five-day, all-expense paid, family getaway trip to some fancy ski resort in the Pocono Mountains for Christmas. A Christmas getaway! Can you imagine? A Christmas vacation . . . to a ski resort in the mountains! And everything is free. Food and drinks, lodging, tobogganing, ice-skating, skiing, all for free. Oh my. Fireplaces, Christmas trees, wine, warm brandy, mountains covered with snow and romantic views of the mountain from some glorious hilltop hotel room. Who knows? Maybe, just maybe, we will not be stuck here for Christmas this year."

I looked over at Mum, who stood there, looking overwhelmingly radiant in her beauty and lost in her wonder of contests and Christmas dreams. Once again, Mum wiped her hands on her apron, set my textbooks back down on the kitchen table, and sighed deeply. I had a feeling that Mum was dreaming of the glory of winning such a fantastic trip. I smiled at Mum's reaction and did not want to be a party pooper and speak my thoughts about that, while only my older sister, Dottie, actually skied . . . the rest of the trip sounded very cool. Dottie was still living at home while she attended a local junior college and she had begun skiing with a boyfriend of a year or so earlier. She was with a new boyfriend now. In fact, that particular chap was about three boyfriends ago, but the skiing remained.

Skippy tugged at me. I am sure his bladder was calling and as I opened the backdoor to head for the mailbox, I said, "Sounds cool, Mum." I pointed at the word "Pussface" written on the postcard under our information and asked, "Why did you write Pussface on the postcard?"

Mum explained, "Oh, well, the rules are to have a secret code word or number on the card. To identify you, just in case that, you are a winner in the contest. I thought that I would use our cat's name because Pussface is the lucky one around here."

I nodded in agreement and said, "Gotcha. Yup, he is lucky for sure. Anyway, ya never know. Maybe we will win. The pickled onions, I totally get. But, the trip? If by some miracle, we actually won, do ya think the old man will really leave the house for Christmas? Ya know 'bout all of his rules and regulations for the season. Staying home by his Christmas village and his tree, listening to his Harvey Crooner Christmas records on the Victrola and listening to station WPAT while he is on vacation from work is a big deal for the old man."

It was true, the old man had off from work every year during the stretch from Christmas until after New Year's Day. It was something that he greatly looked forward to every year. Honestly, I looked forward to it too. Some of my fondest memories of my life occurred during this stretch of time. The old man was a master machinist in a machine shop in Paterson and it was a roundabout tradition of sorts for the shop to close over the holidays, as most manufacturing plants did in New Jersey at the time. Not only was it a tradition, but it was the only time the maintenance mechanics could service and perform extensive preventive maintenance on all the machines.

"Paulie, please, think! This is your father that we are talking about here. If by some incredible chance we won the trip, the key here is that, it is all *free.*"

The word "free" shook me into reality. That one word was all that I, as his son, as well as the old man, needed to hear. My father was one of the greatest dealmakers that the city of Paterson, New Jersey, ever produced. He would barter and argue over a penny and squeeze a nickel until poor Thomas Jefferson screamed in agony. Storekeepers, servicepersons, retail managers, and other purveyors of goods and services in all of northern New Jersey would throw their hands up in defeat and cower in fear at the mere mention of Paul William Henson's name. The old man was a legend and graduated first in his deal making class.

I thought of what Mum had said for a mere half-second or so and answered, "You are right. Skippy and I will be right back."

On the trip to the mailbox, the Henson family's on and off pet tomcat, Pussface the cat appeared out of some remote neighborhood hiding spot. He meowed, rubbed up on my leg and joined us for the journey. Pussface was quite unusual. In many ways. The old cat usually slept in a cardboard box on our back porch and while he grew older, Pussface the cat became more of our pet and less of a wanderer. Skippy and Pussface used to be mortal enemies, but now they had a tolerance of each other. Along the way, I think they signed some sort of truce. Pussface was not a handsome cat. In fact, he was downright ugly, with only half of a tail left, a fur that used to be an orange tabby and now was missing in great chunks, and as a result, Pussface was bald in spots. He had a funny looking cross-eye of sorts, but Pussface sure was smart and loyal. Pussface was smarter than many people that I knew. Plus, he was very fond of the old man and the old man loved the old cat. He really did. They were best friends. The old man saved

Pussface from freezing to death on a Christmas Eve of many years ago, and Pussface never forgot it. In the spring and summer, Pussface patrolled the backyard and kept pests out of the old man's garden and with the combined efforts of both Skippy and Pussface; our backyard was free of all sorts of predators and trespassers. No one, human, animals, or otherwise, messed with either of them. Oh yes, another interesting aspect of Pussface, the cat, was that he loved beer. In reality, the old tomcat was just an old drunk. Every night, the old man would pour some beer in a dish and the old cat would lap it up, run around for an hour or so, then stagger around, climb in his box and sleep it off. Pussface had a glorious life and now he was part of the Henson family.

Just another oddball in our ranks.

We reached the mailbox, I dropped the payments for the bills into the mailbox first, then for some reason, held the postcard in my hand, said a silent prayer for good luck while looking at Heaven and dropped it into the mouth of the mailbox. I closed the metal lid and opened it a number of times and yes, indeed, the postcard was on its way to magical Entryland.

Wherever that was.

Radio station WPAT was a staple for background music in our family home. While Mum seemed to enjoy the station, she occasionally tuned away from WPAT for an "all-news" radio station, but the old man in particular, loved the "easy listening" format and he kept the radio station softly playing from our old tube radio in the background of our home.

Dottie and I were both rockers. Yet, we knew that we had to enjoy our music in the solace of our bedrooms. With headphones on over our ears. The old man would have no part of any sort of rock-and-roll.

Every night, it was the same routine. The old man would arrive home from work around 4:30 in the afternoon and he would want to eat his dinner right away. He left the house at 4:30 in the morning, so by five in the afternoon, his dinner hour was long overdue. Now that the holiday season was bearing down upon us, radio station WPAT would play the occasional Christmas tune between their usual rotation of boring music, and the old man would listen as we enjoyed our dinner. His hope was that his favorite singer, the famous Harvey Crooner would arrive on the air, softly and merrily singing hit songs from his latest Christmas release. Harvey had previously released seventy-two Christmas records, and this year would be no different. The title of his newest record was, "Christmas at Lake Wiffenpoof with Harvey Crooner." The cover of the record album had a picture of Harvey, smiling widely while wearing a Santa Claus hat, smoking a pipe, while sitting in a horse-drawn, red sleigh in front of a frozen lake, with snow all around him and a fresh-cut Christmas tree stuck in the rear of the sleigh. The old man would pick up a copy of the record at the record shop in downtown Paterson and he would rush home to play it on his prize, Victrola record player.

After a few spins, the old man would proclaim it to be, "The best Harvey Crooner Christmas record ever!"

There must have been at least twenty versions of "Silver Bells" recorded by the Harvster, and honestly, to every other person in the world except for Harvey and the old man, they all sounded the same. Regardless, whenever the great Harvey Crooner made a guest appearance on the five-inch speaker, silence ensued throughout 182 Belmont Avenue, so the old man could bask in the golden voice of Harvey and his famous house band, "The Crooning Wiffenpoofs." The house band took their name from the lake. I think. The old man said that Harvey actually owned the lake. Perhaps. After all, he did release seventy-two Christmas records and ninety-seven easy listening records too; therefore, he must have earned a dime or two.

Now, with the great Thanksgiving holiday come and gone, the radio station was in full holiday mode and the contest was in full swing.

A week or so earlier, Mum had proudly announced to the old man that she had entered his name in the contest, and at first, the old man dismissed the entry as, "Bullshit, cuz nobody wins this crap. It is a racket. It is all a phony name game to pull in the stupid listeners and charge more dough for advertisements. The evil, conniving, manager of the radio station pulls random names outta the phone book and never even awards da prizes."

Yet, a day or so later, when the old man heard the name of Bubba "No Neck" Bailey called as a winner of a free lunch card for Lubby's Lunch on the radio one night, even the old man had to fold up his bullshit tent. He worked with Bubba and when Bubba bragged about the win and showed his friends at work the free card, then the evidence was undeniable.

This was a verifiable win!

The contest was real!

Now the tension grew stronger.

Six o'clock became a major event in our house. Since Bubba won his prize, this contest was the central part of the old man's life.

Our Mum's dad, our grandfather, (we always called him, Gramps) who lived upstairs from us in his own apartment, and who generally ate dinner with us every night, along with Skippy, Pussface, Mum, Dottie, me, and even Fritzie the parakeet all stopped, paused, and waited with the old man, for the big announcement.

Every night at six o'clock, the radio station's famous host, Ken Smoothie, would announce the day's winner of the prize. We listened as Ken awarded the prizes in honor and glee. Ken Smoothie pronounced the daily winners with such an air of elegance. A case of Big Bob's Famous Pickled Onions, a ten-dollar pass to the Plaza Theatre movie house, a free lunch of hotdogs all the way and sixteen free pitchers of Big Boulder beer at Lubby's Lunch on McBride Avenue and a free tank of gas and an oil change at any local participating Golf gas station. Mrs. Lawrence Lacalaide of North Haledon, the Jones family of Wayne, Mr. Benito Santoro of Franklin Lakes, on and on the various names of incredibly lucky winners spewed out of that five-inch speaker.

Every day, at six o'clock, silence ensued in the Henson household. We all held our breath and another day of disappointment came and went.

Until it all came down to the wire. The first day of December, the last day of the contest, when in a live, and "on the scene" broadcast, Ken Smoothie would select the grand prizewinner. The event plans included the grand prizewinner selection and announcement of the lucky winner, as well as at six o'clock in the early evening, Ken Smoothie and the Mayor of Paterson would light the grand Christmas tree in front of City Hall in downtown Paterson!

It was finally the fateful day. A Friday night in early December. A day that will live forever in the annals of Henson family history. And believe me, there have been a few winners in there over the years.

The old man burst through the back door of our house at 4:30 in the afternoon on the dot. He slapped his lunch pail on the shelf next to the radio and immediately he fiddled with the radio dial.

"Startin' to snow. Gonna knock the hell outta the radio signals. The electrical waves can't make it through thick snowflakes," the old man proclaimed as his eyes remained glued on the dial pointer of the radio and his fingers finely tuned in the signal. I sat at the kitchen table, along with Dottie and Gramps, and despite the incessant fiddling of the dial by the old man; we really did not notice any difference in the sound.

"What's for dinner?" The old man asked, his eyes

darting around the room and his nerves on an edge. At this point, the old man was out of luck as far as the Big Bob's Famous Pickled Onions and free beer and hot dogs went, but he held out hope for the grand prize. Admittedly, it was a slim hope, but still, he clung to it as a drowning sailor clung to the side of a shipwreck.

"Beef stew, honey. I have been simmering since six o'clock this morning. Please sit down and relax. You still have plenty of time until Ken makes the announcement." Mum entered some relaxation into the mix.

"Since six o'clock! Shit! And the damn house is still standing? Holy tamales! Wondah the stove ain't a pile of molten steel." The old man shook his head and slowly sank into his chair. His amazement that the house had not melted now quickly passed, and his full attention once more turned to the radio and the one person, who was now his nemesis in life, Mr. Ken Smoothie.

While Mum dished out the molten stew to each of us and the table enveloped in billows of steam and hot vapor, the old man stated, "Ya know, da word is out on this here, Ken Smoothie guy. He is full of plastic surgery, like them Hollywood movie star guys. He paints his choppers with all that white stuff and he wears a horrible toupee. Don't want to admit that he is a washed-up old prune. Yup, some of the guys at the shop got the inside scoop on dis bum."

With the strong chance of defeat gliding in on the horizon, the old man was laying the groundwork to discredit Smoothie for being a bum and a phony.

"That's nice, dear," Mum said, while she fought to dish out the stew onto the old man's plate without melting the serving spoon.

I could have sworn that I heard the stew cough.

We usually did not speak too much during dinner, just the usual "Please pass the salt, hand me the ketchup," type of banter. We concentrated on chewing. This dinnertime was especially quiet. It seemed as if everyone was walking on eggshells as the fateful six o'clock hour crept ever closer. Our kitchen clock on the wall seemed as if it transformed into Big Ben, because each tick of the hands sounded loudly and clearly in our kitchen. Pussface had obtained a rare "house" pass for tonight, most likely because the old man thought the old tomcat might be a good luck charm. He might have a point. Any cat that could survive on the streets for as long as Pussface did, must have had considerable luck along with him. Skippy sat on the floor next to the old man. Pussface loomed behind Skippy, with both of them intently watching the old man shovel the molten stew into his mouth. Due to what the old man called a "Bad Army Habit," the old man ate his food as quickly as possible and he shoveled the stew furiously into his mouth. Our pets had a solid chance of catching errant bits and blobs of stew as the food splattered all over the old man's mouth and spun in the air. The old man's eating habits disgusted our prim and proper English-born grandfather, but over the years, he conceded defeat to the New Jersey heritage of his family.

I broke the eerie backdrop of slurping and chewing. The tension was thicker than the steam above the cooker was, "Say, ya know, Dad, maybe this part of the contest is whooey. Ya know, they give away the little, junky prizes, like Bubba won, and pick some phony name for the grand prize."

It might be better to lay the seeds of the plants of discredit right now as a prelude to the looming, crushing defeat.

The old man looked up from his empty plate, with a blob of gravy running down his chin and shook his head. "Nah . . . I don't think so. Not wid such a big deal ceremony down at City Hall. Too many eyes and police around. Even the Mayor of Paterson is there. Too risky, even for a crooked, conniving bum like Smoothie to pull off."

I nodded my head and feigned that I understood the logic of the old man, but in looking over the faces of my family, it was easy to tell that no one else knew what the hell he meant either.

"I guess so, Dad."

Almost on cue, WPAT stopped playing music, and the station shifted to a "live on the scene" broadcast from the front of City Hall with Ken Smoothie's voice cooing out of the five-inch speaker. Ken effortlessly described the Christmas scene, taking place about five miles or so from our front door. We lived in a borough of the old city and our house was actually about fifty feet or so from the city line.

Ken Smoothie was in fine voice tonight.

"What a great night folks! We have some light snow providing a perfect backdrop for our Christmas celebration! It is cold but amazing out here and this fantastic tree in front of us is stunning! What great fun to kick off the Christmas season with the lighting of this amazing tree, and then, the drawing of our grand prizewinner of our annual WPAT Holiday Contest! Live and on the air here, from City Hall in downtown Paterson! We have Mayor Gravely here with me on the podium! The Paterson Police Department is here along with the Paterson Fire Department and the Italian-American Club. To honor America and our freedom, the American War Veterans Club will present the colors and the Marching Blowhards from Southside Paterson High School will play the Star-Spangled Banner. Please remove your hats, put your hands over your hearts and let's pay our respects. . .."

We sat and listened to what sounded as if it was a frozen marching band with ice in the brass and snow on their drums, struggling through an awkward version of our National Anthem.

Mum dished out the last of the stew and I heard the old man mumble, "Geez, the band sucks. They sound drunk.

Must'b freezin' their asses off out dare. Say, Joan, please get me a Big Boulder. Pop, ya want one too?"

Gramps responded that he did and Mum turned to fetch the old man and Gramps two cold beers from the refrigerator.

Mum was leaning into the refrigerator and of course, the question that always came up in our house, Harry's house, and houses across the old neighborhod, left Mum's lips.

"We have Dingleberries. Since it is a special night, would you like a Dingleberry beer instead?"

"Nah, they suck worse than that band does. Too, damn, sweet. Brewed with cow's piss and sugar in the basement of some old farmer's house up in Sussex County. Why the hell do, we even buy 'em?"

As always, dear Mum had no actual explanation for the ever-present rotgut beer that always graced our refrigerator, but no one ever drank. She shrugged and pulled out the Big Boulders.

Poor Dingleberry beer. Forever doomed to exile in dark, cold corners of refrigerators all over New Jersey.

A quick glance at the clock told me that it was ten minutes until six and there was sure to be more blabbing to set the old man off some more. Perhaps the beer would calm his nerves a bit. I hoped. Even Fritzie, our uncooperative and antagonistic parakeet, was quietly sitting on his perch watching and waiting. Usually, Fritzie jumped all over the cage and rang his bell a million times during dinnertime to rile up the old man. Fritzie was not a favorite of the old man.

The parakeet was Mum's pet. . ..

Dottie picked up her plate, took it to the sink, and began to run water in the sink to help wash the dishes. I jumped up to help my sister. We had automatic dishwashers in our house. Their names were Paul and Dorothy.

"Now, a few words from Paterson's most Honorable Mayor Francis Gravely," Ken proudly spouted.

Upon hearing the great news that the good mayor was going to speak, the old man bellowed, "Ya got to be kiddin'! Now, we gotta listen to this blowhard yak his brains out! What the hell is this bullshit? Just get to the good stuff. This guy is just a polished-up Irish mobster! How the hell does he end up always gettin' elected?"

Gramps smiled, took a long sip of his beer and in his glorious English accent entered wisdom into the discussion, "I dare say, Paul, old bean, you answered your own inquiry."

While the cleanup detail began and the old man sat, sipped, and steamed, and Gramps slowly sipped his beer, Mayor Gravely babbled onward, "Blab, blab, blab, and in this great city of Paterson we are proud to, blab, blab, blab."

"Oh, c'mon, for the love of Pete, shut the hell up!" The old man lost it. Steam blew out of his ears and his eyeballs spun in his head with anger.

Mum ran for another Big Boulder, spun the cap off and handed it to the old man along with his prized New York Bugs beer mug. Mum was pulling out all the stops in an effort to calm the old man down. The beer mug reminded the old man of his favorite baseball team and provided soothing influences to his now-rattled spirit. Unless, he recalled that the Bugs finished dead last in the standings last year. For the eighth season in a row.

"Now, calm down, Paul. You will get your stomach all in knots and you will have to take your special, whiz-bang, digestive medicine. Here, honey, here is your special mug. It will bring you luck. And patience. Maybe."

"My stomach is already in knots. I think maybe, ya did not cook da stew enuff."

Immediately, everyone in the entire kitchen glanced first at Mum and then at the old man. Gramps, Dottie, Pussface, Skippy, Fritzie, and me. Mum crossed her arms, stared daggers and a neutralizing beam at the old man and our father immediately realized a resounding defeat was on the horizon.

My eyes caught a glimpse of the wallpaper that, due to the heat of the meal preparation, had dramatically peeled off the kitchen wall near the cooker.

In a hasty and wise retreat, the old man backtracked on a path of correction. "I mean the stew was great. It was really wonderful . . . honey. This contest thing has me all spun around. Thanks for the mug and beer."

Mum smiled at her victory.

In the background, "Blab, blab" and then Ken's golden voice counting down the tree lighting with incredible enthusiasm, "five, four, three, two, onnnnneeeee!" The speaker filled with cheers of joy and awe and the frozen band played, "O Christmas Tree."

I looked at the clock and it was six on the nose. Now it was close. The moment of truth. The grand pooh bah. All the roses. The end of the ballgame. The elusive brass ring. The Holy Grail. There were not enough clichés in the world to capture the feel of this one.

The old man sipped his beer, and his beady eyes peered over the top of his mug. We all suffered through one more horrible delay after the band finished the "song."

Ken planted the seeds of anticipation, but he also added just a little unanticipated and formerly concealed twist to the situation. A twist that the old man's famous "Bullshit Radar" detected right away.

"Now, before we award *a chance* at winning our grand prize to some lucky *contestant* . . . a quick mention and some words from our sponsors of the incredible trip, this amazing contest, and tonight's tree-lighting celebration! We want to thank Big Bob's Food Empire, Fast-talking Joe's Zippymobile dealership in Crooksville, New Jersey, Sal Zucchini's Pools and Tools, Dirty Dick's Funeral Center, Pine-Tree Custom Coffins. . . .."

The old man was a very smart cookie. He did not miss a

trick.

"What the hell is this bullshit? Wadda ya think, Smoothie meant by a chance to win? Does that mean it ain't like the udder prizes and the bum just picks a name and ya win da trip?"

No one wanted to take a chance at this one until finally the wisdom of Gramps ventured into the dangerous territory.

"I would surmise, by Mr. Smoothie's pronouncement of a caveat, to award the grand prize that there might be additional criteria added to winning the final prize. Perhaps, the contestant will need to answer a question or overcome some other such obstacle in order to win."

Our father belonged to the coveted "Chronic Mispronunciation Club" of fellow New Jerseyites and a word such as caveat did not make the cut.

"A cavity? Huh, sounds like ya right on, Pop. Damn, never thought of that. This Smoothie guy is sumthin' else. Crooks and connivers, they are. Bunch of bums!"

Now, finally, the moment of glory crackled out of the five-inch speaker, "And to select this year's lucky contestant for winning the grand prize is Chief Broadchest, Chief of the Paterson Police Department." Even though this was radio, you could picture this in your mind's eye. Ken Smoothie changed his voice inflection, lowered his charismatic voice, and changed it into a "Smooth-talking out of the side of your mouth voice."

"The lucky contestant will need to answer a *very easy* question correctly in order to win the lucky prize."

The old man nailed the situation.

"Ha! What a rip-off! Pop was right! These clowns will make some jerk have to answer an impossible question, the dope won't know the answer and they say sorry, better luck next year. What a load of whooey bullshit this is! Should've known . . . nuthin' for nuthin' No one gives away nuthin' for free."

Regardless of the recently pronounced rip-off status, everyone leaned into the five-inch speaker and held their collective breath.

"Go ahead, Chief Broadchest, reach on in the pail there and pull out a random name! And our lucky contestant for this year's grand prize is, ah, ah, is, okay, yes, ah . . . Mr. Paul William Henson of the Borough of Haledon, New Jersey!"

As the words echoed out of the five-inch speaker and bounced off the peeling wallpaper of the kitchen, Fritzie fell off his perch and collapsed on the bottom of the birdcage, the old man knocked over his beer mug and beer rolled all across the table in great waves and dripped on the floor. Mum dropped her dishtowel and threw her hands up in the air. Skippy ran around and barked madly, and Pussface ran over to lap up the spilled beer. Dottie and I looked at each other. We stopped cleaning the dishes and shook our heads in silence. This was beyond unreal.

Gramps cleared his throat, took another sip of beer and calmly said, "It appears as if you, Paul, old bean, will be the jerk that needs to answer the impossible question."

The radio spewed out the next steps, "Congratulations, Mr. Henson! You have three minutes to call our contest hotline at two-seven-nine-three-five-zero-nine and answer *a very easy* question! Your category is baseball trivia! While we wait for Mr. Henson to call in, our Marching Blowhards will entertain us. Good Luck, Mr. Henson. We hope you are listening and can answer our simple trivia question! We would be soooo sad if the grand prize went unrewarded this year as it has the last sixteen years or so. Yes, so sad. . .."

As the band broke into a rendition of "Silver Bells," the old man jumped out of his chair. His face nearly exploded and his eyeballs virtually burst out of his head.

"HOLY BANANAS! Baseball trivia! I am the world's greatest baseball expert! Get me the number! Dial the telephone!"

The old man ran into the corner of the dining room, where we kept our telephone on a little shelf in the corner of the room and luckily, I had kept my cool during the stunning announcement and had memorized the number, because in keeping with the conniving tradition, Ken Smoothie only said the number once. We all flooded the dining room (all except for Fritzie, who remained keeled over on the bottom of his cage) and the radio continued to play in the kitchen within an earshot of all of us.

"Paulie, dial the number. My hands are shaking."

I carefully dialed the number and handed the telephone to the old man. Our father nodded, took a deep breath and waited.

It appeared as if someone answered on the other end and the old man began to speak, "Yeah, yeah, yeah, this is Paul William Henson calling in. Youse guys just pulled my name outa the pail. Huh? Yeah, I know where I live. I live here. Oh yeah, I get it. Ya need to know to make sure it is *the* Paul William Henson and not just some umpireoster callin' in. Gotcha, well, One-eighty-two Belmont Avenue."

There was a pause and in the other room, we could hear the band stopped playing and Ken Smoothie was back on the air babbling once more.

"Secret code word? Huh? Ya gotta be kiddin' me? What the hell is this. . .."

I stopped the old man before he blew his stack and blew the entire deal. I whispered, "Pussface."

The old man nodded and recovered. "Ah, yeah, my secret code word is Pussface. Huh? Oh, yeah, that's our cat's name. Huh? Yeah, REALLY. He drinks beer. Oh, okay, I will hold on. Huh? Okay, yes, no cussing. I understand."

We all nervously looked in. Our hearts pounding and the tension mounting.

The old man smiled, put his hand over the mouthpiece

of the telephone handset and said, "They are gonna put me on the air now. I got this sucker in the bag. Baseball trivia!"

Now, it was tricky because we could hear Ken's voice in the other room on the radio and we could hear the old man live on the telephone. There was a delay in the broadcast. I guess the radio engineers did not trust the old man and his potential use of "Colorful Language."

No one wanted or needed any notices from the Federal Communications Commission for on-the-air language violations.

"Merry Christmas! Is this Mr. Paul William Henson?" Ken Smoothie asked. "Of, one-eighty-two Belmont Avenue in Haledon, New Jersey?"

"Sure is! Live and on the air. C'mon, Ken, quit the small talk and all that merry Christmas stuff and just give me the question! I am ready to win this trip! I am a baseball expert!"

"Well, okay, Mr. Henson, good luck! You sound very confident! Therefore, without any further waiting . . . here is your *very easy* question. What professional baseball player led the American league in errors during the nineteen-fifty-four baseball season, and exactly how many errors did the player commit? You have five seconds to answer and only one guess. You are now on the clock!"

Even over the radio, you could hear a collective sigh in the crowd as all the air blew out of the situation. Easy question? No way! The question was impossible! More conniving too, because it was actually two questions in one! Nineteen, fifty-four, was a long time ago! Doom!

I studied the old man's face. He tugged at his lips, and without a second of hesitation, the answer spilled out, "Ha! That's the easiest question ever! Plus, ya tried to trick me with two questions in one. There Smoothie. Billy "The Banjo" Hoppleburger, da shortstop for the New York Bugs is the correct answer, and the bum made sixty-two errors that year. The guy is a bum. The biggest bum ever to play the game of baseball. I don't even know why he is still in the big league!"

There was a long pause on the radio and a quiet hush came over the speaker. Both here in our dining room, and on the streets in downtown Paterson, in fact, in the entire world, there remained an eerie and ominous silence.

Finally, the old man said, "Well, ya there, Ken? Ya okay, over there, Smoothie?"

The radio host finally spoke, and for a few seconds his normally perfect and eloquent delivery was rather halting.

Trying hard at a recovery from the shock of the old man's apparently correct answers, Ken's voice shook and stammered, "Well, ah, yes, I am here . . . but, ah . . . no one ever answers the contest trivia question correctly. Yes . . . ah . . . Holy guacamole! THAT IS THE CORRECT ANSWER! CONGRATULATIONS! MR. PAUL WILLIAM HENSON OF HALEDON, NEW JERSEY! YOU HAVE WON OUR GRAND PRIZE! An all-expense paid, five-day, Christmas vacation for your entire family to the world-famous Moose Lake Ski lodge and Vacation Resort in Burgerville, Pennsylvania! Everything is free! Free food, free lodging, free drinks, free skiing and ice-skating. Horse-drawn sleigh rides through the snow! You and your family will have the Christmas vacation and adventure of a lifetime!"

In the end, Ken Smoothie made a nice rebound and lived up to his last name.

The entire world erupted into cheers! In the Oval Office inside the White House, the President of the United States fell out of his chair. In Buckingham Palace, the Queen of England spilled her gin and tonic. The Marching Blowhards broke into a frozen rendition of, "Joy to the World" and Mum screamed, yelled, and jumped into the old man's arms. It was bedlam in our home and on the streets of Paterson, and Haledon, New Jersey. I swore that I heard fireworks going off in the distance. I swear that I did!

The live radio feed now broadcasted only the band playing, and we listened to the old man speaking on the telephone.

"Ha! Of course, I got the correct answers, there Smoothie. It is just like I told ya. I am a baseball expert, Smoothie. Go ahead and ask me a'nudder question or two. I never miss baseball questions."

"Apparently so, Mr. Henson, because they told me this year's question was virtually impossible to answer. No more questions. I am a firm believer in your vast knowledge of such important facts. Please, can you come to the offices of the radio station tomorrow at nine in the morning? We are on Broad Street in Clifton. Number one-nine-six-four."

"Yup. I will be there. Thanks, a ton there, Smoothie. For a chiseling weasel with painted choppers and a bad hairpiece, ya one helluva nice guy. Nice try in working da angles and trying to slip me up. Have a great night and go Bugs!" The old man hung up and his smile was so wide it stretched from one end of the house to the other end.

"Ha! For once, they did not lie, cheat or connive. That *really was* easy," the old man said with an air of confidence and his mastery of baseball trivia firmly entrenched forever in history.

Hoppleburger! Of course! The old man's greatest baseball nemesis in the world! He had done it! The old man won!

Our telephone rang off the hook all night long. We stayed up well past midnight. Gramps and the old man celebrated the victory with gallons of Big Boulder beer and Mum dipped into her stash of red wine.

Harry, Mr. Redmond, Ronzo, the Porters, Cousin Pat, Aunt Alma, long-lost relatives from England, guys from the shop . . . everyone called us. It seemed as if the entire world had heard the radio broadcast! It seemed as if the contest was very popular. All the neighbors came by, even the beat policeman, Officer Hough, and Doctor Salami stopped by and offered congratulations. Big Floyd from the corner liquor store dropped off a free bottle of champagne and a celebratory six-pack of Big Boulder Beer. The old man never drank champagne; instead, he used it to clear the kitchen sink drain.

The old man was a bona fide celebrity.

The next day was a Saturday, and we all tooled down to the radio station in our family car, the famous 1964 Putter Classic Model 200, and picked up the prize paperwork and information. We posed with Ken Smoothie for pictures for the Paterson Evening News, newspaper; even Skippy and Pussface were in the picture. Ken Smoothie was actually a nice guy, but he did wear a terrible hairpiece and no one could have teeth that were quite as white as his were. Yes, indeed, as the old man said, they were "Painted choppers."

Radio station WPAT might never be the same.

Now, the real Christmas adventure began.

Christmas Cocktails

Admittedly, having a celebrity for a father was quite the experience. It is not every day that your old man wins a grand prize in a radio station contest. Even the cool guys and normally aloof gals at school suddenly spoke to me and acted as if I existed within their coveted world. It took a little getting used to. Of course, my best buddy, Harry M. Redmond Junior, always acted as if he was a celebrity and movie star anyway, so Harry played it up big time.

The old man framed the newspaper photograph and article of all of us at the radio station offices, with Ken Smoothie awarding the old man the paperwork for his amazing victory. He hung it up in the living room, directly next to a picture of what was left of our garden shed after we accidently blew it up with fireworks one Fourth of July a few years earlier. That one is a story for another set of pages. It seemed as if holidays were always a challenge for the Henson family.

The weeks leading up to the big vacation getaway and Christmas Day were exciting and unlike any other Christmas season that we ever experienced before this one. Even though, for the first time, we would not be home on Christmas Eve or Christmas Day, our father still insisted on putting up a Christmas tree.

"We are home now and until we gotta leave to go to Pennsservanier, (Pennsylvania was an impossible word for a true northern New Jersey speaker to pronounce correctly) besides, we will be back for some of the holiday week and it would not be Christmas without them," the old man declared and I had to agree with him.

Reluctantly, so did Mum. Once more, we put up Dad's beloved and proudly labeled "fake tree" as well as his famous Christmas village.

Every night after dinner, we sat in front of the Christmas tree and the village and we poured over the full-color brochure for the amazing, world-famous Moose Lake Ski Lodge and Vacation Resort in Burgerville, Pennsylvania (Pennsservanier).

The place was remarkable. A rustic ski lodge was a centerpiece of the resort and property and it appeared, as it was the main hub of activity. It had a full restaurant that served meals all day long, with fine dining, a full bar (Gramps intently studied that aspect along with the old man) and high timber ceilings with a twenty-foot-high Christmas tree tucked in a corner next to a glorious stone fireplace. Full open glass windows looked out on the ski slopes and the trails stopped right outside the door to the lodge. In addition to skiing, there were sled trails and toboggan trails available too! There was ice-skating at an indoor rink and that sure had me itching to give it a spin or two. I was just beginning to think about moving my hockey skills from street and roller hockey to the ice and while I could hold my own on ice skates, I had a long way to go to be an expert skater. I was saving my pennies for a pair of hockey goaltender skates, but in the meantime, I had a used pair of regular hockey skates that I bought second-hand in a thrift shop in Paterson. They would work for now.

Dottie was looking forward to hitting the slopes, and Moose Mountain was not massive in terms of some of the big-name mountains, but in the pictures, it looked awesome. The hotel side of the resort was huge. There were what seemed to be at least one hundred rooms, stacked two floors high, with balconies overlooking the slopes and trails. The hotel rooms were amazing, with king-sized beds, double beds, fine furniture and furnishings and brand-new color televisions in each room. Our excitement was building and all of us were absolutely sure that this Christmas vacation and adventure was going to be marvelous.

Christmas was on a Saturday this particular year and the plan was to load up the 1964 Putter Classic Model 200 and head out early in the morning on Christmas Eve. We would have five days at the resort, with Christmas Eve, Christmas Day, and then we could enjoy Sunday, Monday, and Tuesday. We would head home early on the Wednesday after Christmas and still have some days at home to celebrate our fantastic free trip and the remainder of a wonderful holiday!

The provided information instructed us that check-in was available beginning at three in the afternoon, and we planned to head out of Haledon at eight in the morning. The old man plotted the route out on the map and he estimated that at the Putter's top speed of around thirty-five-miles-per-hour or thereabouts, it would take us about four hours to make it to the resort. The extra time would give us plenty of time to repair the Putter on the way, dig out of snowbanks and other road mishaps and maladies that generally afflicted us whenever we traveled in our slightly unreliable family car. The car had well over three-hundred-thousand miles on it, and the old man had replaced virtually every part and then some on the vehicle over the years, but it generally did better in the winter, then it did in the summer months. The 1964 Putter Classic Model 200 had a terrible habit of overheating every ten minutes in the summer, but once it warmed up for about three hours in the winter, the Putter usually rolled along fairly well. Luckily, in case of a breakdown, our father was the best backyard car mechanic in the Paterson area, having received his automobile repair training in the United States

Army, where he rather quickly made the rank of sergeant by expertly repairing jeeps.

Following a week of packing and organizing by Dottie and Mum, the day of reckoning finally arrived. Bright and clear and amazing. There was a dusting of snow earlier in the week, but it was long since blown away and swept clean. It would be a perfect travel day and the old man was up early, around five or so in the morning, to warm up the Putter. I jumped up out of bed too and Skippy, Pussface and I wandered out to watch the old man start the car. Starting the Putter on cold mornings was a bit of a challenge, but once it kicked over, the car usually ran fairly well. I held my breath, and my two sidekicks stayed by my side for moral support. A click of the starter solenoid, a stomp on the gas pedal, a puff of blue smoke and a cough, and off the Putter's lawn-mower-sized engine went. The old man massaged the manual choke control like a drunk nursing a whiskey before last call and the engine smoothed out and began to hum. One obstacle defeated and Pennsylvania (Pennsservanier) loomed on our horizon.

Both Dottie and I were finished with school as of Wednesday, and while the shop did not officially close until noon on Christmas Eve, the old man's new celebrity status gave him a pass for all of Christmas Eve. His boss signed off on the request for half of a vacation day. The old man seldom, if ever, took a day off from work. He worked at the shop for thirty-seven years and had accumulated more vacation days than the record keeping could even record. Therefore, taking some time out of the vacation bank was no big deal.

The old man and I began to pack the 1964 Putter Classic Model 200, which in light of my sister's luggage was no easy task. Dottie packed a mean arsenal of weapons to lure potential young men who might be vacationing at the resort, and her collection weighed a few pounds too. Perfume, curling irons, make-up kits, a change of clothes for every hour on the hour . . . you name it . . . Dottie packed it. The old man, of course, ranted, raved and howled with complaints at how much stuff that his daughter managed to pack. My sister knew that she needed to turn on the "Daddy's Little Girl" angle, in order to convince the old man to pack one more suitcase in the Putter, because the old man and the rear springs of the Putter Classic Model 200 were both reaching the breaking point.

He pointed at the mountains of luggage stacked on the kitchen floor and stomped his foot in protest and spewed his famous battle cry of, "WHAT THE HELL IS THIS BULLSHIT? A'NUDDER SUITCASE!"

Dottie expertly stepped in and diffused the situation and with a bat of her eyes and a flutter of her golden voice, Dottie laid the groundwork for success by saying, "But, Daddy, there might be some cute guys there. . .."

The old man folded like a cheap tourist's camera, "Pick it up and put it in the trunk, Paulie."

My sister added the frosting on the packing cake, "Don't forget my skis and ski boots, Paulie! They are at the foot of the cellar stairs!"

With a long exhale, the old man shook his head and advised me, "Get da rope out of the garden shed. Ya can tie the skis on the roof of the Putter."

I nodded, grabbed, tugged, and pulled the luggage out the back door of our house.

All of my life fit in a hockey equipment bag. I had to convince Mum that I had a change of underwear and socks for every day packed in there. In addition to the underwear and socks, I had a hockey sweater, a hat, and my vest, a pair of gloves, a rock-and-roll tee shirt, one button-up shirt and one extra pair of black dungarees. That was all that I needed to pack for the vacation. Canvas sneakers graced my feet and for the snow, I planned to grab my work boots out of the garden shed and toss them along with my ice skates in the trunk of the Putter. Cold and snow were where I thrived. This was my time of the year! I might be a hockey player, but in actuality, I was a long-haired hippie, with long blonde hair with red highlights that tumbled over my shoulders. And besides, hippies travel light.

Our grandfather was a seasoned traveler. He, too, packed light. Having traveled all over the world, up and down the east coast to visit his sister, Aunt Alma, in Florida and darting across the pond from England to America and back and forth many times during the big wars, Gramps needed very little. His wool coat, a change of underwear and socks, his pants, shirts, and ties, his ever-present English derby on his head and Gramps was good to go.

Despite a mild protest, our father convinced Mum that Skippy and Pussface would come along on the trip. In retrospect, I think that Mum did not want to step on the old man's greatest victory and after all, the old man's point that the free vacation was for all the family was well stated. Sure, Pussface would be fine out in his usual haven of the backyard and hanging out on the streets for a few days and Harry would take Skippy over at his house to hang with his doggie pal, Harry's dog, the famous, Cocoa Redmond, but Skippy and Pussface *were* family. They had to come along!

After an hour of hauling suitcases and bags and some major grunting and groaning while conducting a strategic jigsaw puzzle of a packing job, the Putter's engine was finally warm and ready to go. When the old man somehow managed to cram a snow shovel, snow tire chains, toolboxes, and spare Putter engine parts, such as hoses and belts and a bag of sand in the trunk, the poor Putter's rear tailpipe was only an inch or so from dragging upon the pavement.

"Have to be equipped to get out of a snowbank, Paulie," was the old man's proclamation. For the Henson family to be venturing all the way out to Pennsylvania

(Pennsservanier) was the effective equivalent of a journey to Jupiter. Our trips were usually once a year to Bug's Stadium over the river in the big city and one excursion to Brady Beach along the Jersey shoreline, for a day trip to the beach. This trip was a big deal. Besides, it was for free, and was the result of the old man's crowning moment. The entire neighborhood arrived at our doorstep to watch us leave, with the skis and ski poles tied up on the top of the Putter, the rear end of the car, virtually dragging along the ground, Gramps, Dottie, and me stuffed like sausages in the rear seat, with Skippy on my lap and Pussface perched on the ledge of the rear window.

I am sure it was quite the scene!

Everyone from the old neighborhood gathered on the sidewalk outside of 182 Belmont Avenue to send us off and on our way. Words of advice from the various neighbors echoed above the din of the city traffic and hung as if they were treacherous icicles in the frozen air.

"Be sure to have lots of dimes for pay phones in case you need to call for a tow truck," and "Make sure you have air in the spare," and "Don't tip the bartender more than ten percent unless you get free beer and drinks!"

For our old neighborhood, this magical trip was one of the major events of the entire year. Everyone was there. Harry, Ronzo, and the entire Redmond clan, along with Cocoa, the world's smartest dog, Vince Barroni and all of his auto-repair mechanics from the corner gas station, and Big Floyd from the corner liquor store, dropped off more free beer and booze. Dottie's best friend and my best admirer, and sort of girlfriend, the gorgeous Maureen Zipperelli and the entire Zipperelli clan were there too. Maureen managed to capture me in order to give me a warm hug that nearly melted me and to give me a sloppy, wet kiss. Even though I was a little younger than Maureen was and we had known each other since we were little kiddies, Maureen was very aggressive in her continual pursuit of me. Her magical kisses always tasted a bit like garlic and red wine. After kissing me, Maureen whispered in my ear how much she will miss me. As an added element of enchantment, Maureen hinted at how she would take care of Fritzie while we were gone, but that she had an extra special present for me when I returned home.

"First, I will take care of Mum's cute little birdie, and then, I will take care of you, Paulie. Very good care."

Oh boy.

She also added how I was not to forget her in and amongst all the beautiful young ladies at the ski lodge.

Although the thought crossed my mind to tell Maureen so, I did not say that for me. It was impossible to forget the gorgeous and captivating, Maureen Zipperelli.

Off we were, to a fun-filled, (free) adventure of enjoying hot toddies and mulled apple cider drinks by the fire, while singing Christmas songs by a majestic twenty-foot-tall Christmas tree in front of the fireplace, in between skiing, ice-skating and enjoying overall, the Christmas glory in a magical land of ice and snow.

Amongst waves and good wishes from our friends as we journeyed all the way to Pennsylvania (Pennsservanier) and between puffs of blue smoke from the tailpipe and the occasional ignition miss-fire of the Putter's engine, we hit the road.

The beginning of our Christmas adventure!

The ride to the resort was in Henson family excursions, largely in relative "Henson" terms . . . uneventful. We listened to WPAT on the radio and the old man whistled along to some Christmas tunes until it faded away into the radio wave world. The old man could not find another radio station that was playing Christmas music, and the speaker was mostly static and noisy, so he shut the radio off. The hills and mountains of Pennsylvania (Pennsservanier) were not conducive to radio reception on the A.M. radio band.

Christmas Cocktails

The Putter ran well, and while the temperature was quite cold, the roads and sky remained clear of snow. We did have to pull over once or twice to allow Skippy to find a tree or two while the old man fumed about "lost time." Dottie complained about the windows being open and the cold air rushing in until I pointed out that the reason the windows were open a crack was to allow the ropes to pass through the car. The ropes that held more luggage and her skis and ski poles on the roof of the Putter.

We also had to pull over while climbing various mountains along the way, especially when we rolled our way into the Pocono Mountains. The Putter did not have much horsepower to begin with, but loaded down with people, pets, and seventy-two tons of luggage, made for a perilous crawl up the sides of the many mountains and hills. The old man would pull over on the side of the road and allow the parade of vehicles filled with irate drivers and sufficient horsepower to pass us by, and then we would crawl to the top of the mountain, fly downhill, and repeat the process. I was the road map interpreter and navigator on long road trips, and this trip was no exception. It was not due to any great skills on my part; it was more of my receiving the assignment by default. No one else in the family wanted the job. Even though the old man remained full of Christmas spirit due to the continued euphoria of his contest victory, he still was the old man. He tended to get a bit cranky on long road trips. Especially, whenever you pointed out that he missed a turn, or did not listen to your directions. Yet, I persevered for the sake of our family and in the name of our free Christmas vacation because the old man usually got lost in the frozen food section of the local Foodworld supermarket.

"Look, Paulie, don't be so damn annoying with all of your perfect directions and stuff. I am an expert driver here and I know the way up here in Pennsservanier. Once, I was the lead driver in an Army Convoy out of Fort Totten up here to these mountains. Well, mostly, I know the way. I don't need ya pointing out all the oblivious things, just the 'portant ones," the old man instructed me as I prepared him for an upcoming left turn. Puzzled at the perplexing old man logic and his twisted words, I looked at my sister, who was generally of no assistance in these matters and she was not stepping up on this one either, because she rolled her eyes and waved her hand in the air. Gramps tugged at his English derby on his head and went back to sleep. Skippy and Pussface snored and Mum remained silent with her eyes dead ahead.

I was on my own and took one for the team.

"Do you mean the obvious things, Dad?"

"Yeah, yeah, yeah, that's what I said. The oblivious things."

"Well, there is a left turn coming up in a half-of-a-mile. Route Four-Eleven."

"Yeah, yeah, yeah, I gotcha. I 'member that one when I studied the map."

Of course, I did not point out the actual turn, waited and then pointed out the road sign when the old man sailed right past the turn.

When the old man realized that he missed the turn and we pulled a U-turn, the old man grumbled loudly during the entire way back to the turn that, "I was a lousy navigator. Smooching it up with Maureen before the trip must'a scrambled ya mind and mixed ya hormones up. Your concencration is whacked, cuz ya got all stirred up down under."

The old man had a special way of expressing certain things, but the funny thing was that everyone understood him.

"Now, now, dear. Remember your free trip and it is Christmas. Please relax. Paulie is very efficient and smart. He is only doing what you asked him to do for you." Mum jumped in on my side and in defense of her son.

Christmas Cocktails

I did not take the old man's comments to heart. When you are the offspring of the old man, you develop a very thick skin. Later on, in my life, the old man's hardening of my soul was a very valuable attribute for me to possess.

About forty-five minutes after missing the turn, my map reading was down to brass tacks and no more miles. I had inked the path with a red pen and the end mark was near.

In fact, according to my navigation skills and the map, we were here! Christmas bliss, whirling about on ice skates, heavenly sunsets over ski slopes, warm fireplaces, singing Christmas carols by the fireplace, beautiful gals, hot toddies and, well, something might be wrong. . ..

"According to the map and my calculations, Dad, world-famous Moose Lake Ski lodge and Vacation Resort in Burgerville, Pennsylvania is well, right here. We are here."

Gramps stirred and woke at the sound of my words. Dottie, Mum, Pussface, and Skippy all looked out the Putter's frosty windows. We were on a two-lane country road. The old man slowed and pulled the Putter off to the side of the road, and his head spun in all directions, while I studied the map intensely to make sure of my proclamation.

"Where the hell is it? I don't see nuthin'"

I had to admit it was puzzling because I did not see too much either. Just some open meadows covered with about an inch of old snow and many rows of various species of trees.

"Geez, Paulie, Ya blew it! This here ain't Burgerville, Pennsservanier!" The old man bellowed.

Mum tapped the old man on the shoulder, leaned over to her side of the car, and pointed out the window to a sign on the side of the road. With a calm voice that hinted that something else was going on here, Mum said, "Ah yes, sorry, dear, but Paulie did not blow it. Look."

A tattered and worn road sign wearily proclaimed, "Welcome to Burgerville, Pennsylvania, Home of the world-famous Moose Lake Ski lodge and Vacation Resort."

The old man leaned over as did the entire crew and the old man's eyes bugged out and once more, he spun his head in all directions.

"Well, whatever. I still don't see no resort! Maybe, the sign is over the boundary or sumthin' and this here is West Burgerville or Cheeseburgerville!"

Gramps cleared his throat and in his glorious English accent, Gramps interjected his wisdom and logic into the madness, "Perhaps, the large metal post dead ahead of us on the side of the road and next to that long path, will be of some assistance in this matter. The post seems to have a wooden sign tilting over and falling off the post. My hope is that the sign might clarify the situation."

While the old man mumbled something about, "Paulie screwing up the directions and we are in the middle of nowhere, wid nuthin' around us but trees," he grunted, and vaguely acknowledged the suggestion. The old man put the Putter into gear and we rolled up the road about one hundred yards to where the post and sign were sitting on the edge of a meadow and the side of the road.

The old man slowed, and the entire car full of people and pets gazed out the passenger's window and gawked at the sign. Skippy was sitting up with his backside on my lap and his front paws on the back of the driver's seat. Pussface jumped off the rear window ledge, bounced off Dottie's lap, and he decided to sit on the front seat next to Mum and the old man. Even Pussface could not believe his eyes! There was a sign mounted on a post, or what one might say was a sign. Sort of a sign. The letters and words on the sign were barely readable; the faded letters did proclaim "Moose Lake Ski lodge and Vacation Resort." Below the title was what might be or had been at one time, an arrow pointing towards a long, long, gravel road, leading up a steep mountain. Next to the arrow, the directions were simple.

"Turn Here."

Oh yes, and the sign was not actually mounted on the post. It was leaning at a forty-five-degree angle. One end of the sign was on the ground, and the other end sat rather precariously on the post.

"Oh, my," Mum said in a low voice, just above a whisper.

I looked at Dottie and my sister shook her head, rolled her eyes, and sank her backside deeper into the seat.

"I must say . . . this establishment's sign is not overly inviting. It could use a bit of sprucing up or a retouch here and there," Gramps proclaimed in his finest proper English language enunciation.

The old man never waltzed around or cared about proper English language enunciation and he cut right to the heart of the matter with a typical, "old man" description of the condition of the sign.

"Sprucing up! Shit! Ought'a take a match to that sucker. What the hell is this bullshit? Turn? Where do I turn? Up that gravel road? Geez, it'll blow the livin' hell outta of the Putter's springs!"

"Now, now, dear, please relax. After all, this is just an old road sign. Perhaps, there is another sign up the road a bit. Perhaps a wayward truck or car hit this one and they have not been able to repair it as yet," Mum injected calming words and an attempt at reasoning to offset the old man's suddenly sour demeanor.

"Truck or car, nah, it looks more like an artillery shell hit this son-of-a-bitch," our father growled and he rolled the Putter forward, turned into the gravel road and we began the long ascent up the side of Moose Lake Mountain.

I began to get an uneasy feeling about this and the word, "Free" resounded loudly and clearly in my head as well as one of the old man's most famous sayings of, "No one gives ya nuthin' for nuthin.'" We slowly climbed up the gravel road and the side of Moose Lake Mountain, within an aura of an eerie and ominous silence; the only accompaniment was the cracking of the springs of the overloaded Putter and the "click-clack" noise of the tires with the frozen gravel underneath them. No other sounds from either man, woman, or beast. There were small plowed piles of dirty corn snow on each side of the gravel road, as well as the same meadows that we saw from the road. Endless meadows and countless trees that dotted the way. Other than that, the landscape was void, empty, and very bland. Despite Mum's previous words of hope and encouragement, there was no bright, shiny modern sign pointing the way to happiness along the gravel road. Only dirty snow, trees . . . and meadows. The euphoria of the old man's amazing victory remained suspended within a fear of what exactly was at the top of the mountain.

The sight appearing in front of our car and before our eyes did not allay our fears, because when the Putter finally made it to the top of the mountain and we finally spotted the magical, Moose Lake Ski lodge and Vacation Resort, the only words spoken came from dear Mum's mouth. In fact, Mum was going to say those same words quite a bit on this trip.

"Oh, my."

This was a disaster.

The building did not exactly look like it did in the glorious, full-color promotional brochure. In fact, it hardly looked like a building at all. A pile of rubble might be a harsh description; therefore, we will go with one of the old man's favorite descriptions.

It looked like a dump.

The first trouble noted was that more than half of the hotel building was missing. In fact, demolished would be a more accurate and complete description. From studying the pictures of the front of the resort and hotel in the brochure, the demolition occurred on the side of the building that had housed the majority of the hotel rooms.

There appeared to be a small section of perhaps twenty or so rooms that were still remaining standing next to the main lodge. The rubble from the demolition remained in place as stark evidence of the spent glory of the facility. The main ski lodge was not the warm, cozy, magnificently rustic log structure shown in the brochure photographs; instead, it was a rundown, worn-out, sad, depressing, paint peeled, ramshackle mess of a structure. The sign hanging askew above the front entrance was barely readable, and it seemed to be a worthy companion to the sign out on the roadside. The main ski lodge had a good number of cracked windows, with the sections of glass held in place with gray duct tape and the ones that remained unbroken were all smutty and dirty. One window held a poorly trimmed section of plywood slapped into an open hole. It appeared as if that particular window was beyond a tape repair. The amazing front entrance displayed in the brochure with colorful flowers and lush landscape and beautiful landscape and entrance lighting was gone. Instead, the landscape was overgrown and ragged and the front entrance portico structure leaned to the port side and one pole holding up the side of the structure had a huge timber tucked underneath it to keep the entire mess from toppling over in a heap of debris. One sad lantern light hung from a post next to the front door.

The light was upside down, but at least it lit up!

I waited for the inevitable explosion of the old man.

Dottie waited. Gramps waited. Skippy and Mum and Pussface the cat waited.

The entire world waited, too.

You could hear all of our individual heartbeats.

We all knew it was coming. I could not see the old man's face, since he was leaning into the windshield with his nose practically touching the glass, but I was quite sure that his eyeballs were rotating around in his head, his temples pounded in anger as if they were tom-tom drums and steam was about to blow out of his ears. Gramps remained fearless, and he stated the obvious as only Gramps could do, "I must say, it does not look as aesthetically pleasing as it did in the full-color brochure. It also appears as if great parts of the facilities are . . . missing. Or is it my eyes?"

BOOM!

Off our father went to the moon without a rocket ship. A successful launch propelled by anger and disappointment! The old man grabbed his overcoat from the front seat. He left the car right in the center of the gravel road in front of the main ski lodge and he shut off the engine. The faithful, 1964 Putter Classic Model 200's engine rumbled to a stop, it sputtered a bit while it wound down and then as if it was sighing at finally making the long trip, the poor Putter choked and coughed out a huge puff of blue smoke. The old man flung the door to the car open, and he jumped out as if his pants were aflame and pulled on his overcoat and tugged some more at the wool hat on his head.

Blue smoke immediately enveloped the old man's head and body.

Undaunted by a little dose of air pollution, he waved the blue smoke away from his face and yelled, "Okay! We are here. Everyone . . . get your asses out of da car!" We all nodded simultaneously, flung our doors open, and jumped out into the smoky air.

Between coughs and chokes, the old man turned to me and said, "Paulie! Remind me to add a quart or two of oil in the Putter and some of Big Bob's, Special Secret Mystery, Lube-O-Oil too. The exhaust smells as if the engine might seize."

I nodded but did not comment. Even in the heat of battling for the honor of his free Christmas getaway vacation, the old man kept his fingers on the pulse of mechanical efficiency. After the doctor prescribed medication for the Putter, the old man took a few steps and then he stopped in front of the main ski lodge and placed his hands on his hips, while he studied the "thing" looming in front of us. Pussface and Skippy sensed the moment and the two faithful pets ran and stood next to the old man, and they sat right there next to his side. He tugged at his wool hat, oddly perched on his head, and then placed his hands back on his hips. We watched and waited, but I knew the famous war cry of the old man was coming. After all, right now, it seemed as if "Free" was a bit of a dubious and strategic word selection by the radio station, WPAT.

"WHAT THE HELL IS THIS BULLSHIT?" The old man's voice boomed and blew away any remaining blue smoke. "Is this some kind of joke or what? This place is a dump! We rode fifty-million miles to come to this dump! That Smoothie guy is a worse bum than Hoppleburger is, was, or ever will be! Con artists, connivers, cheats, and crooks! We are the victims of false advertising! All of 'em are bums and crooks! C'mon, we are goin' in!"

Dottie entered some logic while my sister rolled her eyes and entered into the fray.

"Ah, Daddy, do we really have to? I mean, can't we just get back in the car and ride home? I think we have seen enough."

"Nope. I won the contest fair and square and we are gonna enjoy this free vacation. Let's go, gang."

Up we all marched to the front entrance of the main ski lodge. Or whatever it was. The old man bent into the walk with fierce determination, his shoulders hunched in anger, his wool knit hat now pulled down low over his head and his faithful pets and family in tow. The air was very cold and brisk, and the sky rapidly turned overcast. Something told me that it was about to become a bit gloomier and considerably darker, too. We followed the old man as he tugged on the front door to the main ski lodge and we all stumbled and fell into line in the lobby of the building. Honestly, as all of our eyes scanned the inside of the building, the interior looked better than the exterior did. In relative terms, that is. The reality was that it did not take too much for the interior to be an improvement over the exterior. There were imploding buildings that looked better than these buildings did.

Inside, there was a set of stairs to our immediate left, which presumptively, led to the hotel side of the resort, a large front desk loomed in front of us and to our right was a bar and lounge area, a dining area and the fireplace that was displayed in the full-color-propaganda-filled brochure. There were also the walls of windows shown in the brochure; however, they did not exactly have the same appearance as they did in the brochure. Some front windows had boards covering them up, and some of the remaining windows had broken glass in the frames. Another set of windows faced out to the balcony and ski slopes and they were in rough condition too. Ski slopes that, by the way, had no covering of snow, unless you could count the pile of dirty snow at the base of the ski lift building. There was a Christmas tree in the sitting area of the lodge. It did not require too much of a close examination in order to determine that this tree was not the glorious twenty-foot-high tree shown in the brochure. This must have been the brochure tree's poorer and sadder little brother. The sad tree stood miserably on the side of the fireplace. It looked as if it wanted to run away and hide in a corner so that no one could see it. This mess of a tree was an artificial Christmas tree, or as the old man preferred to call them, "Fake Trees," and it was about six-feet high, bent, twisted, and leaning in a hard, left-hand turn, with eighteen sad glass ornaments on its branches and a set of multicolored lights that remained only half-lit. Hanging on a long string of fishing line that hung from an open timber of the ceiling, at the entrance threshold to the lodge sitting area, was a display of sad, dusty plastic mistletoe. I guess it hung there in hopes that someone would slide under it and share a kiss with their special someone.

I thought, 'Wow! Right now, we could all use a little kiss and love too.'

We stood there with open mouths and shocked looks upon our faces. The only sound was a loud sigh from Dottie when she spotted the barren ski slopes outside of the smutty windows. My sister shook her head, pointed at the slopes and sighed once more. Skippy whimpered and Pussface patiently sat next to the old man, while the old tomcat looked up at our leader and awaited marching orders. Pussface might be just a wise, old tomcat, but even poor Pussface realized that he might have been better off hanging around the old neighborhood and celebrating Christmas with a few chicken bones and licks of stale beer stolen from trash cans. In fact, we all might have had the same thoughts right about now.

Yet this was the legendary old man. A man of fearless courage, stalwart character, and a man who always dug in harder when the terrain grew more difficult. No doubt, this was difficult terrain. However, after all, this was his free Christmas getaway vacation prize and come Hell or high water and aside from Jesus returning, the old man was determined to enjoy his reward for correctly answering the impossible question.

Actually, it was two impossible questions.

With a puffed chest, and a strategic adjustment of his wool knit hat so that he could see clearer, the old man forcibly plowed his way across the coffee-stained, duct-taped and tattered carpet on the floor of the main lobby, making his way toward the front counter. A counter, which appeared to be the main check-in area. It had a sad and dusty Christmas wreath hung on the wall behind the counter and standing under the wreath was a young man, who wore a heavy overcoat and a wool hat not unlike the old man's hat. The man looked as shocked as we did. The young man studied us carefully, as the old man approached, and came in for a landing in front of his main counter. The young man suddenly looked as if he was awaiting execution from the Hangman. For a brief moment, I wondered why the young man was wearing such heavy gear while inside, and then I stopped and realized that you could see your breath in here. In fact, it might have been a little colder inside the main ski lodge than it was outside right now. Another glance in the direction of the bar brought into focus the fact that a man sat on a bar stool behind the counter, at the far end of the bar counter. He too wore a heavy coat. He folded his arms neatly into a makeshift pillow and he rested his pillow on the surface of the counter, with his head tucked neatly into his folded arms. His loud snores told me that the presumed bartender was sound asleep.

Okay, now.

Something told me that our dreams of a fun-filled, (free) adventure of enjoying hot toddies and mulled apple cider drinks by the fire, while singing Christmas songs by a majestic twenty-foot-tall Christmas tree in front of the fireplace, in between skiing, ice-skating and enjoying, the Christmas glory in a magical land of ice and snow, were, a dream indeed. More as if it was all a fantasy.

In the annals of history, there were many classic Henson family adventures, but just by studying the rather abrupt gait of the old man while he walked to the main counter, I knew that this was going to be a good one. I had seen that same stride a few times before and usually, it meant that we were not all going to be sitting around the Christmas tree, holding hands and singing, "Silver Bells."

Christmas Cocktails

"Welcome to the world-famous, Moose Lake Ski Lodge and Vacation Resort!" The young man working the main counter said with a forced smile, filtered in between clenched teeth. His hands gripped the edge of the counter in a death grip as he painfully spit the words out.

"That so," the old man snorted, "and now ya need to tell me exactly what youse pineapples are world famous for. If I had'a guess—it is for having the biggest dump of a resort ever known to mankind."

We all arrived on the scene and we encircled the old man in a team effort of support. Even Gramps had some fire in his eyes as he stared in on the young man and adjusted his English derby upon his head while he zeroed in on the target. With a huge leap, Pussface jumped up on the counter and the old cat stirred around. The horrified young man watched intently while Pussface looked for a good spot to sit. He found one in between some pens and pencils, an open guest register and a coffee mug, and Pussface sat and looked in on the scene too.

"That's just, Pussface . . . our cat. He can't hear as well as he used to and wants to hear whatcha got to say, so he jumped up there for a better look-see and hear-see. I think he smells beer too. It was a long-ass haul from New Jersey to here, so he is thirsty."

"Oh, I see. Pussface, well, hello there, Pussface," the young man said with great trepidation and a gentle wave in the direction of the old cat. "You have . . . an unusual name."

The old man quickly moved on from the introduction of our family's cat and launched into one of his classic diatribes, "On second thought, after lookin' around the inside of this joint, I gotta think ya world famous for being the only hotel and ski resort ever to suffer a direct hit from a meatyzeroid from Outta Space and still sorta be standin'!"

The young man's brow furrowed as he tried to figure out the old man's New Jersey lingo and I leaned in, and offered a translation, "My father means a meteorite."

He nodded and turned his attention back to the diatribe and the verbal lashing that the old man was going to unleash on the young man.

"I mean, for the love of Pete . . . half of the joint is gone, and it is a pile of rubble and the part dat is still standin' ain't worth a shit. Should've just let the bulldoze guy keep goin'. I mean, is this for real? And what is with the ski slopes out there? The slopes are a pile of bare dirt. My daughter here, she is in tears."

I looked at Dottie, and she shrugged her shoulders at the old man's slightly enhanced description of her current emotional status.

"She had her heart set on skiing. We got all her skis and stuff tied up on the roof of the Putter. The slope is nuthin' but bare-ass dirt. This has to be a joke. Right? Or are we on one of those hidden camera shows, and some television guy with shiny choppers and a bad toupee is goin' to jump up from behind that counter there and clue us in on the joke. This place is a dump!"

"Well, I apologize, sir. We are currently, ah, ummm . . . undergoing some extensive renovations."

The old man became even more demonstrative, and he waved his hands in the air above his head and proclaimed, "Renovations? Is that what ya call it? Ha! Ya mean, demonlaytions. That destruction out there is a little different from fixing stuff up, chief! Most of your building is a pile of rubble."

I leaned in and said, "He means demolitions."

The young man nodded and whispered, "I am beginning to understand him now. He seems a tad bit upset. Do you think he will finish berating me soon? I would like to explain what happened here."

It was difficult to study the young man's appearance bundled up in the heavy hat and overcoat, but what I could see of his face, made me feel that he seemed to be sympathizing with the old man, as opposed to taking offense to his words. The young man had kind but weary eyes, a hint of a dark five-o'clock shadow and a warm smile, despite the old man's tirade. I looked over at the old man and our father was oblivious to the fact that we were having this sidebar conversation while he continually ranted and raved. Gramps now stood rather stoically while watching the scene unfold. Dottie let Skippy out the front door to go and check out nearby trees and Mum stood silently next to the old man and nervously held her purse in her hands. Pussface now grew bored with rehashing the same old, same old, and he began to clean his fur.

I studied the old man's face and his body language and watched his hands still waving in the air in a typical New Jersey manner of demonstrative speech.

After a careful observance, I leaned in and whispered to the young man, "He is almost done with the first wave of berating. Try to interrupt him. My mother or grandfather will intervene on your behalf."

The young man nodded and held up one finger to attempt to stop the old man on his long tirade. Right now, the old man was in mid-thought so we would have to wait out just a few layers of anguish in order to hear the young man's side of the story. During this entire episode, and even with the old man's loud yelling and his voice echoing throughout the lodge, the man sitting at the bar remained sound asleep on the bar counter. He did not even move or stir.

"I gotta, ask ya. Where is the fancy, amazing and remarkable dump that is in this brochure that they sent us? Huh? When did they take the pictures? In nineteen-forty?" The old man turned to Mum and waved his hand and said, "Joan, get that stupid brochure out of ya purse and show the guy here what they sent us. Show 'em." Mum nodded, opened her purse, dug out the brochure, and handed it to the old man.

"Look!" This is nuthin' but bullshit! In full-color too! Full-color bullshit! Where are the horse-drawn sleigh rides?"

The young man shook his head and said, "The horses are glue in a bottle by now."

"How about ice skating?" I asked. The young man shook his head to indicate that ice skating was a negative, too.

"The ice melted," he said, but quickly added, "but we could sing Christmas songs by the fireplace. Once we use a pinch bar and pry the rusty damper open."

"Oh, bullshit on Christmas songs and stick the pinch bar up ya ass!" The old man snarled.

Gramps adjusted his English derby to secure it for pending calamities.

He leaned in and said, "The full-color brochure does seem to have been embellished a tad or two. Say, Paul, can you please allow the young man to explain? I am quite curious at how this all evolved. Perhaps, just a brief pause in the berating process would be conducive to hearing his explanation. I am rather curious how we all ended up here within such a massive state of disrepair."

As usual, Gramps and his wisdom laced within his prim and proper English mannerisms were well timed. Gramp's proper manner of speaking English was in stark contrast to the old man's New Jersey speak, as well as his children's deep and hard New Jersey accents. The old man nodded and with a few lower and more inaudible words, he slowly sputtered to a stop. Dottie and Skippy returned. Pussface paused in his fur-licking process and Mum took the brochure back and returned it within the deep confines of her purse.

Mum's purse was always a mysterious place, deep and never ending and able to hold an amazing variety of items, from first aid supplies, to money, to assorted valuables and the old man's stash of Big Bob's Famous Fizzly Whizzly pills for when his stomach turned over. There were homeless persons back in the old neighborhood that lived in smaller places than Mum's purse was.

"I am going to take a wild guess here," the young man finally began to speak, "and say that you are the Henson family."

The old man only nodded, and before he decided to launch back into Outer Space, the young man spoke once more.

"Well, let's start this over. Welcome to the world-famous Moose Lake Ski Lodge and Vacation Resort! I am the owner, general manager, host, cook, housekeeper, ski slope operator, maintenance man, and well, everything else rolled into one. My name is Woodrow Cane. Please call me, Woody. The man, sleeping on the bar over there, is our Head Bartender and Lounge Manager, Mr. Gustavo Melancholy. Please call him, Gus. When he wakes up, that is. Honestly, . . . well . . . right for now . . . we are all of the employees, who are on duty."

"Maintenance man, huh? What the hell do you do? Rake up the piles of rubble into one, neat, pile. I don't see a whole helluva lot of maintenance going on here," the old man spouted while he kicked at a bucket set on the floor to capture drips from a roof leak.

We all scanned the interior of the main ski lodge. High ceilings, with rustic, hand-hewn, timber holding the ceiling in a hard but a powerful slope, the dusty bar and lounge area, with unpolished, but wonderfully, intricate brass railings, and old-fashioned pleated leather on the bar front, torn and patched with more of the same type of gray duct tape. I thought how Mr. Cane must buy the tape by the caseload. The dining area, the broken windows, the grand fireplace with missing stones, the tilted Christmas tree. It was all so sad. Yet, if you looked past the surface mess, you could see that one day in the past . . . in a heyday of sorts, that this really was a grand place. The bones of the resort and the buildings and the operation were still solid. Yes, indeed, the architecture here was within a beautiful concept. There was no question that at one time, this was a remarkable place. A glorious place.

"Well, yes, please, I am so sorry. Please, let me explain. I completely understand your anger and disappointment. I do wish to explain everything. I do need to check you in . . . that is, if you have decided to stay." Woody studied the old man's face and then his eyes met all of our eyes, but no one said anything.

I think deep down, all of us wanted to wave our hands in the air, pick up our items, climb back in the Putter and head home. We might make New Jersey by nightfall and still have some Christmas Eve left to celebrate. Yet, Woody's face longed for something more and we all felt the sadness in his eyes and on his face. I could tell that all of us curiously awaited his explanation. There seemed to be much more to his story than just this horribly rundown dump of a property. The old man did not say a word, but rather, he decided to remain noncommittal on whether we were staying or not. He waved his hand in the air as if to encourage Woody to continue with his story and explanation.

Woody continued to tell his story, "This was my uncle's property. He owned it forever and a little bit more. He passed away three months ago and since I am his only living family member, my uncle left everything to me. My uncle built everything here, and he loved this place with all of his heart and soul. I have such fond memories of visiting here with my parents as a young boy. It was a wonderful place to be, especially so since my uncle owned it. He was my mother's brother, and they were very close siblings. He grew older and older and was quite stubborn. I begged him to begin to either repair it, or sell it all off, but he would not listen. By the time, the place required more repairs and reconstruction as opposed to general maintenance . . . well, it was too late. The heyday of the Pocono Mountains as a popular destination for vacation getaways and such had long since passed, and the money was no longer there. It is so sad because it actually is a wonderful place. The radio station called me out of the blue one day, told me of their contest, and said they would pay me five-hundred dollars to allow them to use a vacation getaway for Christmas at Moose Lake Ski Lodge and Vacation Resort, as their grand prize. I told them that we were under renovations and undergoing construction, and well, they seemed not to care much because they said no one ever wins the contest because the questions are impossible to answer. I sent them that brochure saying that it was from a very long time ago and they claimed they understood and for me not to worry. As you can see . . . many actual paying guests are a very rare thing around here, so I agreed to their offer, mostly, because I need every penny. My savings are fast drying up and I cannot support this much longer. I almost fell over when they called and said you had won. They paid me another eight-hundred in dough and here we are!" Woody shook his head a little as if he regretted his decisions and looked at the old man and said, "It is amazing that you answered that question correctly. It seemed impossible to me."

The old man waved his hand in the air to dismiss the thought and said, "Bunch o' bums they are there at that radio station. Said the vacation was worth two grand. They even tried to trip me up. It was actually two questions in one."

The old man paused in his words, and his anger seemed to melt into a deep level of curiosity. His eyes wandered around the interior of the lodge and then to the front counter and over to the bar, where the sleeping bartender remained fast asleep.

Perhaps Gus was dreaming of spent glory.

The old man piped up again, "Say, Woody, tell us some more 'bout this dump. It . . . well, has some sort of strange appeal to it. I kinda feel, well, I understand where you are at here."

Ah, hah! The old man was softening up his defenses now that he heard the background behind Woody's story!

For the first time, the sadness left Woody's face, and a smile appeared on Woody's face at the thought of the old man's visions and statement, "It does! I assure you, Mr. Henson, Pussface, and the rest of the gang, at one time it was world famous, please, come with me and I will show you."

He enthusiastically waved his hand for us to follow him. Pussface jumped off the front counter, and we all began to follow Woody as he made his way toward the sitting area of the lodge. Woody walked out from behind the front counter area and opened a little door that led to the bar area. He smiled and shook his head a little while he looked down toward the end of the bar and at the currently sleeping Gus.

Woody yelled out to his employee, "Gus! WAKE UP! OUR GUESTS ARE HERE!"

The man stirred a little, then looked up and mumbled, "Guests? Really? We have guests? What the hell?"

It seemed as if to Gus it was a novel idea.

"Yes, guests, Gus. The Henson family that I told you about earlier today is here. Now, wake up please!" Gus stirred; he pulled his heavy coat all around him and rubbed at his eyes.

Once more, a mumble or two came out of the slowly awakening, Gus, "Ya must'b kidding me or what? Are they actually staying? Are they blind guests or what?"

With a warm laugh and a wide smile, Woody leaned into us as he explained, "Gus means well. He has been with us forever. He was my uncle's best friend, and I could never think of letting Gus go. Now, take a look here." Woody pointed to a wall of dusty photographs near the entrance to the sitting area, and it was a glorious display of the heyday of the lodge. You could see famous movie stars, singers and bandleaders, sports stars and television stars all in the photographs with what appeared to be Woody's uncle and the staff of the world-famous Moose Lake Ski Lodge and Vacation Resort.

We all scanned the pot-pourri of history and admired that indeed, at one time, this was the place to be! It was just not right at this time . . . the place to be.

Woody continued to explain, "Now, this is all ours. My wife and I own it together. Except that my beloved Candace took one look at it when we came up after the funeral and the reading of my uncle's will and she said that I was nuts to entertain keeping it, she took off for home in Philadelphia and will not speak to me. She says that when I come to my senses, bulldoze the rest of the buildings and such and post the land for sale, and stop dumping our life savings into this lost cause . . . then she will come back to me. If not, our marriage is over."

The old man mumbled, "Can't say I blame her. Seems as if the wife is the brains of the operation. Woody should listen to her. The place is a dump."

Mum elbowed the old man to keep quiet because it was apparent that his wife leaving Woody was the source of his sad eyes and of his pain. Woody walked over to the edge of where the main lobby met the sitting room, and we all stood there and studied him very carefully. He still wore his heavy overcoat and a wool hat because it was freezing in this place, but for a moment or two, he took his hat off and rubbed at a thick chock of black hair on his head.

Woody spoke again while replacing his hat on his head and seemingly still deep in thought. "In my heart, I know that my beloved Candy is right. This might be a huge mistake, but I owe it to my uncle, to Gus, to the heritage of this place to give it a try. I wish she could join in my vision, but I just dunno any longer."

While Woody's voice trailed off into sadness, I spotted a photograph mixed in with the rest, and I studied it very carefully. Yes or no, it could not be, but upon careful inspection it was! I knew that this could be the ace in the deck. One of the photographs was of the old man's greatest hero, the legendary baseball player, Big Foot Garumba, posing with a pair of skis, wearing a giant smile. A smile almost as big as he was. Almost. If Billy "The Banjo" Hoppleburger was the old man's baseball nemesis then on the opposite side, we had Big Foot Garumba. Big Foot was the old man's baseball hero! A monster of a man, who hit home runs to the moon, and played for the old man's beloved New York Bugs. The greatest baseball player of all time! The old man's hero actually stayed here.

"Say, Dad. Take a lookie here. In this photograph. It is Big Foot Garumba. He stayed here and skied here. Look." The old man circled in and his eyes bugged out.

"Holy guacamole! It *is* Big Foot!" The old man spun and looked at Woody while keeping his finger on the picture and pointing at it. "This is the great Big Foot Garumba! The greatest baseball player of all time. He played for my Bugs! He stayed here?"

Gus appeared on the scene, and he walked over to us while he sleepily wandered from behind his post at the bar.

While rubbing his eyes, Gus explained, "He did stay here quite often. Mr. Henson, I have to tell you that Big Foot was a very frequent guest. He loved the place and was one of Earl's best buddies. He always hung around the bar, drank gallons and gallons of beer, and told great stories of baseball and other adventures. Big Foot is one helluva nice guy. Wish he would come back, but as you can see, ain't much to come back to. We don't even have heat. Freezing our asses off in here right now."

Gus wrapped his arms around his body and shivered a little.

"Earl was my uncle," Woody added.

The old man stood there. His eyes rolled around the inside of the lodge while you could see him ponder the fact that he was standing on holy ground. Ground that the great Big Foot Garumba tread upon so many years ago. His face broke into a wide smile, and the old man tugged at his hat and pushed it back up high on his head.

"We are stayin'! Hell yeah, yeah, yeah, we are! I won that trip and we are gonna stay here. Dump or not! Let's get the gear and unpack! Can you imagine that? Big Foot stayed here!"

Mum sighed and said, "Oh, my."

Dottie rolled her eyes. Pussface and Skippy immediately sat down as if to claim a spot for their butts, and Gramps repositioned his derby, shrugged his shoulders and looked over longingly in the direction of the bar.

"Perhaps, Gus, old boy, has a pint or two that is ready to pour," Gramps mumbled.

"Really? You're staying? What the hell?" Gus asked while mired in deep surprise at the old man's decision.

"Yup, we are staying! Gonna have a great Christmas too! Say, this here is my family. The bums at the radio station said we won a family getaway and, well, I brought the whole crew. This is my wife, Joan. Lots of folks call her Mum. This is my father-in-law, Pop, but most people call 'em, Gramps. I guess ya could tell by the way that they talk so funny that they are from England. My wife and Gramps, that is. The kids and I are from Paterson, New Jersey.

North end of the city. We talk normally. No accents. This is our gorgeous daughter, Dorothy, and our son, Paulie, is the long-haired, super tall, hippie kid there. Might not be able to tell, but he is actually a helluva hockey player. He just looks like a hippie. And you met Pussface and the fox terrier there is Skippy. We left Fritzie the parakeet at home. He is a pain-in-da-ass. Rings that stupid-ass ding-a-ling-a-doo bell in his cage all the time. Drives ya bat-shit crazy. Paulie's girlfriend, Maureen, is gonna take care of the bird for Mum. She has a chest the size of Montana and Paulie will get quite a present when he gets home. I mean that, Maureen has a big chest. Not the parakeet. Fritzie is a boy bird."

Woody and Gus looked over at me, and I shrugged my shoulders. They both smiled and nodded as they carefully listened.

The old man pointed at our family pets and continued with the introductions and explanations.

"Skippy can be grouchy, but he is a good watch doggie. Once he gets to know ya, then he won't bite the livin' hell outta ya hands or the back of ya legs. It is Christmas, and he promised me that he would be nice on this trip. Pussface is a little old now and a little ugly but don't let 'em fool ya cuz, he is smart as hell. Pussface loves beer too. Don't worry. They are housebroken. I mean the pets are. I guess the kids too. Hell, they aren't kids anymore. Dorothy is in college now and Paulie is in a trade school. After too many beers ya might have to worry about me peeing in the corners, but not them."

We all formally greeted and shook hands with Woody and Gus. Even Pussface gave them a leg rub or two and Skippy sat nicely and allowed them to greet and pet him too, without ripping their hands or fingers off.

Suddenly, the old man's face changed as he studied the two men greeting his family, and the previous words of Gus hit home. I had caught them too and wondered how long it would be before I either mentioned it, or asked, or the old man did. The old man beat me to the punch.

Our father waved at the wool hat and the heavy clothing that Woody and Gus both wore and asked, "Say, Gus mentioned that ya have no heat in this dump. Is that why ya wearing coats and hats and cold weather stuff?"

"It is, Mr. Henson."

"Call me, Paul. Ok? After all, ya Woody Cane and ya wife is Candy Cane. What's in a name, right? Still think this is a joke or sumthin'. I kinda expect that television star guy with the bad toupee and gleaming choppers to jump out any second now."

"Sometimes, I think he will too, Paul. Anyway, yes, our main boiler is out along with many other things that obviously require repairs. We have some heat in the hotel rooms. At least in the rooms that are still standing. That is where I was planning to book your family and you. However, most of the main heat is out. There is no heat both here and in the hallways. We have many broken things here. Too many to count. As you have so aptly noted and mentioned to me."

Woody turned around and pointed out the window in the direction of the ski slopes and explained, "The ski lift motor will not spin. All kinds of sparks and electrical sounds come out of a box on the wall and all the fuses pop. Even if I knew how to fire the snow guns or it snowed, we have no way to get to the top of the mountain without the lift working. I am an accountant by profession. Before deciding to run this place and keep it alive, I had my own accounting firm. I have some handyman skills but large repairs are too much for me. The major repairs are way beyond my skills or Gus's skills."

Woody slowly walked over in the direction of the front counter and we all followed him. While Woody walked, he took his wool hat off and once again fussed with his hair before replacing it on his head. A look of disgust formed on his face, and it was the first time since we met Woody that he displayed some displeasure with his thoughts. Despite the situation, he was in and the wretched condition of the property, and facilities, deep down, Woody seemed to harbor some hope and some positive thoughts that everything was going to work out and, in the end, it would be all right.

Woody continued to explain, "Numbers, I know and believe me, they ain't looking too good around these books, but repairs, not so much. Anyway, two weeks ago, I hired a young man to be the chief engineer of the hotel and property, but he quit yesterday. I told him that we had guests coming for the holiday. I explained to him how I needed him to work over the holiday and emphasized that I needed him to fix as much as he could fix and instead, he quit without notice. He said this place was a dump, it was too much work, and that he wanted Christmas Day off. Can you imagine that? To quit a job just like that! This morning, we woke up, the boiler was out, and it was freezing in here. I have called a number of service companies and no one is calling me back as of yet. I planned to check you in and if you stayed, resume my efforts to find a service company willing to come out and service a very old boiler. It is Christmas Eve, and we might be out of luck. However, until we find a service company to make the boiler repairs, we have the fireplace for providing heat. We do have to pry open the flue damper because it rusted shut. I meant to get to it an hour or so ago and have a nice fire burning for your arrival, but I was busy with making endless phone calls."

Woody walked over and reached behind the front counter. There were some random noises as Woody reached over and when he stood up, he was holding a long metal pinch bar.

The old man pulled his wool hat off his head and rubbed his head again in thought.

After some pondering, he piped up, "Yeah, yeah, yeah, the fireplace." The old man pointed at the pinch bar in Woody's hand, and the old man nodded his head in understanding. "Yeah, yeah, yeah, we can pry open the damper. Gonna need heat. It is gettin' colder than a well-digger's ass out dare. Pipes will start popping like popcorn in here. Hired a guy and the young bum up and quit on ya wid out notice, huh?"

"He did."

"We have the same trouble in the shop where I work. It is a shame. The problem with this country today, is that, everyone wants to jump in the back of the wagon and make a few poor slobs pull it. Free rides. It all goes along fine until a hill comes along. Then some freeloaders got to climb out, get off their lazy asses and push. That's when the trouble starts."

Woody smiled widely at our father's wisdom and willingness to tell the truth. Woody now realized that Paul William Henson might talk with a hard New Jersey accent and act all rough and tough, but he was an exceptionally smart and amazing man. Even though his family already knew that he was very special, we were all about to find out just how *exceptional* he really was.

"This here, old boiler. Is it steam or water?" The old man asked while I watched his eyes dart around the lobby and he studied the cast iron baseboard radiators lining the exterior walls of the lobby. From the telltale steam traps perched on the ends of the cast iron, the old man already knew what type of boiler it was, but in his mind, he required confirmation.

Woody looked over at Gus who answered, "Steam."

The old man's eyes widened and he looked over at me and smiled. Oh boy. Trouble. I knew that smile and, more importantly, I knew the look in those blue eyes of the old man. The old man loved steam boilers. Specifically, he loved the hulking steam boiler that dwelled in the dark confines of our cellar at 182 Belmont Avenue. Not as he loved Mum, or Dottie, or Gramps, or me, and Pussface and Skippy. I am not too sure the old man cared two hoots about Fritzie the parakeet; therefore, we will skip ole Fritzie. No, the old man loved boilers as he loved the 1964 Putter Classic Model 200. It was a classic, love-hate relationship. I spent my formative years and beyond working with the old man in the cellar during cold winter nights and days, kick starting and repairing the old boiler, and learning new obscenities. I knew how to add water to the boiler and check the water level in the sight glass shortly after I learned how to walk and talk.

Mum says the third sentence that I ever spoke was, "Check the low water cut-off." The first sentence was, "The Putter won't start." The second sentence, she will not tell me what it was, except that I heard it from my father.

"Ah look, here, Woody. Gotta tell it as it is here. Sorry, but ya shit outta luck. Ya ain't gonna get any plummaar to come out here to the middle of nowhere on Christmas Eve to fix some old relic of a boiler. Besides, it is snowing now."

The old man pointed at the windows and sure enough, the few windows, in which we could see out of, told us that it had begun to snow.

"Fine-ass snowflakes, too. Means business. Gonna be a white Christmas. Paulie and I will look at the boiler. We are experts. Never met a steam boiler that we could not fix. I bet we can get it to fire. Point us in the right direction."

"Oh no, Paul! I cannot allow you to do that. You are on a free vacation and that is very kind of you to offer, but Gus and I will. . .."

"Ah, bullshit! Youse guys work on that damper and get a fire rolling in here before ya asses freeze off and leave the boiler to Paulie and me. Look here, Woody. I know that I let ya have it really hard and mean before, but ya seem like a helluva good guy. A guy who is down on his luck. A guy who is trying as hard as you can to follow ya dreams. We will do what we can to help ya follow 'em. It is Christmas. We are all in this together. After all, ain't that really what Christmas is all about, Woody? Ya know, being in it all together, following dreams and keeping the faith?"

"It is, Paul. It is."

The old man smiled and patted him on the back and said, "Look, here. We are all hungry and thirsty. Why don't ya fix up some food for all of us, Gus can pour Gramps and Pussface a beer or two and find Skippy a soup bone or something to munch on to keep 'em busy? Mum and Dorothy can have some red wine and relax. Kick that damper's ass, put some wood in that fireplace and unload the Putter for us and we will call it square. Deal?"

"Deal. Honestly, I am not much of a cook though, and neither is Gus. We stocked up the entire kitchen with food and supplies, just in case you decided to stay and we were planning to follow some recipes, but I have to be honest. My wife is the cook . . . but Candy is, of course, not here. At least, the plan was for her to be the cook."

The old man shook his head at not only the honesty but also the overall ineptness of Woody and Gus and looked over to Mum and Dottie. Despite Woody's clumsiness, his story tugged at your heart.

Mum smiled and looked at Dottie, who nodded her head to indicate that she was in.

Mum said, "Please, Woody, point us to your kitchen. Dorothy and I will see what we can prepare. As my husband said, it is Christmas. It might cost you a few glasses of red wine but it will be good, wholesome English cooking. It will stick to your ribs."

"Gus and you will need to do the dishes, Woody," Dottie yelled as she followed dear Mum into the kitchen. "I don't do dishes when I am on vacation!"

Gus piped in and waved towards his haven and said, "Hey, remember, it is all expenses paid! We don't have much, but we fully stocked the bar! Red wine coming up."

Gramps removed his English derby and glided off in the direction of the bar, with Pussface and Skippy in tow. Pussface meowed loudly as the promise of the heavenly brew loomed closer.

"Now you are talking the talk, Gus, old boy. What is on tap?"

"Gramps, c'mon and settle in here. We have plenty of drink and light hearts here, but the tales are tall and the barstools are right comfy. On tap, we have Big Boulder, Mistletoe and Mayhem Christmas Stout and Dingleberry. No one drinks the Dingleberry. It is too sweet. Say, does Pussface really drink beer?"

"Why surely, he does. He is quite the feline connoisseur of the brews. He has sampled the finest bottles from tipped trash cans from north Paterson to the North Haledon border. We will have the stout. Please. It sounds festive and intriguing all in one name. After all, it is Christmas and we are on holiday!" Pussface meowed loudly and he circled Gramps' barstool while anxiously waiting for his precious first laps of Christmas brew.

"Okay, Gramps and Pussface, but be warned, this stout packs quite a punch."

It did not take the boiler doctor too long in order to figure out what was going wrong with the boiler. Down in the depths of the basement underneath the main lodge, the old man peered in on the patient and his eyes darted around furiously as he felt and checked the heartbeat of the steam monster. It seemed as if he knew right away what was malfunctioning on the steam monster, and this time, it was a test for the doctor in training.

The old man was in his glory as he looked over at me with his eyes glowing and a smile on his face.

I knelt next to the oil burner when the old man asked, "Whatcha think? This puppy is not half as old as ours is."

I nodded but did not comment that we might have the oldest boiler in the world, but after watching my father make all the checks, and after studying the pilot lights on the control panel, I thought that I knew what was wrong with the boiler.

"It is out on low water. We can add water because it is cold. The boiler has been off for a long time because the temperature gauge is very low. I think the flame failure safety kicked in because this strainer pot clogged with gunk. Woody is a nice guy, but he is down to his last nickels. I doubt he paid for any service on this before they started it when the weather turned cold and the guy hired to do the facility maintenance up and quit on him. We add water, watch the sight glass, clean the strainer, wipe the fire-eye down and reset the low water cut-off."

The old man's face glowed with pride, and he smiled widely.

"Impressive. Very impressive. Right on. Ya got sumthin' on ya mind udder than hockey pucks and Maureen's chest. I am proud of ya. Grown up now. All grown up now." The old man paused and his face became thoughtful. "Ya know more about all that God stuff than what I do, Paulie. I hear ya talk about God's plan, ya know, God puts us in places cuz he needs stuff to happen. Maybe, we were destined to come and help this here, Woody guy. The guy is a helluva nice guy, and he is down on his luck now. Geez, man, he is trying to follow his dreams and his wife took off and left him. Kinda rough to take. Ya know, maybe this is part of a bigger plan. Whatcha think?"

His eyes carefully studied my face for an answer.

I smiled and said, "God's plan is at work. I think you are right on, Dad. Yes, right on."

The old man nodded and waved his hand back over the oil burner and said, "Okay, enuff of that. Let's get to work. First, tie all that long hair back so ya don't get it caught in sumthin'. Then see what ya can find around here to clean the strainer. Rags, sum kerosene or a can of gas or paint thinners. Gotta be sumthin' around here." The old man pointed at a door on the far end of the boiler room and said, "Look over there where it says, maintenance shop on that door. I will add water and reset the cut-off."

"Thanks, Dad. I appreciate all that you teach me."

I stood up and walked over to the door marked "MAINTENANCE SHOP" in block letters. Next to that door was an office with a door that was marked, "CHIEF ENGINEER." When I opened the door to the shop and turned on the lights, I paused and in some type of shock, I took a few steps forward while I scanned the huge shop in front of me. It was beautiful. Magnificent. In front of me stood a fully equipped maintenance shop for the ages. Milling machines, metal and wood lathes, jig saws, band saws, a welder, a wall of hand and power tools, rows and rows of parts, a work bench setup for electrical repairs, a work bench for plumbing. Everything you needed to keep a place such as this was humming along. I could just smell and envision the work and repairs that went on here over the many years. It was amazing because, as Woody told us before, it was a touch of the heyday of when this place was world famous.

"Dad! Hey, c'mon over here. Ya gotta see this shop. It is amazing."

The old man was at my side in a few seconds and he whistled low while taking off his wool hat and rubbing the top of his head. "Geez, it is a thing of beauty. Perfect. Amazing, in fact. I guess that Woody was right. This place must have been sumthin' special in its heyday."

I found a coffee can and some paint thinners and, in a few minutes, we had the strainer cleaned and the boiler fired off on the third try. We waited a few minutes and, sure enough, the steam monster returned to life. Pressure came up and steam trickled into the header. We waited for the pressure and water levels to stabilize and from the looks of the gauges, we would have heat in a few minutes and in an hour or so, the lodge and hallways would be toasty warm. A quick handshake, we stole another look around the shop and off we went to join the rest of the gang. Arriving back on the scene in the main ski lodge, Woody nodded and thanked us graciously because you could already feel the heat pumping up through the radiators and hear the steam traps hissing with delight as the percolation of steam puffed through their valves.

However, the heat was not the only surprise.

There were more visitors standing in the lobby asking to check-in. In fact, it was an entire family! A tall handsome man with a beautiful woman by his side, a tall and younger version of the handsome man, a younger version of the beautiful woman and a little girl. A family! Suddenly, the world-famous Moose Lake Ski Lodge and Vacation Resort not only had heat once again, but it also had guests! The family stood in the lobby studying the humdrum interior of the lodge. Their eyes were wide, and their faces displayed some disappointment. At least Woody, Gus, and the rest of the gang were no longer wearing their wool hats and overcoats. Gramps and Gus were chatting and laughing up a storm at the bar, along with Pussface lapping at a dish of beer set on the floor next to Gramp's barstool. Skippy was off exploring and sniffing around the new visitors, and when he spotted us, the cagey fox terrier immediately sat down and looked at us as if to prove that he was not getting into any mischief today. The fireplace was crackling and the sad Christmas tree, well, it was still sad, but it was there.

Things were improving.

Inside. Outside, it was a different story.

I glanced outside, and it was now snowing really, really, hard.

As in a blizzard type of hard.

And the younger version of the woman, well, she was around my age and very pretty too. And the young man was as handsome as his father was, and he was around

Dottie's age.

Yes, indeed, things had changed in a very short amount of time.

"Ah, ah, yes, thank you, Woody. We are happy to hear that you have rooms available. At least, I think we are." The handsome man spoke with the gentle hint of a German, or perhaps a Swiss or Austrian accent. He removed his hat, revealing a thick chock of pure blonde hair. His eyes moved about the interior of the lodge, gauging the level of disrepair. "We were on our way home to New York from Philadelphia to be home for Christmas. I made an errant turn. We decided to stick to the route when the snowstorm swept in and our car suffered some type of malfunction. Quite a bit of steam from under the hood and the temperature gauge went up. We saw a sign, well, sort of a sign for this hotel and resort and we were lucky enough to make it here. At least, I think we are lucky."

Once more, his eyes, as well as his entire family's eyes, glanced over the interior of the lodge.

I understood their apprehension.

"I am Haus Schmidt. This is my wife, Liza, our son, Nicklaus, our daughter, Isabella and the little, sad, one is our youngest, Eloise. She is quite upset about not making it home for a visit from Saint Nick. It seems as if you are undergoing some type of . . . construction of sorts."

The old man leaned into me and whispered, "I promise to be extra careful with saying their last name. Especially after a few beers." I nodded and the old man added, "Sounds like they blew a hose. No sense in looking at it until the snow quits. They ain't going anywhere tonight.

They got no choice but to stay here at this dum. . ..” The old man stalled and changed his words.

“Stay at this ah, place.”

Even the old man was warming up to the humdrum but somehow very special, Moose Lake Ski Lodge and Vacation Resort.

Woody jumped in and related a modified version of his greeting. “Welcome, Haus, and the entire Schmidt family to the formerly world-famous Moose Lake Ski Lodge and Vacation Resort. Yes, please let me explain.”

While Woody explained the long, sad tale, the old man and I bellied up to the bar and checked in on Gus, Gramps, Pussface, and Skippy. Isabella winked at me as I walked by and she removed her hat and mouthed, “Hello” from a distance as we made our way to the bar. I was too young to drink beer, but I was sure that Gus would look the other way if I stole a sip or two from Gramps and the old man. I was tall and large for my age, well over six-feet-four inches or thereabouts, and with the longhair and hints of a beard and facial hair, I could easily pass for an older age.

Mum and Dottie appeared from the door behind the bar, which led to the kitchen. They both wore aprons, and when the old man pointed to the new visitors, Mum smiled and elbowed Dottie to return to the kitchen. Whatever they were preparing, we now required a few more servings. I saw Dottie’s head spin and her eyes widen at the sight of the handsome Nick Schmidt, and a hint of a smile graced her mouth.

Indeed, things were looking up here.

“What’ill ya have, Paul and Paulie? Thanks for the heat, you two. Your timing was perfect,” Gus warbled as he slid over to us when we sat next to Gramps at the bar.

Gramps made his recommendation, “My glorious drinking companion for this late afternoon on a snowy Christmas Eve, Mr. Pussface Henson, and I do highly recommend the Mistletoe and Mayhem Christmas Stout. It packs quite a punch, is very creamy, and smooth too. I dare say that old Pussface is a bit on the wobbly side and I am not too far behind him."

The old man nodded, smiled, and pointed to Gus to indicate that he would have the stout and then he looked at me and at Gus. The old man made a motion with his fingers to pour just a touch in a glass for me. Gus smiled, closed and covered his eyes in jest as he poured a small glass of the stout and expertly slid it across the bar counter to the old man.

"What the hell—the young man is practically a man. Look at the size of him and besides, it is Christmas and pretty women are all around us," Gus proclaimed as he admired the perfect slide of the glass that the old man rather deftly captured and then handed off to me. Gus wiped his hands on his bar rag that he tucked into his waist.

The old bartender was settling in now and you could see his eyes flicker with joy while he returned to the heyday of the world-famous Moose Lake Ski Lodge and Vacation Resort. His skills as a bartender and a host remained top notch. I had to think that Gus must have poured a million drinks in his career.

I took a small sip of the brew. Gramps was correct. It was very creamy and smooth and it did pack a punch.

From our seats at the bar, we could hear the conversation between Woody and Haus. It appeared as if the family was going to stay. As the old man had said, they had little choice at this point, and despite the initial appearance, they were lucky to stumble upon the resort.

"Well, we will stay. Please, charge this credit card. We are of Swiss descent and perhaps, there will be some skiing available later. Our entire family does enjoy skiing. Since we did not plan this emergency stop, we of course did not bring equipment, but we hope you have rentals," Haus explained while he checked in with Woody.

"The good news is that we have rentals. The bad news is that our ski lift motor is out of service. I am so sorry. We are waiting for a repair service or a new maintenance person, but with the snowstorm and all that is happening . . . we are out of luck for now. The motor sparks and it blows fuses. However, our rooms are cozy and clean, we have a roaring fire, and sort of a Christmas tree, a fully stocked bar and Paulie and Paul Henson, along with Gramps, Pussface the cat, and Skippy, are relaxing in the lounge. Please join them and I will get your bags to your rooms. Here are the room keys," Woody explained to Haus while he handed off the keys and then added, "Oh yes, Mum Henson and Dottie Henson are in the kitchen preparing dinner. They added extra portions for your family. Hot open-faced turkey sandwiches prepared upon toast, smothered with hot gravy, with Mum's homemade stuffing, mixed veggies, and her own recipe of English bread pudding with raisins for dessert. Sounds amazing! It should be ready very shortly."

"The guests have to cook here? Ah, Pussface the cat?" Haus asked.

"It is a long story," Woody answered very strategically. "But it is Christmas Eve and Pussface is quite entertaining. The tomcat enjoys beer. He is quite the interesting one, as are the rest of the family. Go along now. It is going to be wonderful! We will do our best to enjoy it all!"

"Yes, I guess you are correct. A beer-drinking tomcat? Interesting. Thank you."

Haus and his family wandered over and after a round of introductions, Haus settled in on a barstool with his son and the rest of the family sat at a table in the dining room. The little girl, Eloise, was very cute, but quite sad at what she perceived to be a derailed Christmas, and Mrs. Schmidt and all of us did our best to comfort and encourage her. I guessed Eloise to be around five or six years of age, and at this time of her life, Christmas was very important. Isabella was quite the beauty, with long blonde hair and wide blue eyes. Once she removed her coat, I noticed she had a nice figure too! She lingered for a long time when we shook hands and she smiled widely at me. I hid my now empty beer glass by sliding it over to the old man's side. I did not want her to think that I was a teenage lush. The old man playfully tapped me on the back of the head when Isabella wandered off. I guess he caught me checking out her rear view.

The old man now had a few sips of the high-test stout floating around in him, and Gramps loosened up once he found out that the Schmidt Family were of Swiss descent and not of German heritage. Ah yes, all remained well in the world. At least for a little while. Ya know, the entire peace on Earth, good will toward men sort of thing took shape.

"Say, there, Haus . . . it seems as if your name is kinda backwards. Ya know what I mean? Should it be the udder way around?"

Upon hearing the old man's words, I almost spit out a sip of another small glass of the stout; Gus held back a laugh, Gramps waved Gus down for another refill, and Haus did not get it.

Luckily.

Nick got it and he smiled and took a sip of his beer and laughed at the old man and his mannerisms.

"Well, no, my name is Haus Schmidt. Always has been. I am not sure what you mean, Paul."

"Hey, fuggetabout it. I gotta tell ya how I won this here trip to this great place for free. Answered questions in a radio contest. Da bums tried to trick me. But, anyway, look, it sounds as if ya popped a hose on that rig of yours. I am a pretty good car repair guy, along with a boiler guy and 'udder stuff that I tinker with and Paulie here, he is learnin' the trades but he is sharp. Tomorrow, I bet we can take a lookie once the snow stops and fix ya up good as new. This place does not look like much but it grows on ya. Relax and have a few cold ones here and all will be well. This here missile shot and mix-up stuff is pretty good. Strong as hell, though. Grows hair on ya ass."

"Well, yes, very well. That is nice of you, Paul. I do want to hear of the contest. Sounds . . . different. Thank you. Right now, my wife is trying hard to cheer up our youngest. She is heartbroken."

The old man's eyes wandered out to the dining room, to the table where the little girl sat on her mother's lap, with tears in her eyes, while clutching a little stuffed teddy bear in her little hands.

"Yeah, yeah, yeah, I see that," the old man said. I knew that look in his eyes.

Our father had a plan.

"What did you say the name of this brew was, Paul?"

Gus jumped in to clear up any, "New Jersey influenced," misunderstanding, "Mistletoe and Mayhem Christmas Stout."

"It is outstanding, but very strong. I can understand the mayhem part of the name. This drink can cause some mayhem."

"Bet after sucking down a few of these here suds, that ya, are looking for some missile shot and a pretty gal to smooch under it with," the old man commented, and my father winked at me. I looked over in the direction of Isabella and then to the dusty old mistletoe hanging from the fishing line at the entrance to the lounge. I smiled. She sure was pretty.

Mum and Dottie appeared while proudly announcing that dinner was ready. After additional introductions, we all pitched in to serve the food and the drink, and we took our places at the dining tables to enjoy what promised to be a glorious meal. The old man took a spoon, tapped his beer mug, and stood up.

He cleared his throat and said, "I think we ought'a say a

little prayer here. After all, it is Christmas Eve and while things don't always go as ya plan 'em, we are thankful that we are all here. Safe, warm and dry. The shi . . . I mean Haus and his gang and all of us. And thanks to Woody and Gus too. I ain't the guy to say prayers, but our son here, Paulie, he knows all 'bout God and prayers. So, I will get him to say a few words. Paulie will keep it germenic so he don't offend no one. We are Lutherans, but don't know what ya religion is. I guess on a night like this one is — it really don't matter much what ya are or who ya might be."

Haus smiled widely, lifted his beer mug, and said, "We are Lutherans too!"

Gus looked at Woody, and they both shrugged their shoulders.

"Tonight, we are what you are," Woody answered.

"Good! Paulie, please, do ya stuff and say a few nice words," the old man said as he sat in his chair.

With a nod, I began, "Please, let us bow our heads, fold our hands, and give thanks and praise in prayer. Father in Heaven, on this most holy of nights, where the greatest gift ever given, arrived within the heralds of angels, we gather as one family under Heaven to thank you for the greatest gift. To thank you for being safe, warm, and dry, and for the food and drink in front of us. Most of all, we thank you for the love. Your love. Our love. For there are many gifts, but love is the greatest gift of all. In Jesus' name, we pray. Amen."

When I finished praying, and I opened my eyes, all I saw was glowing Isabella. Oh yes, and Maureen's words echoed in my head, "Do not to forget her, in and amongst all the beautiful young ladies in the ski lodge."

Until a few hours ago, the only things in here were cobwebs and memories. And a sad Christmas tree and dusty mistletoe (missile shot) hung by a fishing line.

"Beautiful prayer, Paulie. Stunning," Mrs. Schmidt said.

I thanked her and without any further delay, we dug

into the food. We were all very hungry. It had been a long day. Mum and Dottie received countless thanks and continual compliments for an incredible meal. The best testimonies of how wonderful a meal it was seemed to be that everyone asked for second helpings and all the plates were clean. Skippy and Pussface gladly assisted with any additional cleaning of the plates. After the main meal, then there was the fabulous bread pudding! Followed by the beer, the wine, the soda, the tall tales, and the glorious laughter! What a great and grand Christmas Eve meal and wonderful time together this turned out to be.

Mum proclaimed how the kitchen was old but very functional and efficient and they even found that the dishwasher worked! Therefore, we were all off the hook for dishwashing duty too!

We had cleared all the tables, and I found myself chatting with Isabella, and Dottie had cornered handsome Nick, as we shared tea and coffee in front of the fireplace. Outside the snow intensely fell down. Inside, it was warm and dry, and Woody tuned some Christmas music in on the sound system in the lodge as a holiday backdrop. It seemed as if we were all settling in for a silent night and holy night.

All is calm and well, and merry and bright and, ah, well, not really. You see, on this Christmas Eve, ole Pussface the cat had a bit too much of the stout to drink. The old cat wobbled, teetered, and tottered, and in a rush of drunken Christmas joy, Pussface decided to celebrate by trotting around the sitting room. Skippy barked at him and decided to chase poor Pussface for an encroachment of territory. Mostly, Skippy was chasing poor Pussface because he was being the obnoxious version of Skippy. Obviously, the dog forgot his holiday promise of good behavior to the old man, and resorted to the fact that he had to be mean to Pussface, at least once a day. To everyone's amazement, Pussface ran across the lodge floor, wobbling and staggering and then to everyone's horror, the old cat jumped in the sad Christmas tree and climbed the branches to the top!

The old man jumped up, waved Skippy off and scolded Pussface, "Ya, old drunken bum of a cat. Get outta the Christmas tree! I'm having Gus cut ya off on the beer drinkin'! Ya had too much of that fancy beer now!"

Pussface poked his head out of the branches near the top of the tree, right under the star, and with one leap, the old cat jumped out of his hiding spot and the tree, well, it all came crashing down! Lights popped and exploded and the eighteen sad glass ornaments crashed, popped and scattered, and electrical sparks flew as Pussface ran off to hide from the disaster!

Immediately, little Eloise erupted into tears at the sight of the now destroyed Christmas tree.

It was not too swift of a Christmas tree to begin with, but now it was a pile of Christmas tree rubble. A strong whiff of ozone and electrical sparks filled the air as the lights on the toppled Christmas tree, shorted out, flickered, and then they slowly dimmed and sputtered to a slow death.

"Now, we don't even have a Christmas tree! Saint Nick will never find us now! Our tree is gone! That crazy kitty cat broke it!"

Mrs. Schmidt did her best to console the little girl, and I looked at Isabella, who factually stated, "I think your cat just ruined the tree." Then, with a puzzled look upon her face, Isabella asked, "Is he really bombed from drinking too much beer?"

"Yes, I am afraid so. He usually holds his beer a little better, but that stout is no joke. Yes, he did break the tree. Oh, boy. I am so sorry that your little sister is so upset. He did not mean to break it. I will see if I can fix it."

I stood up to walk over and gather up the remains of the tree, and give it my best shot at resurrection, when the old man stood up and shook his head at the sight of the destroyed tree and the tears of the little girl.

"Now, now, please, don't go crying here, Eloise. Not on Christmas Eve."

The old man slowly walked over to where the little girl sat on her mother's lap.

"But, Mr. Henson, I want to go home. Saint Nick will pass us by here and we will miss Christmas! Pussface broke the tree!"

"Yeah, yeah, yeah, I know, and he feels bad about it too. He did not mean to break the tree. That missile shot and mix-up beer stuff was too much for him. He is bombed. Look at him over there. Pussface is sad, but ya gotta 'member that Santie Claus knows everything. I bet right now, in his workshop, he is working on a new tree for here. Yup, Santie and those little guys that work for him. Wadda ya call 'em?"

"The elves?" Eloise asked.

"Yeah, yeah, yeah, da elves, guys. They are working hard and ya gotta believe that when ya wake up tomorrow and come in here, there will be a brand-new fresh Christmas tree right here, and a few gifts under the tree for ya. Most of ya stuff will be at home, but Santie Claus will drop sum stuff here too. Cuz ya gotta have faith. Yup, faith and love, just like Paulie said at dinnertime. Love is very important and Santie Claus, well, he loves you."

The little girl's eyes studied the old man, and I held back a laugh when Eloise asked, "Is Santie Claus the same as Saint Nick?"

"Yeah, yeah, yeah, same guy. In New Jersey we call him Santie Claus and in Austrich, youse guys call him, Saint Nick."

Eloise nodded. I guess that she spoke New Jersey.

I had stopped walking towards the destroyed Christmas tree and I realized now that all eyes in the room were on our father as he spoke to little Eloise. I also realized that Isabella had followed me and she was standing next to me.

Isabella leaned in and motioned for me to bend down so she could whisper in my ear.

"My goodness, you are so tall. Your father has a unique manner of speaking, but he is very kind and very smart too. He is an amazing man."

I smiled and for some reason, I took her hand in mine and said, "Thank you. He is. Very special and amazing. In many, many ways."

We stood together and continued to listen.

The little girl was about to put the old man on the spot.

"I understand about love. I love Mommy and Daddy and my sister and brother, and Saint Nick and even you and Pussface, but I don't understand about faith. What's faith? Mr. Henson, how will Saint Nick find us here?"

The old man's mouth twitched nervously, but no words came out and his eyes darted around in his head. He looked at me, and then to Mum and Gramps and Dottie. He checked on Pussface and Skippy. Everyone in the room stared at the old man, waiting for an answer. Gus dashed from behind the bar and handed him another mug of liquid inspiration. A mug of missile shot and mix-up . . . ah, I mean a mug of Mistletoe and Mayhem Christmas Stout.

Gus was one helluva great bartender.

Never had I experienced the old man become tongue-tied before this and he had been in many difficult situations and always wiggled out of them, unscathed. However, right now, this little girl might have pinned the old man down with one of the toughest questions of all. There was an eerie silence in the room, just the crackling of the fire and a stirring rendition of the Christmas classic "We Three Kings of Orient Are" playing on the backdrop music system. The old man tilted his head and caught a few bars of the song; he took a sip of stout and smiled.

The music seemed to have struck a chord and off he went, "Well, faith is sorta like believing but it is a lot stronger. It is like the story from the Bible 'bout those Three

King Guys. Do you know that story?"

Eloise shrugged her shoulders and said, "Sort of. Please tell me."

The old man pulled a chair up next to where they sat; he placed his beer mug down and waved his hands in the air.

"Well, on Christmas Eve a long time ago, in a far-off land somewhere on the other side of the Indianier Ocean, there were these, very important, Three King Guys. They lived in the same neighborhood, but they all were kings of their own places. They were from Chiner, Indianer, and Cereal. Their names were ah, ah, King Gasseous, King Blabberous, and King Molasses. Or sumthin' like that."

I felt Isabella squeeze my hand tightly, and she looked up at me and smiled.

"Ya can look it up in the Bible. Anyway, they were sittin' around on the porches of their tents, drinking beer one night, and they see this here bright star in the sky. A really bright star. And King Gasseous, he was smart, and he had a sore neck cuz he always looked up all the time and he says to his pals, 'Hey that's a new star up there.' So, they get out their microscopes, barameasurers and sky checking-out instruments and studied the star. After a few more beers and a shot or two of whiskey, they decided that the star is an important sign. A sign from God. They jumped on their camels and started to ride in the direction of the fancy star. After a long ride, they found the star shining down on a horse stable in a barn. Next to a cornfield and a racetrack. That is where they have that famous race every year. The Indianerappleous five-hundred. There are lots of cornfields and racetracks near Indianer. Anyway, they found one of them old fashioned sawloon-type gin joints with the swinging front doors and they tied up their camels to a telephone pole next to the gin joint and walked over to the barn. When they got there, they found that the star was shining down on baby Jesus and his mother, Mary, and his father. . .."

The old man's voice sputtered out. He looked over to me for help, and I mouthed "Joseph" to him.

"Yeah, yeah, yeah, his father's name was Joseph, and he stood off to the side because fathers don't know what to do with a baby except to smile and then go off to work to pay for all of it. The Three King Guys realized that the star guided them here, and that Jesus was super-important. The most important baby ever born because he was God's son. The Three King Guys knelt down, prayed, and said lots of nice things. The Three King Guys gave the gang presents. King Gasseous gave them some spare coins that he had because money is always good to buy what ya need. King Blabberous gave them extra diapers because they only had swaddler clothes to wrap Jesus up in and a baby needs diapers. King Molasses gave them wine and beer. Not for the baby to drink. For the mother and father to drink, because a baby cries a lot and the parents need the beer and wine to get through it all, until the baby grows up and moves away and gets a job or goes to school or gets hitched and has their own babies."

The old man paused and looked around the room. Everyone still had their eyes riveted on him and he took another swig of stout and finished, "But ya see, da point is that all that the Three King Guys had was a strange star in the sky to look at and follow. Now, they could have just drank more beer, got totally bombed and gone back to bed and forgotten 'bout it, but they did not. They had a thought that the star meant sumthin' important and without anything else happenin' or anyone tellin' 'em to do it, they followed the star and found a wonderful thing!" His voice lowered, and the old man picked up a napkin from the table and gently wiped the tears away from the little girl's eyes.

"They found the greatest gift of all. The gift that saved all of us. They found love."

Eloise smiled and said, "They had faith! They found the

baby Jesus, Mr. Henson. I understand. Thank you."

She gave the old man a little kiss on the cheek and he turned a hundred shades of red.

"Well, that is enuff of that now! Off to bed! It is late and Santie Claus might be flying around in the sky soon."

I was never prouder of my father, as the little girl happily scampered off to bed. She stopped and said good night to all of us and, most importantly, there were no more tears. Mum walked over, gave the old man a big smooch and hugged him.

I stood there holding Isabella's hand and mumbled, "Yes, indeed. He is very special and amazing. In many, many ways."

Christmas Cocktails

"Hey, wake up, youse two guys. Pop, Paulie, c'mon, I can't do this Santie Claus stuff all on my own."

I rolled out of the bed and was vaguely aware of a voice from the hallway and some knocking on our door. We had all retired to our rooms for a long winter's nap and now, the clatter in the hallway was the old man. There was a hotel room with two twin beds, so Gramps, Skippy, Pussface, and I bunked in together. Mum and the old man had their own room and Dottie had a king-sized bed and room all to her own. Despite the rest of the mess here, the hotel rooms that were still standing were clean and neat. The rooms were very outdated, but very warm and quite functional. Gramps stirred, and I looked at the clock on the end table. It was just a few minutes after midnight. It was now Christmas Day in the early morning. The very early morning. The only ones up were Santa Claus, some elves, and apparently, the old man and now me, too.

And Gramps.

Pussface and Skippy did not move a muscle. They were three sheets to the wind and Pussface was sleeping off too much, celebrating.

My feet hit the floor, and I made it to the door and swung it open. There stood the old man all dressed in his winter gear and he had snow all over him. Lots of snow. He stomped into the room and Gramps switched on the light.

"By Jove, Paul. What the devil is going on? Paulie Boy

and I just nodded off an hour or so ago. It was a very long day."

"I know, I know, but that little girl. We can't let her down."

Gramps nodded and swung his legs and feet over to the side of the bed while saying, "Oh yes, indeed. The Gospel according to Henson. Somehow, the story of the Magi will never be quite the same."

I suppressed a laugh, and instead of commenting on the old man's unique version of the Visit of the Magi, I started changing into my work clothes and then set out to find the work boots that I wisely packed.

"Hey, Pop, it might not have been entirely correct, but youse guys all got the storyline and meaning."

"Oh yes, yes, they and we did. It was very impressive but the good book also says, thousest that come upest with stupid ideaest, needeth to carry out on themeth by themselevest."

The old man screwed his face up and asked, "It does? Well, look, I will buy ya a few beers to make it up to ya. I found a tree that we can cut down. And in the maintenance shop, there are extra tree lights and a box of ornaments. I also found lots of stuff that we could use to make some simple toys. Ya know, old-fashioned toys. Simple but fun. I just need ya help. Paulie, I need ya muscles and ya brains with the electrical. The lights don't exactly all light, and Pop, I need ya wisdom and ya skills. Ya know tools, machines and stuff too."

Gramps nodded as he pulled off his pajamas and dressed into his clothes. "I do, but I am retired. Long since retired. A fact that you seem to have conveniently forgotten. Yet, it is Christmas and we cannot disappoint the little lassie. Especially after, you spouted off that story as if you were a wise Biblical scholar. What name did you give the third king?"

"Molasses."

"I believe his name was Melchior."

"Yeah, yeah, yeah, that's what I meant to say. But, what the hell, I was kinda close. In New Jersey, we changed his name to Molasses."

Now dressed and ready to go, Gramps slipped into his overcoat, looked at our sleeping pets and waved his hand as if to not even worry about them, plopped his English derby on his head and pointed at the door. "Lead onward, Ghost of Christmas Present. I know that you mean to do me well! Lead onward," Gramps paraphrased from his favorite author.

Within a few minutes, I found myself in the middle of a snowy field next to the rubble that used to be the other half of the hotel, kneeling in about twenty inches or so of fresh powdery snow and sawing at the base of an evergreen tree. Gramps held a flashlight and the old man held the tree as I worked through the trunk with a saw. I had mentioned that perhaps we needed to check with Woody before cutting down one of his trees and the old man quickly dismissed me for being an "Old Lady."

"There are fifty-two million trees here. Ya really think that he is gonna miss this one?"

Even Gramps said not to worry about it. And to think that a few minutes ago we were all cozy and snug in our beds and now. . ..

Snow was still falling very lightly, but it looked as if it would stop soon. It was a gorgeous Christmas morning. Simply breathtaking, but it was cold. The top of this mountain must have allowed for a ten-degree drop or so from what the temperature was down along the road. I wondered what the temperature was at the top of the ski lift. Within a few minutes, we had cut the tree down and carried it into the main ski lodge. Woody was here somewhere. He might be asleep in the back office. The lodge was open and the check-in available, but the chances of a visitor would be very remote. The chances were high that the main roads were unplowed, as was the path leading to the resort from the main road, and that would make for an interesting drive. However, you never know. Gus had his own room, and he retired to it shortly after we left. Walk-ins to the bar were rare. The bar area and sitting room were dark and quiet. While we cleaned up the old tree and salvaged what we could from the destruction enacted by our family cat, Gramps went to work, setting the tree up and filling it all out. The old man and I went down to the maintenance shop and my father showed me the Christmas lights.

"See, Paulie. Not all of them light up. This shop has everything. I found spare bulbs, fuses, and this electrical meter. While you get them lit, I will work on some toys. There is the box with the extra ornaments."

I went to work and so did the old man. I heard some machines spinning and turning and sawing and cutting going on. The old man was a master machinist and machines were putty in his hands.

Within an hour or so, I had most of the lights working and I delivered them to Gramps, along with the ornaments and a stepladder. When I repaired another string, I brought them to Gramps, until on my last trip up to the main lodge; we had a breathtaking and spectacular tree. Gramps had done a magnificent job! The tree was amazing, and it smelled good, too.

"I do confess, Paulie Boy, to sneaking in the rear of the bar and pouring a pint or two more of that stout! It proved to be rather inspirational in its influence. I dare say this is quite the Christmas tree. The little lassie will be thrilled. What is your father up to?"

"He is busy being, Santie Claus, as he calls him. He is down in the maintenance shop working on toys. It is a very cool shop. C'mon, I'll show you."

I sat for a few hours and had the immense pleasure to watch two master craftsmen at work. My father and my grandfather. Gramps had worked for a great part of his career in the repair and maintenance of looms, silk weaving machines, and garment weaving machines. He also had great skills with machines and power tools, as well as amazing plumbing skills. The old man had already fashioned a wooden camera that I felt was a piece of creative genius and a little rocking horse with a stick figure riding on it. Gramps, in a very short order, worked some genius on the wood lathe. He made one of those toys that had a stick with a cup on the end and a ball tied to a string attached to the cup. The trick was to catch the ball in the cup. My job was strictly in the finish work. I was in charge of sanding, filing and then applying a sealer to the toys. The old man explained that the sealer was latex-based and would dry rather quickly. This maintenance shop was amazing, and it really did have everything imaginable within its shelves and corners.

When the clock told us, it was three-thirty in the morning; we had assembled quite a little variety of simple toys. There was a little doggie made of wood that you pulled around on a string, and the old man turned a couple of quick wheels on the metal lathe for the doggie to roll around the floor on. I painted some eyes, a nose, and a smile on the dog. Gramps put the finishing touches on a wooden maze of ramps and tracks that you rolled marbles down and tried to have them fall into holes. We could not find any marbles, but some steel ball bearings worked just as well. These toys were all simple but lots of fun. I was playing with the ball and cup toy too!

After cleaning the shop up, we snuck upstairs to the lodge and placed the toys under the Christmas tree and I thought that we were finally done. I thought wrong because Santie Claus had one more thought before we could seek safe havens under those warm covers. My eyelids were dragging on the floor now. But Paterson's most famous grand prizewinner had one more trick up his sleeve!

"Ah, youse guys, I was thinking. Do you think we could get that ski lift going? Ya know how Dottie has her heart set on skiing, and with all that fantastic snow out dare . . . it sure would be a shame to waste it. Think about it, if Woody opened the mountain for skiing. The dough he could make! All these here rustic guys up here in Pennsservanier love skiing! It might make this joint popular again and maybe his wife, ya know, maybe, ah, she would come back."

The old man was tugging at our heartstrings on Christmas Day.

Just what we needed at three-thirty in the morning on Christmas Day, when you have only slept for two hours in the last forty-eight hours . . . a softie, Santie Claus.

"I dunno, Dad. From what Woody said about the motor, it sounds as if it is a bad scene. Sparks and blown fuses. That motor is big-time stuff. High voltage, three phases. I am only in my third year of the electrical trade. Just a student apprentice."

I looked at Gramps. He was shaking his head, and he frowned at me. I sensed his disappointment with my testimony and lack of ambition.

With an air of teaching wisdom laced within his voice, Gramps said, "Listen to me, carefully, Paulie Boy. Please, never harbor a doubt of your abilities or your intelligence. You are a brilliantly smart young man with a bright future and I am somewhat surprised at your lack of confidence and your defeatism. Believe me when I tell you that your genes and your heritage do not allow for such an attitude. Furthermore, do not forget that not all my machines ran on waterpower or pedal power. I am old, but not that old. We had electrical motors in the lace factories and garment mills, too. Let's give it our best shot. After all, it is Christmas."

I nodded my head and smiled and said, "I apologize. You are correct, Gramps. Let's give it a whirl, eh?"

Goodbye, warm and cozy bed. Hello, dangerous and deadly high voltage!

A few minutes later with an electrical V.O.M. meter in my hand that looked as if Edison used it in his lab, Gramps and I peered into a huge motor control center in the machine room for the ski lift. I never saw such a motor. It was huge and the drive pulley that towed the cars along was huge too. I still felt as if I was out of my league on this one, but Gramps dug in hard. The old man held the flashlight and coached encouragement.

"How many fuses are blown, Paulie Boy?"

"Two. A phase and B phase."

"Double-check the main power and make sure it is off, then check it once more. I think we can read the motor wires to ground and see if they are shorted to ground or not."

I nodded and dug in and after the checks; we determined the motor was in good condition. When the old man flashed his light on the main controls, I spotted some burn indicators, along with a trace of an arc-over of carbon and what I thought looked like it could be the source of the electrical trouble.

"Gramps, take a good look at that motor contactor. The copper contact lug on the end is arced and the end of the metal is missing."

"By Jove, good eyes, Paulie Boy. That is where the trouble is. I bet that arc blows the fuses."

"I guess, but where are we going to get a new motor contactor like that? It is older than dirt and it is Christmas Day."

"We will not replace it. We will repair it. We just need to drill that out, mill a new piece of copper, and slip a new piece of copper in there and rivet it back into place. We just so happen to know that Santie Claus here doubles as a master machinist and milling machines are his specialty." After Gramps spilled the plan, we both looked up at the old man. My father sauntered over confidently with the mission clearly in his sights.

The old man leaned into the motor control center, peered in with his flashlight, smiled and said, "Youse guys need me to make that piece there? That little copper whoosie? Piece of cake. I can make that sucker, in fifteen minutes, while blindfolded with one hand tied behind my back. Pull that piece out and meet me in the shop. I will fire up the milling machine. I even saw a stash of copper blocks in the electrical shop that I can mill down to the right size."

It was about five minutes to five in the morning when we had all new fuses in place and the new copper machined and installed on the motor contactor. I had the honor of flipping the switch and I confessed to closing my eyes and praying as I approached the motor control center and prepared to turn the power back on and push the start button for the lift motor.

Gramps waved at me and motioned with his hands while instructing me on safety, "Stand to the side, Paulie Boy, when you flip the main switch."

I nodded in acknowledgment of the instructions and did stand to the side as I wrapped my fingers around the switch handle.

"CLUNK!"

The electrical disconnect switch made a loud thump as I flipped the switch and applied the main power. Now, a little push on the start button, and I held my breath as I pushed the glowing red button.

Wow! No smoke, no smell, no arc, but the motor turned, and the pulleys, and the cars too! Shouts of joy! Hugs! Backslaps and handshakes! It was a thing of beauty. Woody was going to faint when he saw this.

We all snuck back into the bar for a few more pints of the beloved, "Mistletoe and Mayhem Christmas Stout."

The old man and Gramps poured me a big boy glass. They said that I earned it. That stuff sure packed a punch. It was not as if I needed it to sleep, because I think I was snoring before my head hit the pillow.

"Hey, wake up, youse two guys. Pop, Paulie, c'mon, it is almost seven-thirty. Eloise is going to go to breakfast at eight. C'mon, ya don't want to miss it!"

Upon hearing the clatter from the hallway right outside our door as well as Santie Claus's voice, my eyes opened wide, and I heard Gramps groan. The old man persisted at the door.

"Bloody well! What is it with your father? Even Father Christmas sleeps," Gramps moaned as he tossed the covers aside.

"Therein lies the problem. We are dealing with Santie Claus and not Father Christmas," I explained to Gramps what the old man's secret identity really was.

Pussface and Skippy both stirred. Sure, they had a good night of sleep because they were not lucky enough to be part of the Saintie Claus team.

"Is this the part of the story where Scrooge repents, Gramps?"

"I bloody well hope so. That will mean it is near the end and I can go back to bed."

Gramps made it to the door and let the supercharged, insomniac, Santie Claus in our room and then without another word, Gramps headed for the bathroom.

"Your mother and Dottie are already down there cooking breakfast, and Woody and Gus are up too. What's wrong, ya look tired? Merry Christmas!"

"Yes, merry Christmas, Dad. No way, are we tired. I

mean, why would, Gramps and I be tired? No, not at all. Sure, sure, sure, we will be down there as soon as we can."

"Okay, well, don't be lard-asses! Youse guys are gonna miss out on Christmas! I will let Skippy and Pussface out. They will do their thing and run right back inside. It is colder than a well-digger's ass out there." The old man waved at our pets and said, "C'mon, you two pineapples. Follow me. And, Pussface! I am telling ya old ass right now that ya drinking only Big Boulder beer today. No more of that missile shot and mix-up stuff. Packs too much of a punch. Made ya crazy in the head. Ya ain't wrecking a'nudder tree on Christmas Day!"

I heard Pussface loudly meow in protest, or in acknowledgement. It was difficult to tell. My cat language interpretation skills were still in bed.

Where I should be.

Our faithful pets followed Santie Claus out the door and the door closed with a hard slam.

I had all that I could do not to fall back into the bed. It was sheer agony being a blood relative to Santie Claus. However, we could all use a glass or two more of that, Mistletoe and Mayhem Christmas Stout.

Besides, Isabella did have rather captivating eyes and some other rather intriguing attributes too.

The joy of little Eloise when she spotted the beautiful tree and the toys underneath it made up for the lack of sleep. The Christmas joy filled the world, and she felt Christmas faith and love.

It was definitely worth it.

Sort of.

I kept telling myself how amazing this all was while I yawned continuously. Gramps sat at a table with toothpicks in his eyelids to keep them open, and he was sucking down tea and coffee by the pot. Even with all of that, he nodded off in his breakfast plate once or twice.

Santie Claus, or I mean the old man, was a bundle of

Christmas energy. He proudly showed Eloise how each toy worked, and told her a captivating tale of a loud thump on the roof, followed by some strange noises. He jumped out of bed and when the old man ran out of his hotel room and came to the lodge, he caught a glimpse of a red suited man slipping up the chimney. He was amazing. I think he was running on Christmas adrenaline.

Later on, today, I was sure that his fuel would be some "missile shot and mix-up stuff."

Woody and Gus were near tears when we showed them the now working ski lift. Poor Woody could hardly stop shaking with joy and pouring out the emotions because he could not even imagine how this all had happened overnight.

"Just a little visit from Santie Claus and his helper guys," the old man spouted.

Woody and Gus joined Eloise and legions of other believers in the man in the red suit named Santa Claus, or I mean Santie Claus. Dottie, Nick, and the rest of the Schmidts (minus Eloise) were already on the slopes. They hit the slopes right after breakfast, and the old man babysat and played with Eloise.

Woody made a phone call to the local radio station and proudly announced that Moose Lake Mountain Ski resort was open with twenty-one inches of fresh powder. That opened the floodgates. Gus fired up an old tractor with a plow on the front of it, and the old bartender did his best to make a path in the deep snow to the main road. The path was a bit crooked because old Gus was already partaking in a nip or two of the Mistletoe and Mayhem magic — but what the hell — a path is a path. After plowing the main roads and parking areas, Gus fired up an ancient trail groomer, and he groomed the slopes for the first few runs down the mountain.

When the skiers came flooding in, it was all-hands-on deck. Gus ended up manning the lift tickets and ski rentals.

Christmas Cocktails

Dottie worked as the ski patrol officer, and Nick manned the lift at the top of the mountain. I handled the controls and the boarding of the skiers at the ski lift at the base of the mountain. Mum and Mrs. Schmidt and Isabella worked the kitchen and Gramps, assisted by Pussface, tended bar. Mr. Schmidt was serving the tables and slinging drinks and beer. Skippy was security. He growled at anyone who did not pass his watchful eye and discouraged any evil doers.

And you might ask where the old man was? Well, he provided the entertainment. He told fabulous stories with his famous Paterson, New Jersey accent in full voice and his hands waving in the air in a glorious demonstrative manner of his best display of his New Jersey heritage. In dramatic fashion, the old man told stories of his amazing victory over the "radio station bums" and how sparks flew out of the ski lift motor and bounced off the walls of the machine room! Stories of baseball folklore and how his hero, Big Foot Garumba hit tape-measure home runs and skied Moose Mountain and how he drank gallons of beer at this same bar while he visited this fantastic resort. He told one of his favorite Christmas stories of how he met the glorious "giant chief guy" who sold Christmas trees at a corner lot in Paterson so many years ago. The old man captivated his audience while he explained how big the giant was and how his laughter sounded, as if it was a sonic boom. He also played with all the toys with Eloise. After a few glasses of his favorite missile shot and mix-up stuff, he could finally beat Eloise at the marble roll, but the ball in the cup was not working out so well.

Around two o'clock or so in the afternoon the remaining hotel rooms were now booked solid. A little light snow drifted in and everyone took a little breather from the business of the day. Woody announced that he would not turn the lights on for any night skiing and we all breathed a sigh of relief. We were taking Christmas night off!

The old man sauntered up to Woody and put his arm

around him. With quite a bit of the beloved stout flowing around in his veins, the old man walked over to the front counter telephone and handed the receiver to Woody.

"Give your wife a call. Tell her that Santie Claus came last night and from here on in it is going to be okay. Tell her 'bout faith and those Three King Guys."

The old man stopped speaking, rolled his eyes, and shook his head.

"Nah, on second thought, ya better skip that one. Tell her 'bout the greatest gift of all. Love. Tell her that ya love her with all of your heart and soul. Love is the best gift of all. I think that right now that is what ya should give 'er. Betcha she will be here in an hour or two. The roads are pretty clear now. That light snow is just a Christmas kiss on the scene. She is in Philly-del-fee-er, right?"

"She is, Paul. Ah, I think she is. I mean wherever it was that you said. However, we are not world famous yet. We still have a very long way to go."

All eyes were on the conversation, and the old man nodded. "I know, but Woody, think 'bout it. Maybe ya ain't got to be world famous. Maybe, being world famous is not too swift after all. Betcha Big Foot Garumba would agree with that. Why don't ya just try to be Pennsservanier famous? That might be just good enuff."

Yes, indeed, the old man was a special guy. Very, very special. Very special and amazing. In many, many ways.

A few hours later, the first kiss, under the dusty mistletoe hanging by a fishing line, was between Candy and Woody Cane. Yup, sure was. Then the Schmidts, and then Mum and the old man. Nick and Dottie stole a smooch, and I never told Maureen, but Isabella and I shared a smooch, or perhaps, two, or three. A few of the new guests and skiers enjoyed the mistletoe too. That old dusty mistletoe regained some lost glory while it broadcasted its power.

That evening, we all sat around the fireplace toasting

marshmallows and popping popcorn in the fire, with some new overnight guests joining us, while sharing laughs and telling tales of Christmas glory. Thankfully, Pussface stuck to the Big Boulder beer and stayed out of the Christmas tree and away from the mayhem. Little Eloise drifted off to sleep amongst her scattered toys underneath the Christmas tree, and shortly thereafter, we all hit the hay. I never slept as well as I did on that wonderful Christmas night. Gramps put a chair under the doorknob of our room in case the old man (Santie Claus) decided to stop by.

On Boxing Day, Woody had managed to recruit new workers from some skiers and Candy worked in the kitchen. We were officially off duty and finally on vacation. The old man and I fixed the hose on the Schmidt's car, they packed up, and we had a joyful but tearful farewell.

We all promised to stay in touch, but you know how those things go.

We did not see Gramps until two in the afternoon on Boxing Day. Gramps took up his stool at the bar next to the legendary Pussface and along with Gus and other guests; the gang whiled away the rest of the holiday.

The only keg of the precious Mistletoe and Mayhem Christmas Stout lasted until late Tuesday night, when Gus sadly announced that the tap finally ran dry of the precious brew.

On Wednesday morning, we added a few quarts of oil to the Putter as well as Big Bob's magical formula and the old man warmed the car up for an hour before he declared the Putter good to go. We all packed our luggage and our minds and hearts too, and prepared to make our way back to New Jersey. It had been a remarkable holiday. Woody, Candy, and Gus, all walked us to the Putter, and all of us exchanged hugs, handshakes and warm wishes. Woody walked over to the old man and gave him a big hug, just as the old man was climbing into the driver's side of the car.

"Paul, you and your family, well, all of you, changed

our lives and our fortunes too. I cannot thank you and your amazing family enough."

The old man waved his hand in the air as if to dismiss the thought and said, "Nah, it is just as Paulie says. The big man upstairs. Well, he has a plan. It all came together. You can ask, Paulie 'bout how it works. I am retired from Bible stuff. All in all, we did not do that much."

Woody shook his head and Candy leaned into him. She gently kissed his cheek and hugged him tightly.

Woody continued to expound his thoughts. "Well, that might be how you see it, but not from our side. Anyway, thank you and thanks to everyone. And to think, it all began with you answering an impossible trivia question."

"Well, actually, Mum, mailed the postcard and besides, it was two questions. The bums tried to trip me up," The old man said while he leaned on the open door of the Putter and his face became thoughtful.

After a few seconds, the old man said, "It was not really impossible, Woody. Nuthin' really is impossible if you put your mind and your heart in it. Especially at Christmas time. Ya just take the i and the m outta of the word and make it possible." The old man smiled at his simple formula for success and then said, "Youse guys take care and watch out for that missile shot and mix-up stuff. It packs a helluva punch."

The old man patted Woody on the shoulder, climbed in the Putter, and we were off in a trail of blue smoke. My last views of Woody, Candy, and Gus were of all of them waving to us while enveloped in a haze of blue smoke. They did not seem to mind at all.

When we rolled down that gravel driveway and made our way onto the main drag, we rolled back to New Jersey with Christmas joy and love in our hearts. I had to think that there was more than just Mistletoe and Mayhem in that Christmas Stout. I think there was some magic in that mixture too. Christmas magic.

Poof!

The screen went dark and the scenes that were so vivid just a few short minutes ago and projected upon the screen in front of me . . . disappeared.

The ghosts floated away, too.

All that I could do was to rub my eyes and grasp at the reality of where I actually was. I was no longer in the 1964 Putter Classic Model 200 making our way back home after a strong dose of Christmas joy. No, no, no. I was back in my office and it was late in the day.

How late?

I turned and looked out the window and realized that darkness was settling in on the city. I had daydreamed the afternoon away! My goodness.

What time was it? Almost five!

Oh no! I will be stuck in traffic forever on the crawl up Route 21 and then to Route 3 and to the split for 80 and 46. Black Friday's traffic in New Jersey. Goodness. It was hardly worth even trying. I stood up and stretched and then leaned in and clicked the "shutdown" button on my computer. Oh well. I did have the best of intentions, but the ghosts had a different plan. My mind danced with the memories of our glorious Christmas adventure, and I strolled back over to the window and gazed down upon the glory of the city. The activity. The Christmas lights. The joy of it all.

The old man and dear Mum received a Christmas card

every year from the Cane family for as long as I could remember. They had two boys, and the resort did capture some of its past glory. They finished all the renovations and rebuilt the hotel side in order to add more rooms. They also added summer activities and some pumpkin picking, hayrides, and such for the fall of the year. I think the old man's wise advice worked out quite well. It might not have been world famous, but it was famous enough.

"Pennsservanier famous. That might be just good enuff."

Dottie, Gramps, and I never returned to the Moose Lake Ski Lodge and Vacation Resort, but Mum and the old man visited for a reunion of sorts. They said it was a wonderful visit, and the place was a marvel. Old Gus had sadly passed on, but his spirit was still there. I think Woody and his wife are retired now and the boys run the operation.

I, for one, was rather glad that I never returned. Instead, I wanted to keep it in my mind's eye exactly as it was. It was a special place, and that Christmas was a very special time in all of our lives.

My ears perked up while the radio station began to play a stirring rendition of "We Three Kings of Orient Are." In fact, it might have been the same version that played on the radio in the lodge on that fateful Christmas Eve and inspired the Gospel according to Henson. I sat on the edge of my desk and listened to the entire song, and when it ended, I stood up, walked over to the radio, and shut the radio off. I grabbed my vest and thought that instead of fighting the traffic home, I might head for the "Elusive Lion Pub" visit with my close friend, Janet, the gorgeous bartender, to have dinner and a few brews.

Kill some time.

I wonder if by chance they might have some of that "Mistletoe and Mayhem Christmas Stout."

You never know.

If not, I will enjoy whatever Janet pours and maybe, just maybe, I will tell her about those Three King Guys. You know them, King Gasseous, King Blabberous, and King Molasses.

The Three King Guys.

I might just enter that radio contest too. With any luck, the trivia question will be, "What are the names of the Three Kings of the Magi?"

I would have that one in the bag.

I smiled, pulled my vest all around me, shut off the lights, walked out in the hallway, and locked the door behind me. I rode the elevator down to the ground floor, bid a good evening to the lobby security officer, and disappeared into the maze of the city.

Into the Mistletoe and Mayhem.

Into the joy of it all.

THE END

Waltzing at Christmastime

"Paul John, I think you need to have a long chat with your son. Before dinner," my gorgeous wife, Binky said to me as I opened the back door to the parsonage and took about one half-step into the kitchen. Oh, no. Seems as if we have a little uprising on the home front. I looked at Binky and she shook her head, went back to stirring whatever it was that she was cooking in a large pot on the stove and she dug her left foot into the floor while she stirred the contents of the pot. That left foot digging in is always a sign of determination. From the glorious smell wafting about the kitchen, I surmised that it was a beef stew that my wife prepared for dinner today. Binky was an amazing cook and on a cold December day, after fighting through another Advent season dilemma as the Senior Pastor of Reunion Lutheran Church, a hearty beef stew was just what I needed. From the sound of Binky's voice and her using my full name as well as her mannerisms, I might also add a cold beer or two to the dinner wish list.

"Oh, okay, Binky. I will, sure, sure, sure. Why, what's up? You might break that wooden spoon on the side of that pot if you do not ease up on the stirring." I tried to break the tension a little, and that did not go over so well.

Binky turned around and glared at me and added, "I know very well how to stir a stew, dear Paul. I might also add a tidbit of testimony about your lack of culinary skills."

I threw my hands up in defeat and surrendered. I tried a different method. It was worth a chance. I waltzed over to Binky, leaned in and gave her a long kiss and she met my lips and the warmth of her body filled my soul. I knew she was not angry with me.

In fact, far from it. . ..

"Okay, you melted me. You always do. Later, after dinner, you can melt me some more. Right now," Binky playfully pushed off on my chest, "please, go and speak with *your* son. It seems as if he ended up in Mr. Flanker's office this afternoon for making rude remarks about Irene Goldstein and her lack of dancing skills."

"Oh, I see. Irene Goldstein, eh? She is that big gal, right?"

I finished my words and question with a demonstration with my arms and hands of a person who was rather immense.

"Yes, she is, and that seems to be part of Paul William's issue. The teacher paired Paul William off with Irene for dancing lessons for the upcoming Christmas show and she is, sort of clumsy and *your* son took issue with her dancing skills and was unkind to her."

I nodded and made a note that this was the second time in this conversation that Binky referred to Paul William as my son rather than our son.

"I will speak to him and take care of it. What was his punishment with the principal? Flanker is the principal. Right? I think."

Binky nodded to confirm Mr. Flanker's lofty position with the local school system and added, "No lingering punishment, other than a good talking to by Mr. Flanker, an apology to Irene and a note to take home to us. I mean .. . to you." Binky aggressively tapped her wooden spoon on the side of the stew pot and then she sat it on the spoon rest on the top of the cooker. She whirled around and with more than just a bit of intensity, Binky said, "Furthermore, he took an attitude with me when I questioned him about the details! I exiled *your* son to his bedroom and told Paul William to stay there until you came home from work."

"Oh, I see. Okay, well, I am on it. Where is Heather Sarah?"

"Oh, *our* daughter is in her room doing her homework."

I nodded as Binky clearly drew the lines of parenting.

"I am on my way to take care of this. Keep the stew warm."

"Oh, and my dear, twenty-seven," Binky said as I took a few steps to go upstairs, "I meant what I said about melting me later on tonight." Binky winked, fluffed her long blonde hair, and posed rather seductively.

"It's a date, my darling, Binky."

A few bounds up the stairs, a knock on the door, and I was sitting on the edge of the bed in Paul William's room. He sat at the top of the bed, on some propped-up pillows, and he rather glumly looked at me while thumbing through a hockey magazine. Paul William was in eighth grade now, tall, lean, and athletic. He was the spitting image of me. When he was younger, he resembled Binky, but as of the last few years, he seemed to change as his face filled out and his frame grew larger. He too wore his blonde hair long, as I did. Paul William's long hair flowed down past his shoulders and he often tied it back in a hair tie as I did. Binky would never entertain either of us cutting our hair. He also was a hockey fanatic, just beginning to play some serious ice hockey in a local league. He too, wore number twenty-seven and, much to the chagrin of his mother, was a goaltender.

"I hear you had a rough day, eh?"

"Yes. The whole thing was not fair, Dad. And Mom did not even give me a chance to explain. She read the note and went totally nuts on me."

"I see. Okay, well, maybe that is because you never go to

the principal's office, you are generally a straight A type student and your mother might have been shocked and disappointed at the note and testimony. Mom also said you copped an attitude and I sense you still have it. Sometimes, you need to take ownership of your behavior, Paul William. So, give me the scoop. What happened?"

Paul William nodded, closed the magazine, and set it aside on the nightstand next to his bed. A nightstand, with a lamp emblazoned with the New York Rovers hockey club's logo on the lampshade.

"Well, Miss Bigly went to my gym teacher, Mr. Kneeknocker, and asked if I could be part of the dancing class instead of gym class. Miss Bigly is the music teacher. She is in charge of the stupid Christmas pageant at school this year. Mr. Kneeknocker did not even ask me and sent me over there! I think the old coot has the hots for Miss Bigly. And we are just starting to play floor hockey in gym class."

I held back a smile at his disdain for the yearly extravaganza of holiday huff n puff that the Charles T. Lumpkin Memorial Public School produced every year. Every year, our children always seemed to be reluctant participants and Binky would insist on a one-hundred percent support for the production. Everyone in our family and all our friends would attend the show, my best buddy Harry M. Redmond Junior and his wife Rose and daughter, Blue Cloud, along with the old man, Mum, and my in-laws, Senator William T. Hobnobber and Mrs. Hobnobber and my brother-in-law Tinky Hobnobber and his wife and family. I have to admit that it was sheer agony. Last year, the old man fell asleep on Senator Hobnobber's shoulder. My father-in-law did likewise, and they both snored so loudly you could hear it on the stage. When Mum, Binky, and Mrs. Hobnobber woke them up, it was hell to pay.

Afterwards, Mum and Binky would not speak to the old man for a week when Miss Bigly greeted us and asked the old man, "What part of the show did you enjoy the most, Mr. Henson?"

The old man replied, "The end."

Paul William most likely was correct about Miss Bigly and Mr. Kneeknocker. The music teacher was very cute and Kneeknocker was an old coot.

I refocused on the problem at hand. This story suddenly sounded very familiar, and I found my mind wandering back in time to a very similar situation in my own life. I wrote in one of my writings somewhere that life is often a circle. It seems so. In order to concentrate on helping Paul William and dealing with this current dilemma and his behavior, I tabled those thoughts, but I knew they would surface later on.

"I see. Well, okay, I think that Mr. Kneeknocker should have asked you first. Did you voice your concern, or tell any of the teachers, or Mr. Flanker that no one even asked you if you wanted to dance?"

"No, I just went over and did it."

"I see. Well, the fact that you did so, might be sticking sideways with you then and it still is now. Perhaps, you should have stood up a little harder. Respectfully, of course, but at least had a voice in the matter."

Paul William nodded his head, but he did not comment.

I waved my hand in the air and continued, "Okay, it is what it is. Then, what happened?"

"Of course, Miss Bigly paired me with Irene Goldstein. Miss Bigly said that I was a very good dancer and Irene needed my help to be a better dancer. Meantime, Steve Lapworth got a chance to dance alone with Suzie Biggles. I get tubby, Irene, and Steve gets Suzie. Irene does not even celebrate Christmas. She is Jewish!"

"That is not nice to say that about Irene. And this is about the holiday season, not necessarily just Christmas. I taught you all about Hanukkah and the Jewish holidays. Irene is a little large, but that is not nice. Irene is a very sweet gal. I take it that you are a little jealous of Steve. Suzie is cute, eh? You have your eyes on her, eh?"

Paul William's face turned a little red. He toyed with the pillow behind his head, hid his face from me and said, "Yeah, she is."

"Hey, it is okay, Paul William. I understand. Right now, life is all about girls and hockey. I get it. You can tell your old man. I have been there too."

"Yeah, Dad. She is really cute. I want to ask her to the holiday season dance," Paul William admitted as he pushed his long hair behind his ears.

"Well, then go ahead and do it. Or, Steve might beat you to it."

He nodded, and I again waved my hand in the air for him to tell me the rest of the story.

"Irene stepped on my toes at least a hundred times and she weighs a ton. I got frustrated, stopped dancing, stormed off, and sat on the sideline. When Miss Bigly came over to me and asked me what was wrong, I lost it and said some stupid and mean things."

I did not comment, only stared at Paul William for him to reveal what he said. He was an honest kid, and he willingly spilled the beans.

"I said that an elephant could dance better than Irene Goldstein can and probably weighs less too. Miss Bigly marched me off to the office and I think Irene overheard my words and she was crying, cuz of them."

"Ouch."

"I know, Dad. Not good, right?"

"No, on the mean scale . . . that one is pretty high, Paul William. I am surprised at you."

"Dad, honest, I am ashamed of my behavior and my mean words. I let my frustration get to me. It is just like Uncle Harry and you try to teach me about hockey and playing goalie. Your frustration can beat you if you let it."

I smiled at his young wisdom and sensed his remorse

and his sincerity.

"Mr. Flanker lectured me for a long time, he let me ride with the note and I apologized to Irene and to Miss Bigly."

I stood up and nodded at the testimony. There was not too much more that I felt I could add. I think Paul William learned his lesson here. If I jumped into the fray and beat on him some more, it would just be counterproductive.

"What did Irene say to you after you apologized?" I asked. Paul William turned red again, and he slid off the edge of the bed without answering me.

"Ah, okay, Paul William, I asked you a question."

"I heard ya, Dad . . . it is just a little embarrassing."

"Okay, then, well, you can keep it to yourself. As long as Irene accepted the apology, then we are good. You apologized, learned your lesson and I am sure you can move on from there. C'mon, down for dinner now. By the way, you better make it right with your mother too."

Paul William nodded, took a few steps, then spouted, "Irene said she forgave me because I am the most handsome boy she has ever seen and she loves to dance with me. Even if she steps on my toes."

I smiled at the fact that Irene had a crush on her dancing partner.

"Well, then I guess it is all fine and well and good. Look, you do not have to dance. You can make an appointment with Miss Bigly and Mr. Flanker and politely and honestly, tell them what happened and that no one gave you much of a choice in the matter. I admit that would be justified because the situation was a little unfair to your feelings," I said, as I put my arm around his shoulders and led him out of the room. My goodness, how tall he was now. He might be taller than I am before he finally stops growing.

I could tell that Paul William was pondering the offer.

While we shut off the light and made our way downstairs to eat dinner, Paul William said, "Nah, Dad. I am gonna stick it out. I think that if I quit now, I will be a quitter. If Irene and I can dance together and make it not so half-bad and she does not break my toes, then it will be like a shutout in hockey."

I laughed aloud at Paul William's analogy. It actually made a great deal of sense to me.

"Okay, cool. Your choice, son. I like the fact that you do not want to quit. Say, what is Miss Bigly making youse guys dance. I mean, what kind of dance is it?"

"Waltzing. She calls this part of the show, 'Waltzing at Christmastime.'" I stopped dead on the stairs, shook my head, and smiled before walking the rest of the way down the stairs. Now, the memories came rushing into my head in a giant deluge of Christmas delight mixed with some humor and a touch of apprehension, too.

"Well, stick with it. By the time the show arrives, Irene might just surprise you with her moves."

Paul William patched it up with Binky. We enjoyed a glorious dinner of beef stew, and I enjoyed a few beers too. After helping Binky clean up, I retired to my easy chair in the living room. I had built a nice fire in the fireplace. I planned to sit next to the fire, light up the Christmas tree and relax for a while. Heather Sarah asked Binky for some help with her homework, and Paul William retreated to his room. I think he was feeling better now, but still licking his wounds a little.

The quiet time would do him good.

I sat in my easy chair, but the words of Paul William would not leave my mind.

She calls this part of the show, 'Waltzing at Christmastime.'

Once more, the ghosts swirled around the room and off. I went again to a time and place long ago. A memory of when, I too, had to experience a wonderful adventure of my own, "Waltzing at Christmastime."

"Now, Paul John Henson, I know that you are best friends with Harry and that you two are extremely close, and I do not want to put you on the spot here, especially so in front of your best friend."

Mrs. Woodford furrowed her brow at me and stopped pacing in front of us. She wagged her finger at me. Despite her words, she *was* going to put me on the spot in front of Harry.

Harry M. Redmond Junior wiggled nervously in the seat next to me. I could see the big dope out of the corner of my eye. As usual, Harry's spurious antics had put us in, as dear Mum would say, "A bit of a sticky wicket."

"However, Paul John, I am afraid that I will need to punish you too, unless you tell me exactly what happened. After all, you were the one that Miss Pilgrim caught with your hands on the picture. I feel that this is unfair but you will leave me little choice in this matter. Since September, you have been an exemplary student. I checked with all of your teachers and you are a straight-A student. It would be a shame to have such a blemish on your record."

Mrs. Woodford poured a little roundabout empathy on my situation as she moved in for the kill shot.

Harry and I sat together in the office of the Vice Principal of County Technical and Vocational school. Mrs. Woodford held that Vice Principal title tightly within the grasp of her hands, and she was a master at manipulating the truth out of a sticky wicket situation. Right now, it was not looking too swift for either of us. We were in our freshman year of trade school. It was the first week of December, and in the back of my mind, I knew that since school began in September, this was already Harry's third time sitting in front of Mrs. Woodford. Harry squirmed nervously once more. I remained silent . . . for now.

Since we both were trade school students enrolled into the vocational programs, we had our trade classes for the majority of the day, but the State of New Jersey mandated certain subjects for all students. The mandated subjects included four years of English, Health, Physical Education and two years of mathematics and United States History.

Miss Pilgrim was our English teacher and her timing today was perfect. Perfect for Miss Pilgrim but imperfect for Harry and Paul. She walked into the class, just as I had jumped out of my seat, in order to switch the picture mounted over the classroom door, of a bikini-clad woman, posing on the beach, back to the original picture of President Abraham Lincoln. I was tall enough to reach it without a chair and if I had been a few seconds quicker, all would have been well. Harry had put the bikini-clad chick up there in place of Honest Abe, and I was trying to save his ass. Miss Pilgrim caught me red-handed, I remained mum on the details, but Harry's snickers and the fact that the picture of Honest Abe was sitting next to his desk, caused Miss Pilgrim to decide to send, both of us to Mrs. Woodford's office to sort out the details of this particular Harry and Paul adventure.

I studied Mrs. Woodford very carefully while she began, once again, to pace in front of us. Somehow, she was going to extract the truth from us. The pacing was an interesting ploy as it built the suspense factor.

Mrs. Woodford was a widow. She lost her husband to combat in the Pacific during World War Two. Her husband was a Marine and the third wave of landing on the Island of Palau did not go as planned. His honor and his blood remain forever in the ocean waves that now gently touch the sand of that island. Mrs. Woodrow always wore an American flag pin and a United States Marine Corps pin on the lapel of her dresses. You could see the pins there, shining in honor and worn as such. She was, in my opinion, a very nice woman, very fair and obviously very strong in her courage and will. She was still quite attractive, yet she never remarried. I think it was the honor that hung over her heart that prevented her from doing so. Her honor was actually a shroud to her soul. I felt awful for not telling the story, but as much as I liked Mrs. Woodford and wanted to spill the beans, I still felt extremely loyal to Harry.

"Well, I guess your silence speaks volumes. It will be a punishment for both of you. I suspect that Paul John is protecting you, Harry. Paul John, I understand your loyalty and I do not like to do this, especially at this time of year. I know that you are working hard as a volunteer on the scenery and lighting on the upcoming Christmas pageant for the school, but you leave me little choice. I will assign you both detentions and Paul John you will need to advise Mr. Grossi that you will not be able to. . .."

"I did it, Mrs. Woodford! I put the picture of the beautiful chick up there and Paul was trying to switch the picture back to Abe Lincoln when Miss Pilgrim caught him. He was just doing the right thing. I am to blame, not Paul. I am sorry for my stunt. It was wrong. I love Honest Abe Lincoln. But man, oh man, that chick was a knockout. Did ya see the picture? Her chest and backside are amazing!" Harry burst into the conversation and spilled the truth in a billowing crash of emotion. Talk about an epic fall. It was as if all the wheels rolled off the Harry blabber bus at once. After doing so, Harry looked at me and said, "Thanks, Paul. I can't let ya hang for my crime. I know how you are such an old lady and how much you enjoy that Christmas pageant stuff."

Mrs. Woodford held back a smile and with great effort, she forced it from her lips.

"Okay, Harry. Thank you for the confession and no, I did not see the picture. I do not need the intricate details and will simply take your word for it."

"Yeah, yeah, yeah, poor Honest Abe. He didn't stand a prayer. I was just tryin' to liven up the class. Dangling particles are not too interesting."

"It is dangling participles, Harry. I would not think volunteering for work at the Christmas pageant qualifies, Paul as acting as if he was an old lady. I would apologize to your friend for such a remark and find his volunteering for the work, quite school-spirited." Mrs. Woodford waggled a finger in the direction of Harry once more, and Harry whipped up the most insincere apology in the history of the spoken word.

"Sorry, twenty-seven, it is not only that particular kinda volunteering that makes ya an old lady, though."

I nodded and said to Mrs. Woodford, "It is fine, Mrs. Woodford. Harry has called me that since we were ten years old."

"Well, moving on . . . since Harry has confessed to his actions, and has been painfully honest, perhaps, too honest with some of his words . . . I will not punish Paul John for trying to correct Harry's attempts to divert an English lesson. I also will not assign detention to Harry or any suspensions."

Mrs. Woodford zoomed in close to Harry just as the big dope broke into a wide smile. Something told me she was about to wipe that smile off his smug puss.

"However, Harry M. Redmond Junior, I want a five-hundred-word minimum essay composed on the life and accomplishments of Abraham Lincoln. After all, you just said how much you love, President Abraham Lincoln. You will compose the research paper with intense research, footnotes, bibliography, and proper formatting and the paper will be on my desk by next Tuesday at four in the afternoon."

Harry tried to force a smile, and I held one back. Mrs. Woodford caught me out of the corner of her eye, and she winked at me. She was very cool. With one finger in the air, Mrs. Woodford sealed Harry's fate for another day or two.

"In addition, I want ten perfect examples of dangling participles. All used in sentences and clearly identified. And no help from Paul John!"

Harry bowed his head and in a voice of defeat, Harry whispered, "Yes, Mrs. Woodford."

I thought, 'Ha! No help from me! Harry did not know a dangling participle from a spaceship. This was going to cost the big lug. Big time.'

"Let this be a warning! Harry, if you return to my office for any further adventures, and if you implicate Paul John into any more of your sideshows, then that will be it. A note will go home to your father and sisters and I will suspend you. Perfect behavior, Harry. Perfect. Please listen carefully. Absolutely. Perfect. Behavior. Cooperation and respect with capital letters. No more lewd comments about women, no outspoken critiquing of female body parts and no outbursts of lust. Is this all clear to you?"

"Yes, Mrs. Woodford."

"Good, you are both dismissed, and Harry, I will look forward to reading and reviewing the paper and your English work next Tuesday. I can assure you that it will be the highlight of my day. Now, I think you two can still make your physical education class. I will write notes to Mr. Gatemann and Miss Pilgrim and drop them off in order to explain the situation," Mrs. Woodford said with a wide smile.

We both thanked Mrs. Woodford, and she nodded and signaled for us to stand up. She led us to the door and opened the door. With a wave, she released us back into the world.

At least Harry waited until we made it out of the main office and about halfway up the hallway before he said what I already knew he was going to say.

"I am gonna, need ya help with that work stuff. No way that I can do that stuff. Mrs. Woodford knows that, right?"

I kept my eyes straight ahead and at first did not answer Harry. I figured the least I could do was to let him boil a little for what he put me through today.

"Um, Paul. Um, twenty seven. Ya are gonna help me, right?"

"Maybe."

Harry playfully pushed me and we stopped at the end of the main hallway.

"C'mon, man, I apologized and confessed to doing it. That ought to count a little."

I smiled and said, "It does, yes, but this is still going to cost you big time."

"Whadda ya mean? I mean . . . by big time? I can put in a good word for ya with Linda Alcatraz. She thinks ya hot and man, her chest and ass are amazing!"

I shook my head and dismissed the thought.

"I don't care about Linda. I have Maureen and Maureen is a hundred times better looking than Linda is. I want one year of you promising that you will never call me an old lady. One entire year."

Harry's mouth dropped open, and his eyes bugged out.

"Shit, Paul! That is friggin' impossible! One year! C'mon, we gotta talk 'bout this. After all, I mean we are like brothers and it is nearly. . . .."

Mr. John Gatemann was our Physical Education instructor. The man never met a whistle that he did not like. He came out of the womb with a whistle in his mouth. He went to bed with a whistle hanging around his neck, and took a shower with it, went to church with it and blew the whistle at the pastor to, "Speed up the sermon! Come on lard-ass, double time those words!" As a little babe, I do not think he actually spoke a first word; or cried out; instead, he blew a whistle at his poor mum whenever he needed a diaper change.

After a twenty-five-year career as a drill instructor in the United States Army, Mr. Gatemann, or "Sarge" as some of his fellow teachers called him, (we were about to find out that there was one teacher who had a pet name for good, ole, Sarge) somehow managed to utilize the G.I. Bill and go to college. There, he obtained his teaching education and certification and now, his main objective in life was screaming "incentives and motivational words" at a group of losers, lazy, lard-ass, trade school students (or so he called us) and blowing that incessant whistle.

Thank you, G.I. Bill. . ..

Political correctness and hurtsy-wurtsy feelings did not exist in our school, nor did these feelings exist in our day and age, and if I did ever complain to my old man about how tough Mr. Gatemann was, my father would go to school, thank, and then congratulate Mr. Gatemann for beating our silly asses. After comparing "Army Stories," the two of them would go out for beers together. The two of them were from the same exact mold.

Mr. Gatemann's chest and shoulders were as wide as the State of Montana. His muscles had muscles and his waist was narrow and tight. He looked like an upside-down bowling pin. He shaved his head and face until they were raw from a razor burn. A hair did not stand a chance of existing on the man's face or head for more than ten minutes without getting razor-whacked. Mr. Gatemann's skill at screaming at helpless recruits in the military for all those years and calling them horrible and offensive names carried over quite well into his civilian career. The man was an incredibly talented multi-tasker, who could yell general gibberish, insult you and all of your relatives, blow a whistle, and speak a string of ten consecutive cuss words all in one breath.

Our first meeting in September did not go too swift. Mr. Gatemann assembled us in formation, scanned our sad-sack group, took one look at my shoulder-length hair and budding beard and facial hair, and immediately targeted me as a "Hippie." I was used to it and I had an answer for it. The old adage of, "Don't judge a book" . . . you know the rest. I was still many years away from realizing my dream of becoming a professional hockey player, but I was a solid athlete. It only took Mr. Gatemann a few sessions of screaming at me, running me, blowing his whistle in my face like a steam locomotive, push upping and pull upping me to near death and general physical abuse to realize that he could not break me. After an initial assault and relentless pounding, he eased up and our relationship changed for the better. It came down to long, impassioned lectures in front of my locker that generally all began and ended the same way.

"Henson, sooner or later you will have to cut all that hair off. Why not do it now? People misjudge you. They look at you and see a wild, long-haired, hippie freak, weirdo, and in reality, you are one of the finest natural athletes that I have ever seen. You should consider college or playing football or the military."

"No, thank you, Mr. Gatemann, but I am not going to cut my hair. My family cannot afford college and I am going to be a professional hockey goaltender and I plan to learn a trade as a backup until I can turn pro."

Mr. Gatemann persisted.

"Ice hockey! C'mon, Henson, that is a pipe dream. This is New Jersey not Canada. Does your long-haired ass need a geography lesson? Ice hockey is a brutal sport, best left to barbarians to beat the living hell outta each other. That is a waste of a gifted athletic body. You will be a basket case of injuries by the time you are twenty-five. Football is much better or basketball. You are already six-feet-five, or something or other. Ya taller than trees. Even better yet . . . you should join the Army! With your leadership skills, athletic skills and smarts, you will be an officer in no time. Of course, you will need to cut your hair and shave that beard and facial nonsense."

Those chats became commonplace. He did not give up easily.

Harry was also a superior athlete and although Harry always had that famous "Smart-Ass" reputation, Mr. Gatemann generally left Harry alone. Jeffrey Porter, who was our other friend, and who was the final third of our boyhood trio, was also a fine athlete and Jeff received a free pass from most of the more brutal "lessons" inflicted by Mr. Gatemann. Often, we found that Mr. Gatemann would pick Harry, Jeff, or me to demonstrate some physical education technique or for us to lead the rest of the class in exercises or calisthenics.

Thankfully, Mrs. Woodford had already delivered the explanation note by the time that Harry and I arrived in the gym or our reception would have been even worse than what it was.

"Henson! Redmond Junior! You two losers have exactly forty-three seconds to change into your gym clothes and sneakers and get your lily-white asses out here to show the rest of these losers how to do a rope climb," Mr. Gatemann shouted as Harry and I burst through the gymnasium door. Mr. Gatemann then blew his whistle, pointed in the direction of the locker room, and shouted, "Triple-time! And Henson, tie that mop of hair back!"

Harry and I nodded and sprinted to the locker room to change. We caught a glimpse of Jeff standing in line with the rest of the class and while Jeff was not in the same English class as Harry and I were, the word of Harry's latest antics spread quickly throughout the masses. Jeff smiled and waved his hand in our direction, as if to wish us good luck.

"Geez, Paul! Where the hell did he pull the forty-three second time frame bullshit out of? Random ass time, huh?"

I nodded and I am not sure of the exact time frame, but it was a quick change for the two of us. We sprinted out to meet the class just as Mr. Gatemann was coaching poor Joey Dexter up the rope. Joey's arms were straining and shaking and his face was so red it looked as if he was about to pop a blood vessel out of his head. We were lucky because we joined the formation around the ropes and Mr. Gatemann hardly noticed us because he was embroiled in "coaching" Joey.

"Oh, c'mon, Dexter. I mean, for the love of Heaven, you have only managed to climb two lousy feet off the floor! Arm strength, Dexter! Suck it up! Use your feet! Someday, Dexter. Someday, your big ass will make it up that rope and ring that bell! C'mon, Dexter. Suck it up, man!"

Another ear-piercing blow of the whistle sounded just as poor Joey lost his grip and hit the floor with a loud "thud."

Mr. Gatemann shook his head, turned and looked at me, and as someone gave Joey a hand and pulled him back up on his feet, our fearless, whistle-blowing leader said,

"Henson! Get your long-haired ass up that rope, ring that stupid-ass bell at the top and show these bananas how to do it!"

"Yes, sir, Mr. Gatemann," I said.

Just as I scrambled over to the rope, took it in my hand, and prepared to climb to the top of the gym . . . it happened. There was a knock on the door in the wall. There was never a knock on the door in the wall. Ever. Moreover, even more shocking was the fact that the door opened and through it walked the stunning and gorgeous Miss Penelope Wigglesworth. Miss Wigglesworth came through the door!

The wall was a huge, accordion type folding door contraption that divided the "boy's side" of the gymnasium from the "girl's side" of the gym. Our school was a county school and while we had our trade side, and the vocational arts, the school also taught typing, business administration, office skills, hair styling, cosmetology and other such types of professions and skills on the "girl's side." While our mandatory classes were coed, classes such as Music, English, Health, History, and some other classes such as Art, Music and the Culinary Arts, our Physical Education class was separate. The other side of the wall was the Holy Land. That was where the girls were! In their skimpy gym clothes! And when they ran around, fantastic "parts" jiggled and bounced!

Even holier to all of us was, "Up on the Hill." That was where the county college preparatory high school was located. They were entirely separate from us. That was where the incredibly beautiful people attended high school. We heard that all the young women up there walked around in mink coats, sleek black dresses, high-heel stilettos and pearl necklaces. All the young men had fancy watches, wore the best sneakers, had expensive school jackets, and wore gold braces to straighten their choppers, and all the upper-classmen drove brand-new sports cars.

Christmas Cocktails

We walked to school or took the city bus and had crooked choppers. It was the way that it was. Crooked choppers and slightly dull, yellow teeth were some sort of a rite of passage. We were poor kids, and they were rich kids. It was a simple formula.

The county of our residence had the poor cities and the rich towns. Up on the Hill was where the rich kids attended school, from the affluent communities. It was strictly off-limits to us poorer schleps.

I froze with the rope in my hand and stopped dead in my tracks at the sight of Miss Wigglesworth. The woman was so hot that she could melt a glacier in mere seconds. Mr. Gatemann stopped in mid-whistle, his face turned red, his eyes bugged out of his head and the one hair that the razor missed on the top of his head stood straight up in the air. I swear that I saw that one hair doing pull-ups. I swear that it did.

All the guys in the entire class froze, too. We all remained frozen within an aura of shock, awe, and intense admiration. A goddess walked amongst mere teenagers. Male teenagers, full of raging and somewhat wild hormones and growing imaginations.

"Yoo, hoo, Johnnie!"

Johnnie? Who the hell is Johnnie?

Every single guy in the gym class turned and looked at a red-faced Mr. Gatemann.

The one hair on his head stopped doing pull-ups, push-ups and squat-thrusts, and it slowly floated back into place on his scalp.

"Ah, ah, sorry, I mean, Mr. Gatemann! Please pardon the interruption!" Miss Wigglesworth spouted as she melted hearts while strolling across the gym floor in our direction. The alluring wiggle of her glorious backside kept time, as if it was a perfectly calibrated metronome.

I thought, 'Ah, okay, please go ahead and interrupt all you want!'

Out of the corner of my eye, with the rope still tightly held within my hands, I spotted a weak-kneed and open-mouthed Harry M. Redmond Junior. Jeff was not faring much better, but I think Harry was bracing his massive body on Jeff for support. I wonder if I recall the specific details of that lesson in resuscitation. . ..

Miss Penelope Wigglesworth was the women's Physical Education Instructor. This gorgeous woman was the object of every man's desire. Young and old. Far and wide. Perfect teeth, perfect facial bone structure, perfect ocean-blue eyes, flowing auburn-colored hair that fell in graceful tresses upon her shoulders. A glorious glow of intoxicating beauty flowed from her perfect face. Miss Wigglesworth had a perfect hourglass type of figure. Her legs began somewhere near Houston, Texas and ended just before Butte, Montana. Her hips flowed, other parts jiggled and bounced, men's hearts fluttered and her chest arrived about twenty-seven seconds before the rest of her did.

There she went, strolling across the gym floor, strutting her stuff in her tight athletic shorts, her tanned, long legs glowing, and a whistle on a chain tucked between her amazing twin peaks of glory.

Lucky whistle.

All she had to do was to ask any male to jump and collectively the answers would resound in a gentle roar, "How high? How far? Where?"

Mr. Gatemann was a mess.

I looked over at him and then at Harry and then scanned the eyes of my classmates. I swear Mr. Gatemann's left eye rotated clockwise in his head and his right eye spun counterclockwise. Our fearless leader managed to regain control over his eyeballs; he looked over at me and waved a hand in the air as Miss Wigglesworth walked closer.

"Stand down, Henson," Mr. Gatemann mumbled. While nodding and dropping my grip on the rope, I suddenly thought that Mr. Gatemann's statement had a double meaning.

Covertly, I checked just to make sure.

No, I was good.

Mr. Gatemann cast a stern eye and a fierce look at the rest of the class and he warned us with a single word, "Menssss." Mr. Gateman always added multiple s letters at the end of the word men. Then he followed it with a glance at Harry and a foreboding waggle of his finger in Harry's direction. In a voice just above a whisper with a hint of his trademark growl, Mr. Gatemann said, "Redmond Junior. I am warning your horny and sorry-ass. Remain. Under. Control."

Harry nodded in acknowledgement. This was going to be good.

"I am so sorry, to just barge in here," Miss Wigglesworth said as she flipped her hair and smiled that glorious smile as she arrived in the circle of testosterone and bouncing hormones gathered around the rope climb. "But something glorious has just come up and I need your help."

All of us groaned at her words and their hidden but exact meaning.

"I promise it will be very exciting! I have a proposition."

Every single guy's right arm and hand went up in the air at exactly the same time.

"Oh my, such a willing group of young men," Miss Wigglesworth said with a coy giggle and a flutter of her eyebrows.

"No apologies required. Why, yes, of course, this class is ready for a mission assignment at a moment's notice . . . Pene . . . le . . . ah, I mean . . . Miss Wigglesworth. This is an upstanding group of finely tuned, athletic young men," Mr. Gatemann made an outstanding recovery and elevated us from our previous low standing. Losers to an upstanding group of finely tuned, athletic young men in the flash of an eye, within a glorious wiggle of an amazing female backside and a bounce of some female breasts.

"How might we be of assistance?"

While posing and flipping her hair, Miss Wigglesworth explained, "As you know, it is the most wonderful time of the year! This is going to be a glorious Christmastime. As our beloved Christmas pageant looms ever closer, Miss Redbud approached me today and proposed a joint effort between the Physical Education Department and the Music Department. Miss Redbud would like to introduce a musical interlude of an elegant display of ballroom waltzing during one of the highlights of the Christmas pageant." She stopped speaking and scanned the eyes of the class for a reaction. We all vaguely heard what she was saying. Something about a waltz, and the Christmas pageant, and that old grouch of a music teacher, Miss Redbud, but mostly we remained focused on other aspects of Miss Wigglesworth. Much more interesting aspects than mere words. It did not much matter what Miss Wigglesworth was proposing to us. I knew that we were in.

Off she went once again, explaining this glorious opportunity, "As you might recall, I was a dancing champion in college and waltzing and dancing is a wonderful, cardiovascular exercise. I thought we might join forces, instruct our classes on the finer points of waltzing and then pair off the young men with the young women and those that prove to be good dancers and would like to participate in the pageant . . . might do so. After all, we have to do our best. Up on the Hill, is having a full-scale Broadway quality presentation of A Christmas Carol, complete with their one-hundred-member choir and a seventy-two-member backing orchestra. The word on the street is that they hired professional musicians, screenplay writers, music directors, set designers and costume outfitters. We will have, well, Miss Redbud on the piano and our little Christmas presentation and now, our waltzing class."

Miss Wigglesworth paused with her words in order to

flip her hair and wiggle her hips a little and with a renewed coyness to her voice; the gorgeous woman finished the invitation.

"And of course, we will have *me*. I plan to wear this darling little Santa Claus outfit, with a red mini-dress that I found."

In unison, the entire class gasped, and Harry almost collapsed. Off once again went Mr. Gatemann's eyeballs with the curious rotation issue. I bet that he could make the medical books with that affliction.

Once more, after making a remarkable recovery from a Santa Claus outfit and red mini-dress induced vision of lust, our fearless, whistle-toting leader spouted off like a boiling teakettle, "I think this is a fine idea, Miss Wigglesworth. I am all for superior cardiovascular exercise, of all sorts, in order to whip these loser bums, ah, I mean, my class into shape. We are all devoted to supporting our school and my men are ready for the mission at hand! Besides, we cannot allow an upstaging of our beloved school by a mere professional production, induced by a superior budget allocation and the majority of the taxpayer's monies going on Up on the Hill! After all, we have Miss Redbud and her piano, you in that Santa Claus outfit and red, ah, ah, I mean, your outstanding . . . ah, dancing skills, and besides, it is Christmas and we have our honor!" He blew his whistle loudly, waved his arm and hand in an assembling command, and yelled, "Mensssss! You heard, Miss Wigglesworth! We have a mission. Lead on, Penel . . . ah, Miss Wigglesworth. We will follow."

Oh yeah, we will follow.

"Oh, goody, this will be such fun!" Miss Wigglesworth said as she wiggled off in the direction of the door.

We stormed the door like a stampede of rampaging buffaloes while Mr. Gatemann frantically blew his incessant whistle in an effort to have us fall in and march through the door in an orderly semblance of a military formation. After realizing the futility of such an endeavor, Mr. Gatemann, too, broke into a double-time hustle that slowly progressed into a full-out sprint. We popped through the door like corks bursting from champagne bottles on New Year's Day; we emerged on the other side of the wall and scanned the wonderful view of the Holy Land that appeared before us. A glorious land, populated by young women . . . all dressed in skimpy gym clothes! This sure beat the living stuffing out of the electrical shop and soldering wires! Rope climbing? Never heard of such a thing. What the hell is a rope?

At the head of the gym floor was a well-worn piano, which a custodian just finished rolling out onto the floor, while another custodian carried the piano bench. Miss Marigold Redbud carefully instructed the maintenance crew on the exact positioning of her beloved musical instrument.

Miss Redbud was the epitome of a spinster. If you opened the dictionary and looked up the definition of a spinster, I was quite sure that there was a picture of Miss Marigold Redbud, right there next to the explanation. Around her neck was the obligatory stringed necklace of white pearls that rested upon her huge bosom and competed for space with her stringed eyeglasses whenever Miss Redbud did not wear the glasses over her eyes. She dyed her hair a bizarre yellow-gold color that was hard to classify and her hair looked as if it was a molded football helmet upon her head, but the top of her hair went up in great layers similar to the swirls of ice cream on top of an ice cream cone. Miss Redbud always had a gaudy costume jewelry brooch pinned to her paisley-patterned, high-necked dress, and today's brooch was a musical note embellished with a Christmas wreath. From her ears dangled some earrings that actually were miniature Christmas ornaments. Red, gold and green, the earrings aggressively tugged and pulled at her ear lobes. She had the remarkable talent of being able to tinkle the keys while simultaneously glaring at us out of the corners of her eyes. She was the type of woman that you never saw her teeth. When she spoke, when she sang, and on the rare occasion that she smiled, Miss Redbud hid her teeth. Honestly, her face remained in a perpetual frown and I guessed that she built the frown over a perilous lifetime of trying to teach a team of business and trade school students how to appreciate music, to keep time and to sing.

No wonder she frowned so much.

"Now, now, ladies and gentleman, please let's have the ladies on the right side of the piano and the gentleman all over to the left. Please, let's create orderly lines," Miss Wigglesworth explained as she tried to form us into some organized fashion. We were too busy gaping at the view of legs and tight gym shorts and the ladies were too busy gaping at the muscles and tight gym shorts on the guys.

"Stand aside, Penol . . . ah, Miss Wigglesworth! I will handle this!" Mr. Gatemann stepped in with his ear-piercing whistle and a few loud commands. Within seconds, he had the newly joined gym classes lined up in a perfect military formation.

"Oh, Johnnie, I mean, Mr. Gatemann, I love how you are always in command of everything," Miss Wigglesworth praised her comrade.

Commence eye spinning.

Harry strategically used his ever-diligent "chick" radar to seek out the voluptuous Linda Alcatraz and by trampling, pushing and otherwise rolling over classmates, Harry strategically managed to line up directly opposite Linda. Jeff was just past the center in the middle of the guys and I was dead last in one of the lines, all the way on the other side of the row of young women.

And I was very happy to be right where I was. Surprisingly, I was an experienced dancer. My sister Dorothy was a fantastic dancer, and we were both music fans. From the time we were little children, my sister and I danced together and Dottie was so good that I think that I learned to be a decent dancer by attrition. Dottie and I won a dance competition at our church last year, when we pulled off an awesome Foxtrot, and while I was not nearly as gifted a dancer as my sister was, I could hold my own. Still, I had no actual intentions of standing out in the crowd here. I wanted to blend. As if a six-feet-five, long-haired and slightly bearded hippie could actually blend.

Miss Redbud spoke in a loud voice, but it was a bored monotone. A voice, refined over many, many years of leading boring music classes filled with obnoxious and bored students. Her voice was similar to the sound that your car's tires made when hitting the asphalt on the highway. At first, you paid full attention, and then it became rhythmic, constant, but ultimately unexciting.

"We are going to perform the basic steps required for a waltz while being led by Miss Wigglesworth and under the command of Mr. Gatemann," Miss Redbud instructed us, "I will play the Skater's Waltz, Opus number one-hundred and eighty-three. This is a magnificent piece, composed by the French composer, Émile Waldteufel. This is a Christmas pageant and our interlude will mimic skaters gliding upon a frozen pond. The waltz is in three-quarter time, about thirty bars per minute. I will play a sample so everyone gets a feel for the music."

Miss Redbud sat on the bench, flexed her fingers, and loudly cracked her knuckles. Of course, Harry was flirting with Linda Alcatraz the entire time and not paying any attention to Miss Redbud, until Mrs. Woodford strolled into the gym, to check out the buzz about this incredible event. Vice Principal Woodford stood directly in front of Harry. She folded her arms across her mighty chest and cleared her throat. Linda stopped Harry within mid-flirt, and she pointed at Mrs. Woodford. Harry glanced over and immediately straightened his back and nodded.

Mrs. Woodford first pointed at her own eyes, then in the direction of Harry and she mouthed, "I am watching everything you do, Harry. Everything."

After playing a few introductory bars and notes of the Skater's Waltz, Miss Redbud turned the instruction over to Miss Wigglesworth, who directed us in the first steps of the simple box step.

This was a piece of cake.

It utilized the same basic steps as many dances did. The guys all delighted in watching Miss Wigglesworth as she delightfully bounced around in front of the class and told us, as well as demonstrated, all of the basic steps.

"Very simple now. Left foot, one, right foot, two and then left foot, three. Back right foot, four and then right, left, here we go now. Come along, Mr. Gatemann and I, will dance together and please, all of you dance in place and follow along. Miss Redbud, please, here we go, one, two and one, two, three."

Lucky man that Mr. Gatemann was. There were many starts and stops, laughs, and stumbles, but at the end of a half-an-hour or thereabouts, some of us were looking pretty snappy.

When Mr. Gatemann blew the whistle to end class and send us back into exile to the dark side, I must admit it was with just a touch of sadness. This was a most enjoyable Physical Education class. It surely beat watching Joey Dexter struggling up that stupid rope.

Off we sprinted, our fearless leader marching behind us, blowing his whistle, bellowing at us to move double-time to the showers, as Miss Wigglesworth waved to us, flipped her hair, and posed while telling all of us, "Yoo, hoo! Thank you, young men! It was a wonderful first session! We will see you all tomorrow!"

We dashed off at double-time with a spring in our steps, a touch of romance in our hearts, and I do think we were all propelled by more than just a touch of Christmas magic too.

"Will I see you all tomorrow?"

Oh yes, you will!

"Very simple now. Left foot, one, right foot, two and then left foot, three. Back right foot, four and then right, left, here we go now."

Christmas Cocktails

Lunchtime in the cafeteria was a sacred time for us. Time to eat, time to relax, time to have arm-wrestling competitions to declare a table champion by the end of the school year, time to talk sports, time to talk about the young women, and time to be with your friends. It was time out in the busy life of a trade school student. Reserved only for freshmen, sophomores and a handful of juniors. All too soon, we would look back fondly on that time. For the majority of the last two years of the trade program and vocational schooling, we no longer would have our lunchtime meetings and social time. The school would launch us off to our actual workplaces, to find our niche in life and within the trades, young men rushed into manhood and a lunchtime break in the cafeteria would no longer fit into a crammed school and work day. Looking back, perhaps we all grew up way too soon. Right now, lunchtime had a different subject, and to Harry M. Redmond Junior, it was time to boast and engage in his favorite hobby. Working the angles to court the latest young woman in his life.

"Oh, yeah, yeah, yeah, of course, while I am checking out Linda's tookus, and figuring out how when we dance that I can accidently steal a squeeze, Paul is over there making out like he is the world's greatest waltzer. He is some kinda twinkle-toes. All I care 'bout is the chicks and Miss Wigglesworth. Did ya see her chest bounce when she showed us those dance steps? Anyway, ya gotta give, Paul, a break. He can't help it cuz, he is an old. . .."

I approached "our table" with my tray, and Jeff elbowed Harry in the ribs when he spotted me. Harry stopped in mid-proclamation and I smiled.

I was going to relish this year of bliss.

Thank you, Mrs. Woodford.

"Hey, don't stop on my account, there, number thirty-five. It will be very lonely writing that paper on Honest Abe and doing English assignments all by ya lonesome. Something tells me that Linda Alcatraz and her fine backside and a huge chest, will only go so far."

"Hey, sorry, twenty-seven. I did not finish it. Besides, ya can't expect me to stop on a dime after a lifetime of spewing my insults."

I nodded my head, slipped my tray on the table, and sat down.

"I gotcha, Harry. Do not forget that while all of you clowns call me an old lady and are chasing these young women . . . I have Maureen. Every. Single. Night. Talk about a woman! So, exactly, who is the old lady here?"

I hit them where it hurt.

My girlfriend, Maureen Zipperelli, was not only older than we were, and of exotic Italian descent, but she was beautiful beyond description as well as very voluptuous. The entire table sighed at the mere thought of the gorgeous and captivating Maureen Zipperelli.

Case dismissed.

Harry leaned in as I grabbed my sandwich and took a bite of it. He wanted advice, as did the rest of the table. Despite the good-natured insults and kidding, the perception was that I was a leader of sorts. It was obvious that the waltzing with the young women was capturing all of our spirits.

With an air of sincerity in his voice, Harry asked, "Say, Paul, in all seriousness, where is this waltzing stuff going? I mean, what do ya think our chances are of Miss

Christmas Cocktails

Wigglesworth picking us? Ya know, what do ya think of our chances to pair up with a gal and dance at the pageant? Chances are you have it nailed, cuz ya ass can dance, but the rest of us are lead foots. You don't care 'bout picking out a chick, cuz ya got, Maureen, but the rest of us are in our glory. I am counting on dancing with Linda and getting a date with her after all of this is over. Been chasing her for a long time."

"Then, I guess youse guys need to quit messing around, pay attention, buckle up, and get it done. Especially you, Harry. Mrs. Woodford has her gun sights on you, and she is not letting you go. One mess-up around these gals, one rude comment about their bodies, one supposedly slipup grab of Linda's ass and you are history. Honestly, it is really not that hard to do. A few steps. Pick a chick you want to dance with, set your sights on her and do it. You might want to keep in mind that the gal that you want to pair up with might not be too swift at dancing. Some other chick out there might just fool you. The way that I figure it is that Miss Wigglesworth will pick at least ten couples out of our group. That is only a guess. Hey, Mr. Gatemann has a solid point. It is about our honor. Those hot shots, Up on the Hill have everything. However, we have some stuff too. Besides, they do not have Miss Wigglesworth, and for that matter, Miss Redbud too. She might be an old grouch, but she can sure play the hell out of that old piano. We can't let them rich guys and gals outshine us. Now, can we? We can pack the gymnasium for our Christmas pageant too!"

I struck a nerve.

This was not only about the young women, but this was about a challenge.

This was about our honor. Honestly, in addition to our honor, it was about the young women and Miss Wigglesworth in that Santa Claus outfit and red mini-dress too.

After all, honest is honest.

For the next few days, Miss Wigglesworth worked us near to death. We sweat up a storm waltzing in our little boxes. There was no doubt that waltzing and dancing were great exercise! Miss Redbud played her heart out and Mr. Gatemann blew his whistle and danced with Miss Wigglesworth.

Lucky guy.

After five or so days of practicing steps in our little boxes, and being able to play all the beats and the notes of the Skater's Waltz in our heads and with our hands, the atmosphere began to change. Slowly and rather elegantly, the entire scene took on a surreal magic to it all. No longer was it about guys, gals, Miss Wigglesworth, and Mr. Gatemann and his incessant whistle.

It was about doing our best.

It was about our honor.

As the countdown time, to the Christmas break and to the Christmas pageant slowly wound down and the big day loomed closer, Miss Wigglesworth hinted at the day of reckoning on the horizon. The day where we would pair off and actually waltz with our partners.

"Have a great weekend! Next Friday is the pageant, so on Monday, we will select partners and pair-up for the final practices before the pageant," Miss Wigglesworth announced with a seductive pose and a flip of her hair. It was now a Friday about ten days before Christmas and a week or so before the Christmas holiday from school.

Oh boy, the pressure was on now!

Over the weekend, I finished the essay on Honest Abe and gave Harry eight examples of dangling participles. The big lug could figure out the last two.

I was in a unique position because I was still working with Mr. Grossi and the electrical crew from electrical class on the technical support of the pageant. As a result, I had a behind the scene's insight into the Christmas pageant. As far as Christmas presentations went, it was much of the standard fare. A small choir, a few secular songs, one or two religious' songs, (this was still the day and age where you could mention religion in a public school without the world crumbling and a slew of lawsuits filed), a reading or two of some emotional Christmas-themed pieces and a small skit about sharing and giving to those who need it the most. The interlude for the waltzing was, in my opinion, well timed between some winter-themed readings and the skit. Miss Redbud might have been a one-woman-band with some late-in-the-game assistance now from Miss Wigglesworth, but together, they did a fine job. What our school lacked in numbers, we made up in dedication and hard work. We might not have the financial backing, professional clout, or the horsepower that the school Up on the Hill had, but we were going to give them a run for the money.

Moreover, we had an ace in the deck with Miss Wigglesworth in that Santa Claus outfit and red mini-dress!

However, we also had one more hidden ace in the deck.

Miss Margaret Wally was for lack of any other description, like the side of a mountain. A very large mountain. There was no way around describing Margaret. It was not about being mean, instead; it was simply being factual. Her arms were huge, her head was huge, her legs were huge, her breasts were huge, her belly was huge and when she navigated the floor, it was in great, thunderous, colossal steps that shook the very walls and floors of our old school. Margaret had long black hair that she always tied in a ponytail. She might have been the only person around our school that had longer hair than I did. Her face was bulging and her giant jowls shook and wiggled when she walked, moved, and talked. Her eyes were deep in her head and you could see them in there somewhere. Behind the layers of human skin and huge rolls of extra flesh, there were eyes.

Somewhere.

Margaret was in the typing class in business school and by all testimonies and accounts; she was a wizard of the keyboard. For a person with giant fingers, the word was that no person could out type her. Her fingers flew on the keys, and even the typing teacher, Mrs. Buckholtz, could not keep up with her. The word was that Margaret could hit the keys at a speed of well over eighty-five words per minute without error.

A record setter.

I found it all very interesting because there was another aspect of Margaret Wally that was beyond compare.

Her voice.

She could speak and sing like an angel.

A record setter in typing class and a show stopper on the stage. I am not kidding that the world stopped turning when Margaret spoke, or she belted out a song. Naturally, she had a long solo during the musical set of the Christmas pageant. Miss Redbud knew talent when she heard it. I would venture to say that people would pay good money to hear Margaret Wally read and sing the telephone book.

Miss Wigglesworth in that Santa Claus outfit and red mini-dress and Miss Margaret Wally with the voice of an angel. Two secret weapons!

Oh yeah, take that, Up on the Hill rich kids.

Monday morning arrived, and with nervous anticipation, we launched into the waltzing madness. When Miss Wigglesworth announced that we should split up and find a waltzing partner, it seemed as she did so with an air of joy in her voice. As if she released a bunch of young people to find not only their partners but to find a destiny of some sort. Known boyfriends and girlfriends, quickly paired off, and for the unattached, it was sort of a haphazard courting process. I was not too sure about it all and approached the crowd of eager young women with an air of slight aloofness. As if I needed to select a waltzing partner very carefully. I was not sure of why, because beforehand, I had explained to Maureen the entire situation, and my girlfriend was completely at ease with the circumstances. Maureen had full intentions on attending the Christmas pageant with Dottie and with my parents, whether; Miss Wigglesworth selected my partner and me to waltz at the event or not, so there were no layers of jealousy for Maureen attached to this at all.

For some reasons, yet unknown to me, I made my way through the frenzy and I encountered numerous gals posing and batting their eyes at me and waving while mouthing, "Hi ya, Paulie" to me. I was quite sure that many of them knew that I had a steady gal, but still they batted their eyes and posed for me. Much to the chagrin of Harry, Linda Alcatraz paused when I walked by as if she wanted to see if I stopped and asked her to be my partner as opposed to Harry. Fat chance on that one. When I continued on my way and walked by her and it was clear that I had no intentions toward her, Linda took Harry's hand and they ran out to their position on the floor. I saw Jeff meet up with and select a short, cutie with dark black hair from the hair styling class and after a brief discussion, the gal nodded and took Jeff's hand and off to their position they ran to await the next instructions from Miss Redbud, Mr. Gatemann, and Miss Wigglesworth.

There was something strangely archaic about this situation, yet in its own way, it was wondrous and beautiful too.

Before too long, there were no young men left and only two or three young women left standing on the sideline. An odd number of young women versus available young men. Miss Wigglesworth had that figured out with herself and Mr. Gatemann, Mrs. Woodford, and such as extra dancing partners. When I realized that a certain Paul John Henson was still standing alone on the sideline and I looked over and saw a very sad faced Miss Margaret Wally standing all alone, then I knew that my heart spoke to me. Without hesitation, I quickly strode across the floor and approached Margaret.

She had her head down and more than just a hint of tears in her eyes, and Margaret almost jumped out of her sneakers when I stopped in front of her and said, "Hello there, Miss Wally. Would you do Paul John Henson, a favor and waltz with me?"

Her eyes widened (yes, they were in there) and she said almost in a whisper, "Ah, ah, are you really and actually speaking to me? Did you just ask me to be your waltzing partner?"

"I did. I do think that you are the only Miss Wally here."

"But I am the ugly, fat girl left on the side that no one wants to waltz with and you are the incredibly handsome, and amazing, Paul John Henson. You are supposed to pick the most beautiful girl here. You are not supposed to waltz with some ugly, fat girl that no one wants."

I looked all around and all eyes and ears in the entire gym were on us.

The silence was deafening in the gym.

I smiled and said, "Funny, but I don't see any ugly, fat girls, nor do I see any handsome and amazing young men. I only see Margaret and Paul. Therefore, once more, I need to ask you, because I do think we are holding up this show. Do you want to waltz with me? It would be my honor to have you join me and for you to be my partner."

Her smile could have cracked ice. To say that her smile was a mile wide would be a gross understatement. In order to settle the matter, for all of time, mine was just as wide and just as powerful. Maybe even more so. I held my hand out. Margaret grasped it, and with a quick dash, we ran out to claim the last remaining position on the gym floor. We posed, and we took our positions. I waved to Miss Wigglesworth to indicate that we were ready to go. Miss Wigglesworth blew me a kiss, and Mr. Gatemann smiled and saluted us. With a loud blow on his whistle, and instructions from Miss Wigglesworth, followed by those now familiar notes on the piano. As Miss Redbud struck the first few notes, we broke into our steps.

This time with our partners.

"Very simple now. Left foot, one, right foot, two and then left foot, three. Back right foot, four and then right, left, here we go now."

We grasped hands. Miss Wally was shorter than I was by just a few inches, and heavier by quite a few pounds. She smiled and so did I. I grabbed a hair tie and tied my hair off in a ponytail and Margaret did the same. Within the first few steps, I knew that we were as one. A perfect pair. Margaret Wally, despite her huge and immense size, was as light as a feather on her feet. She virtually floated in the air. Her timing was immaculate, her steps were light and gentle, and we flowed as one. Surprise! Surprise! Miss Wally was an absolutely amazing dancer!

"Oh, Paul, you are a great dancer," Margaret said to me as we took off across the floor.

"No, I think that you are leading me, here, Margaret. You are remarkable!"

Off we went, and we did not stay in our box. We waltzed across the floor, into the nooks of the gym floor, over to the wall, past the other dancers, and off on our own. Waltzing as if we were on clouds sent from Heaven. Miss Redbud continued to play, and little did we know or even realize that all the other dancers had long stopped waltzing.

Regardless, Margaret Wally and Paul John Henson continued to waltz.

Up, down, and all around, until Miss Redbud finally ended the Skater's Waltz. It was then that we realized that we had waltzed off on our own, off to some unknown place full of Christmas waltzing magic. When we finally stopped and looked around in embarrassment, the entire class broke into loud applause. Loud and continual applause. Miss Redbud stood up from her piano bench, smiled, and applauded. Miss Redbud actually smiled! She was happy! I saw her teeth! Miss Redbud does have teeth! Miss Wigglesworth and Mr. Gatemann applauded. And Mrs. Woodford applauded too!

"I think we should do something, Paul. How embarrassing! I think we might have become overly ambitious with this. Do you think we should bow?" Margaret whispered to me, and I nodded in acknowledgement. We held hands and bowed, and after we did so, I leaned in and kissed Margaret's cheek. When I did so, the applause grew even wilder! Poor Margaret must have turned eighty different shades of red!

After recovering from the dramatic interlude, Mr. Gatemann smiled, blew his whistle and Miss Wigglesworth said, "Very simple now. Left foot, one, right foot, two and then left foot, three. Back right foot, four and then right, left, here we go now."

Word spread fast in our neighborhood. Our performance was on a Friday evening about two hours or so after the Up on the Hill performance ended. Regardless, the facts and figures stood for themselves. The attendance for our meager and comparatively, budget less, Christmas pageant trounced the major production going on "Up on the Hill." Oh yes, indeed, the fact that Miss Wigglesworth wore the now infamous Santa Claus outfit and that incredibly short red mini-dress to the pageant, combined with Margaret's magical voice and our flawless waltzing moves, might have contributed to the fact that our pageant attendance was standing room only, but hey, we nailed it. The choir sounded awesome, the skit was well acted and very effective. The stage had plain but effective sets and backdrops, designed, constructed, and installed by the students and instructors in our woodworking shops, and painted with glorious designs by the art department students and instructors. The sound system, special effects and lighting by the electronic and electric students and Mr. Grossi created a wonderful atmosphere, and they were a major hit. Miss Redbud, who came with her loosely cracked knuckles and brought her "A" game, demonstrated some fabulous piano playing and remarkable music. That piano was old and well-worn and it was not a full, seventy-two-piece orchestra, but Miss Marigold Redbud wore that sucker out. In addition to the white pearls and eyeglasses, she wore a Christmas wreath brooch pin with a piano inside of the wreath. It was very cool and I swear that we saw her smile twice. Aside from all the other fantastic elements of the Christmas pageant, (including Miss Wigglesworth's amazing outfit) the unquestionable highlight of the evening was Waltzing at Christmastime. The guys wore black suits, the gals wore red dresses, and luckily, for me, the only suit that I owned was a black one. Margaret and I both agreed with Miss Wigglesworth, and her suggestion of letting our hair down worked. We flowed across the floor, our hair following behind us for a few seconds. Of course, the old man had some fun with that, kidding me later that my hair was longer than Margaret's hair was, but it worked for the effect that Miss Wigglesworth was looking for. There were twelve couples, if you included Miss Wigglesworth and Mr. Gatemann, who waltzed together.

Lucky guy.

Mr. Gatemann looked stunningly handsome in his black suit, his trusty whistle still around his neck, along with his necktie.

Harry and Linda made the final cut, as well as Jeff and Debbie. Debbie was Jeff's new cute little new gal pal, and she certainly was a beautiful gal! Jeff played his interest in Debbie very close to the cuff. We had no idea he had his sights set on her and apparently the feelings were likewise. Debbie was petite, bubbly, with dark features and a great smile. At this point in this magical evening, we had no idea that their waltzing together was the start of a romance for the ages.

When the lights dimmed and then came back up as my fellow electrical students worked the special effects, and then Miss Redbud tinkled the keys for the opening notes of the Skater's Waltz, a quiet hush came over the crowd, in fact, over the entire world. A spotlight bounced and danced on the gym floor and then it found Margaret and me as we made the grand entrance and took the opening whirl across the floor.

I whispered to Margaret that she looked gorgeous and she smiled and blushed as she whispered, "Thank you and that she was afraid her hands were going to melt because I was too hot to hold."

Miss Wigglesworth's choreography was amazing, and as the waltzing couples gradually flowed in and joined us, we all elegantly floated across that old wooden gym floor. Near the middle of the song, within some glorious piano interlude where Miss Redbud pulled out all the stops and improvised on the melody with a bridge of some sort, the spotlight found Margaret and me once more, and while our fellow waltzing couples circled us on the outside, Margaret and I waltzed in the center. It was magical, and Margaret was amazing. She was in superior form, floating as if she was lighter than air. What an amazing athlete she was! What a beautiful young woman she was, too! Then, in an improvised and unplanned moment, Mr. Gatemann and Miss Wigglesworth waltzed to the center, bowed and "cut in" on Margaret and me! We switched partners and suddenly, I had a feeling that Maureen Zipperelli was not going to be too happy about this one. Off we went for the final whirls and steps and Miss Wigglesworth was a fabulous waltzing partner. Honestly, Margaret was a better dancer, but my goodness, Miss Wigglesworth, was stunning!

Now, I was the lucky guy!

She smiled that perfect smile and as I floated on the heavenly scent of her perfume as well as the feel of her glorious body next to mine, Miss Wigglesworth whispered to me, "Too bad, Mr. Henson that you are not about fifteen years older."

She then winked, and I almost missed a step.

We ended the Skater's Waltz. The crowd erupted into a ten-minute standing ovation, and as they would say, "We brought the house down!"

Afterwards, there were refreshments, remarkable food cooked and served up by our culinary students, and their expert instructors, and we all mingled and posed for pictures. I met Margaret's parents, they met mine, as well as Dottie, and of course, Maureen arrived to, "Reclaim me from all these gorgeous women." Maureen did so by planting a big kiss on my lips and lip locking me for quite a long time in front of the entire world.

Maureen was so aggressive.

I certainly was the envy of many of the males in attendance this evening. First with Margaret, then Miss Wigglesworth, and now the gorgeous and captivating Maureen Zipperelli hung on my arm.

The old man kidded me that I was quite the, "Lover Boy."

It was an enchanting and magical Christmas pageant evening. Full of glorious memories and spirit.

Mrs. Woodford walked over to me after the show while we were enjoying the food and drink and congratulated me on the performance, my efforts on the waltzing and with the work on the electrical lighting. With a coy smile, she added that I wrote a helluva good paper on Honest Abe. She also added with a wink and an arm around my shoulders that all of my English examples were perfect. All eight of them, but two were incorrect and old Harry was back to the books. She winked at me and laughed. Geez, Harry! The big lug could not even get two answers correct!

The local newspaper coverage by the entertainment reporter noted, "How the college preparatory side of the Passaic County High School certainly put on a glorious spectacle of a nearly professional version of Dickens's *A Christmas Carol*. It was professional in all aspects, but rather cold in nature. However, for pure wholesomeness, honest Christmas spirit and entertainment value, it was impossible to beat the Christmas pageant performed by the business, trade and vocational side of the school. The performance featured a single, old, piano played by the incomparable Miss Marigold Redbud, stage sets and backdrops constructed by the trade students and beautifully painted by the art students. The show featured great special effects, sound, and lighting, all assembled by the students, this time, from the electrical and electronic classes. The show itself was an amazing production, written and produced by Miss Redbud and Miss Penelope Wigglesworth and assisted by Mr. John Gatemann. The music was outstanding and flawlessly performed by a small choir and highlighted by a grand solo performance by Miss Margaret Wally. Her singing was the performance of a lifetime, and her voice brought the house down. The skit performance was full of emotion and well-acted. Certainly, the highlight of the evening was a performance by the coed physical education classes of *The Skater's Waltz*. There, once again, the incredibly, multi-talented, Miss Wally, stole the show along with her very talented and strikingly handsome waltzing partner, Mr. Paul John Henson. Afterwards, we all enjoyed incredible food cooked and served by the culinary department. It was the best Christmas pageant that this reporter had the pleasure of ever seeing and attending. This reporter extends a hearty thank you and a merry Christmas cheer for a job well done to all! The college preparatory side, sure had the budget and the flash, but the business, trade and vocational students had the heart."

That night never really ended.

It exists forever in many of our memories and it was a bridge for many other things in our lives. Jeff and Debbie went on to be a romantic couple. They eventually married and still are to this very day, raising two glorious children and living in the proverbial and very real, happily ever after.

Harry and Paul resurrected our waltzing careers when we first dated the two women who eventually, someday, would become our wives. It was at a fancy nightclub and while Harry initially forgot his box steps, it all came back to us rather quickly.

That is another set of memories.

Occasionally, I would hang out with Margaret Wally. We remained good friends, sitting for lunch here and there, even going out occasionally for sharing some slices of pizza and some sodas. We drifted apart in our senior year; I went off to my trade apprenticeship and Margaret went off to her job at a major local insurance company's main office. I heard down the road that Miss Wally eventually ran the entire office, went off to college, obtained multiple degrees, and became a high-level executive in the insurance world. I am not surprised because that young woman could do anything that she set her mind to!

She signed my yearbook, and I signed hers.

Her signature had a little emotion tied to it as Margaret wrote, "To the amazing, Paul John Henson. I will love you forever because you saw into my heart and did not just see the outside of me, but you saw the inside too."

What a beautiful person Miss Wally was! Inside and outside too!

Unfortunately, we never recaptured the magic of that particular Christmas pageant. I worked the electrical and lighting duties every year, until my senior year, when my job and apprenticeship requirements made it impossible to do so, and the pageants were good, but none of the successive performances ever came close to what we achieved with our show.

Sadly, Miss Penelope Wigglesworth left our school the following school year. Every male, young, old, and in between, both at the school and for miles around the area, cried at the news. Rumor had it that she went off to follow her dream and become a dancer and choreographer on Broadway. I never saw, heard, or followed her after that, but I am sure she was a success.

Miss Marigold Redbud retired after that school year. The school finally bought a new piano, and while the new music teacher, who was a handsome young man, with perfect hair and perfect teeth, was talented, he was no Miss Marigold Redbud. No one could fill those shoes, tinkle those whites and blacks or crack knuckles like her.

Ever.

Mr. Gatemann was never the same after that night. Oh sure, he still blew his whistle and yelled at us here and there. However, he was kinder and softer in nature and I do not think he ever called us "Bums" or "Losers" after that night. That old gym did have one more standing ovation in it that I was present for, involved in, and will always recall fondly. One gym class, in our junior year, after years of struggles and failed attempts, Joey Dexter finally climbed all the way to the top of that blessed rope, rang the bell at the top and made it all the way back down safely. That was worthy of a standing ovation! As a further qualification for Joey's outstanding achievement, Mr. Gatemann awarded him with his own solid brass whistle, and for the remainder of our school years, Joey Dexter was an honorary coach and "Mission" leader.

I can still hear that ear-piercing whistle and Mr. Gatemann's voice bellowing across the gym floor, "Now, hit those showers. Double-time menssss. . .."

Double-time indeed.

I woke up and found that I was in my easy chair and my family was all around me. Paul William and Heather Sarah sat on the floor watching a Christmas show on the television. Binky sat in her chair next to me; she too, was watching the show while knitting some handwork. The Christmas tree was all aglow, and the fire in the fireplace still crackled. Binky must have tended the fire while I was off with the ghosts waltzing through my past. Sleepy-eyed, I rubbed my face and tried hard to focus. Everyone turned and smiled at me.

I smiled back and said, "I am so sorry. I dozed off and was off somewhere."

"Wherever it was, dear Father, you sure did enjoy it. We had to keep turning the volume up to drown out the snoring," Paul William explained with a laugh.

I kicked in the footrest on the easy chair and leaned in to see what the show was all about on the television. It was some Christmas variety show and remarkably, to my luck, shock and awe, the singers and dancers on the show broke into a Christmas Waltz! The familiar notes of the Skater's Waltz echoed throughout the room and I jumped out of my chair as Paul William moaned at the sound of the music and the thought of waltzing. I stood up, walked over to my lovely wife, bowed in front of her, and extended my hand.

"Will you be my waltzing partner, Mrs. Henson?"

Binky nodded, smiled, and set aside the handwork. She took my hand and to the laughs, smiles, and enjoyment of our two children, Binky and I waltzed throughout the first floor of the parsonage.

My wife is a glorious dancer. Here we are, together and enjoying such a glorious time.

Waltzing at Christmastime.

While we hugged and kissed as we waltzed, I heard Miss Wigglesworth's glorious voice very clearly in my head. "Very simple now. Left foot, one, right foot, two and then left foot, three. Back right foot, four and then right, left, here we go now."

THE END

In the Window

It was a dark, dull day before Christmas. In fact, it was about three weeks or thereabouts until the big day. It was a Monday evening, and it seemed as if the city exploded into a massive Christmas rush tonight. I carefully walked the city sidewalks along the busy streets of downtown Newark, New Jersey. I was making my way through the madness of the city at quitting time for the local businesses and at the beginning of the rush hour. Rush hour during the Christmas season in northern New Jersey is the real deal. I stayed late at my job as the Lutheran Bishop for the Northeast District of our Lutheran Synod, and now, I was paying the price. My faithful assistant of all these many years, Mrs. Martha Wiggins, warned me not to stay too late, but I lost track of the time as I answered emails and worked on wrapping up some end of the year projects. Martha continued her track record of being much smarter than her boss was. Martha left early. I stopped on the busy street corner at the first cross street next to our office building and waited along with many others for the "DON'T WALK" sign to give permission to proceed. I parked my old jeep in a rented spot in a private lot a few city blocks away from our workplace and, honestly, I had no actual plans for the evening. I even debated stopping at my favorite dining and watering hole, "The Elusive Lion

Public House" and drowning a few pints, grabbing a bite to eat and chatting with my good friend Jennifer, who tended bar there. However, I was a bit tired and thought it best to head home to the townhouse. These days the townhouse was a quiet place.

Perhaps it was a little too quiet.

Since my beloved wife, Binky, left us, what is now many years ago to be a saint in Heaven and my best friend or more accurately, my brother of a different mother, Harry M. Redmond Junior joined Binky a few years ago, my life was very, very different. My work kept me busy, and I buried myself in it whenever I could do so. As of late, I also returned to writing, so when I was not Pastor Paul John Henson or more accurately, Bishop Paul John Henson, I dabbled as an author.

Our parents were both gone now, as well as my in-laws, and I remained very close to my sister, Dottie, and her family, but Dottie lived in south Jersey and I stayed up north. For a few years, I had our daughter, Heather Sarah and our granddaughter, Sarah both staying with me, living at the townhouse, but they moved out this past summer as Heather Sarah prepared to remarry in the spring of the upcoming year. Her fiancé, Vance Howard, was a professional hockey player for the Boston Bears. Ironically, he was a goaltender, as I was, in what now seems as if it was another lifetime. Obviously, Vance was on the road a great deal of the time during the hockey season, but as a prelude to the wedding, Heather Sarah and Vance decided to purchase a brand-new home in order to settle their lives before the marriage. The home was gorgeous. It was a custom building and once it was completed, Heather Sarah and Sarah moved into their new home and prepared for a new life.

I loved the townhouse for many reasons, and I especially loved my private office and my huge deck off the rear of the home. The townhouse was a custom building too, and it was only a few years old, but right for now, it was too big, it was full of too many echoes and honestly, too many ghosts.

Perhaps a little too lonely.

I always had mountains of love and support, and Heather Sarah and Sarah were often at the townhouse. In fact, they were just visiting at the townhouse this past weekend. They stayed over Saturday, and Sunday since Vance was on the road. We all were very busy when they insisted on decorating the townhouse for Christmas and we decorated the outside and inside of the townhouse. Then we all decorated our huge ten-foot-high Christmas tree in the family room that stood proudly and gaily next to the fireplace. We had quite the tree-decorating party and a wonderful time. Their new house was only a few miles away, but it was not the same as when they lived with me.

Our son, Paul William and our daughter-in-law, Blue Cloud, were always checking on me too, and they visited often. As well as Harry's widow and my best friend in the entire world, Rose. Paul William, Blue, and Rose, all joined Heather Sarah, Sarah, and me on Sunday evening for the tree-decorating party and it was a great time and a glorious memory now. Yet, for me now, with all the things that have changed in my life, this time of the year, despite the good times and the love and joy of my family, has such a different feel to it. This is the time of the year when the ghosts of the past haunted me the strongest and in the most powerful ways. As much joy as Christmas brings to our lives, it can be painful too.

Paul William married Harry and Rose's daughter, and Blue Cloud was an amazing woman. I love her with all my heart and soul and we are very close in many, many ways.

There were many influences playing with my emotions right now. It was Christmas; the ghosts were powerful and relentless, as were the memories of my loved ones, and it all was in my mind and deep within my soul. In addition, as of late, my relationship with Rose had taken on some new twists, too. We were always very close, but now there was something else growing within our relationship. It was more than just the love we had as close friends for each other all these years; it was a love of a different type. Powerful, romantic, and immense. I felt it and I know that Rose did, too. I prayed every night for God to reveal the plan to me, and I knew that in these cases, patience was indeed a virtue. If there was one golden rule that Pastor Paul John Henson learned by now, it was that God's plan is powerful and all encompassing, but God chooses when to reveal the plan to us and only faith allows you to understand that and wait for it to become clear. Faith and a dash of patience too!

The "DON'T WALK" signal left the sign and the "WALK" signal happily blinked at us. I stepped off the curb and hustled across the crosswalk along with the waves of my fellow humanity as we all made our way to the next intersection. The street light poles glowed brightly with Christmas and seasonal decorations and the storefronts happily displayed Christmas decorations, Christmas trees, tinsel and lights, along with their products and wares. It was an enjoyable time to walk the streets. There is something quite special about a Christmastime in a downtown city setting. The glow is different. The world has a kinder and gentler feel to it and no matter what your religion or your beliefs might be there are many magical things that do happen at this festive time.

I stomped my feet on the cold ground and watched as the puffs of warm breath from the various waves of humanity hit the cold air. A few days after Thanksgiving, it had snowed about six inches of snow or thereabouts, but we only had some flurries here and there since then. The remnants of that previous snow hung on gamely in some dirty piles here and there, but for the most part, the snow was gone now. Yet the cold lingered. It was around twenty degrees now and after the sunset; the temperature was rapidly dropping. Another street corner and another stop in the journey and a repeat of the previous corner. I looked around at the jewelry store window, all merrily lit up now and decorated with holiday fluff. I was not too much of a window shopper and I paused for just a moment or two when some engagement rings caught my eye. With my feelings brewing strongly with Rose, I had better keep on moving. Too many beers one night during the holidays might lead to an errant and premature move on my part!

'God's plan, Henson, God's plan,' I repeated the thought in my head.

The dry cleaner's store window had a Christmas tree and light display, as did the Main Street Coffee Shop and Bakery and Lopworth's Deli, then Kowalski's Pork Store, and the First National Bank and Trust on the corner. The beauty of this time of year is difficult to surpass. One more block to walk and the holiday displays of the next block appeared more subdued in holiday gaiety. The store window of Buckley's Hardware Store was awesome. In an outward stroke of optimistic genius, they even wrapped snow shovels with multicolored Christmas lights and had an electric train chugging around train tracks in their window, with the toy locomotive working hard to pull along a string of open freight cars carrying tiny replica snow shovels loaded in them. I thought about how the old man would have loved that one! Actually, other than the hardware store display, the opposite of the street from where I was walking had more festively decorated window displays than this side did. However, as I approached the seedier end of the main drag and left the more affluent and gaily lit stores and the window displays of Christmas now behind me, something in front of me caught my eyes and caused me to pause in my steps. Most of the waves of my fellow "City Walkers" peeled off, the sidewalk was not busy with footsteps, and I was only a half of a block or so away from where I parked my Jeep, but I needed to stop and pause here. I was not sure of why . . . but I did so.

There it was, directly in front of me, "Clyde's Pawnshop." The small storefront window of "Clyde's Pawnshop" had a string of multicolored Christmas lights blinking above a display of goods and they blinked rather sadly, a handful of the lights in the string did not illuminate and the string of lights hung in a rather disorganized and haphazard manner over the displayed goods. The "Clyde's Pawnshop" sign perched above the storefront just above the steel roll-up security door that protected the glass and the goods on display after hours, buzzed in the cold air, some lights in the sign were weaker in illumination, with the letter, "P" and the letter, "O" barely lit.

However, it was not the sign, nor the letters in the sign, nor the rather sad Christmas lights in the window, or the store in general that captured my eyes and my thoughts. It was the young woman standing in front of the smutty window, her hands in her coat pockets and her eyes glued upon the display in the window. She had a wool hat pulled down over her head, and her long, black hair hung out from under it and tumbled over her shoulders and down her back. The long overcoat that she wore seemed a bit ragged and her shoes were not the type of shoes that a woman should wear outside on such a cold evening in December. I was certainly not an expert on women's footwear, but the shoes on her feet seemed to be the slip-on type of shoe, with very thin soles. These shoes were more aptly suited for warmer weather and casual strolling as opposed to walking city streets on cold evenings. Something alerted the pastoral instincts in me, as well as harkened my mind to return to my younger years of growing up on the hard and difficult city streets of north Paterson, New Jersey. I knew the look of despair and I knew the look of a person down on their luck and in trouble.

I had seen it a countless number of times.

Too many times.

This young woman was down on her luck and when she took her one hand out of her coat pocket and slowly and reverently, placed the bare palm of her hand against the glass. I felt my soul shake. She held her palm on the surface of the cold glass of the window for a bit, and then as I took a few steps toward her, she spotted me, turned, and looked at me.

I stopped in my steps, smiled, and said, "Hello."

Despite the wool hat pulled down low over her head, and in spite of her sad demeanor, I could see that she was very pretty and her wide, doe-like eyes blinked a few times in the cold air and then I watched while her gaze slowly continued over me. She was studying me. I wore no overcoat, unless the temperature lowered to the mid-teens or thereabouts. That was the norm for me. The cold weather did not bother me too much. This was my favorite weather and time of the year. My long hair hung over my shoulders and I saw her eyes study my pastor's collar and then my face and my hair, and full-facial hair, and then to my tall frame and large size. At six-feet-five or so, with all the long hair and the pastor garb, I am sure this young woman was not quite sure of whom or what I was!

"Cold out tonight," I said, and followed it up with a wave of my hand and a point of my finger in the direction of the window and then, I asked the question that I longed to ask since I spotted the scene, "has something caught your eye in the window?"

She blinked again, looked at the window, removed her hand from the glass, and quickly placed it back in her coat pocket.

Her eyes quickly flashed over me once again and her mouth twitched a bit before the words arrived.

"Yes, cold night. No, there is only some pain on display

here."

I went to answer, but for some reason, the words stalled and she quickly spun on her heels, turned and walked quickly away.

"Oh, I see. Ah, ah, well, stay warm," were the only words that I could think of to say right now. While she disappeared into the night, I stomped my foot on the sidewalk in protest of how stupid that was to say and for my inaction.

I mumbled into the cold air, "C'mon, Pastor Paul John Henson! Geez man, you must be getting old and suffering from some brain fade. No doubt, I blew that one big time."

I walked up to the window. The warmth of the young woman's hand remained on the surface of the glass, and an outline of her palm glowed in the dim light of the sad Christmas lights as well as the city lights behind me. I needed to know what it was that she focused upon in the window.

I might have missed an opportunity to help the young woman, but I still needed to find and see the pain.

In front of where the rapidly fading palm print was, there was a display of odds and ends, but the majority of the items on display on the opposite side of the glass were women's jewelry. My eyes quickly scanned the mass of goods directly in front of me. I saw a woman's brooch with some elegant gemstones set within it, a spectacular necklace, graced with some clear diamonds, and multiple sets of earrings, some rings, including what appeared to be numerous wedding rings matched to engagement rings, women's watches, and other assorted jewelry. I stuck my hands in the pockets of my suit pants and sighed in defeat. As much skill as I lacked in women's footwear, I remained an even worse critic of fine jewelry, or costume jewelry, or otherwise. I did not know a real diamond from a blob of glass, but to me, all of these pieces looked as if they had some value. It was impossible for me to tell what piece or pieces in which the woman set her soul upon and caused her such pain. My eyes scanned around the remainder of the store window display and there was a selection of radios, a few televisions, some cameras, some assorted kitchenware, and even an acoustic guitar and an electronic keyboard. I shook my head, looked around to see if by chance the young woman decided to circle back and tell me her story, but only a young man in a business suit with a laptop bag slung over his shoulder hustled by me. I looked at my watch and decided it was time to brave the roadway madness. If I was lucky, I might make it back to the townhouse before eight or so tonight. It was a good thing that I stocked my freezer with plenty of frozen pizzas on my last food shopping adventure. There was always a remote chance that Rose or Heather Sarah stopped by and slipped some fantastic culinary delight in the refrigerator for me. Both of them are fantastic cooks, and in some vain hope of a text announcing the delivery of some incredible feast, I pulled my smart phone out of my pocket and checked for messages or texts.

Nothing. Oh, well.

You never know if they might have stopped by and left me an unannounced surprise, they both had keys to the place, but considering the fact that I might not sample some fine home cooking tonight, combined with the fact that I was the world's worst cook, a sale on frozen pizzas at Foodworld was a gift from Heaven.

Christmas Cocktails

It would be nearly impossible to calculate how many times that I walked by "Clyde's Pawnshop," on my journey back and forth from the Bishop's Office in the high-rise office building a few blocks south of the store. I suppose I could check with dear Martha and she could do the rough calculations, but considering that, I didn't even know how many years that Martha and I worked together in the office, then suffice it to say it was quite a few times.

My best guess was that I think we were going on nearly twenty-five years or thereabouts, of working here together, but whenever I asked Martha how long we were together in the office, all Martha ever responded with was a roll of her eyes, and a statement of, "Too long, Pastor Paul. Much too, long."

Martha followed the staged drama with a coy wink to assure me that it was all part of her persona.

I sure loved me some Martha Wiggins. Her bark was most certainly worse than her bite was.

In all of those many journeys, I often wondered why it was that I never paid much attention to the pawnshop. It was there as long as I worked in downtown Newark, and now and then, especially in the warmer months, I would see the owner standing on the stoop of the store's entrance enjoying a few puffs on a cigar. Honestly, it *was* a man who I saw standing there and a man that I assumed to be the owner, but I had nothing to go on other than my assumption. Perhaps the man was Clyde. I do not know, but other than a nod of the head or the occasional "Hello" or "Nice day," type of exchange, I never actually met him, nor did I ever enter the store.

Pawnshops and Lutheran bishops did not exactly mix too well.

That experience all changed for me now. I found myself lingering late in the office and timing my walk to my jeep at around the same time that we first met, all in hopes of seeing the young woman once again standing in front of and staring into the window of the pawnshop. It was a nagging feeling and each night, when I walked by and saw no one standing there, I felt a pang of sadness at how I missed an opportunity to help her. After all, I might be the Lutheran Bishop of the Northeast District of our synod and rarely preach, or conduct worship services, except as a special guest of a congregation or on special occasions, but I was still a Lutheran pastor. On the night of our meeting, I did not do my job, and I prayed each night for another opportunity to meet her and learn her story. Especially more so at this time of year. Christmastime is a time of great joy, renewed hope, and of much happiness, but it is also a time when want, need, pain and loneliness are intense emotions within many people's hearts and souls. I knew the pain. I felt it too.

The pain was in every picture of Binky on the walls of my office, and it was in every corner of every room of the townhouse. It was in the ghosts and in the voices and the shadows that danced on the wall. I felt the pangs of loss and sting of pain when my eyes landed on the special, homemade Christmas ornaments that we bought one day at a local craft store, and we hung together every year on our Christmas tree. It was in the sound of her voice that still echoed in my head, in the flash of her smile and beauty in my mind's eye, in the memories of Christmas Days of the past, and most of all, it was in my heart. If you add to the pain of the loss of Binky that Harry was gone now too, and my parents and most of my family . . . my goodness, it was hard to focus on Christmas joy. Yet, I put my head down and did my best to shut it all out and carry on with the holiday celebrations.

Now, I longed to know more about the young woman and to see if I could help in some way.

All I had right now were my prayers for a second chance. For ten days or so, each night was the same and there were no window shoppers at all in front of "Clyde's Pawnshop." No young woman, no window gazers, unless you could count Pastor Paul John Henson in that group. I found the window to be a magnet and each night, when I passed by and each morning too, I glanced over the items in the window. It seemed to be in hopes of taking an inventory of the goods to try to figure out what it was that the young woman focused upon that evening. I guess that I thought that if I saw her once again staring in the window, then I would know the item or items did not yet sell, and maybe there remained a chance of helping her. One day, the elegant necklace was gone and a few watches and then a set of earrings that I saw there for a week or two. All sold, or at least that was my assumption.

One cold evening, about ten days or so before Christmas, my heart jumped in my chest when I neared the section of the street where the pawnshop was and I saw her. Standing in the same location, the same spot, the same coat, the hat . . . all the same! Her hand once again rested upon the glass and her head was down. I picked up the pace, no in fact, I broke into a sprint, the sound of my footsteps startled her, and when I stopped a few feet away, she once more looked at me, shook her head, and quickly turned to walk away.

I ran closer and said, "Please . . . don't leave. I want to help. I want to know more. There is so much more than the pain behind that glass. There is still hope and there still is love."

She slowed and then stopped, but she shook her head again and mumbled, "No. There is nothing really left. Thank you for caring but there really is nothing left."

"Please," I pleaded, as I finally stood next to her, "I am a Lutheran pastor. I am Pastor Paul John Henson and I want to help you in any way that I might be able to do so." I reached out my hand and in the light of the window, I could see as the tears tumbled down her cheeks, and I fought away my own tears.

"Please, here is my business card. If you want to leave, of course, I cannot make you stay, but please, my office is just a few blocks away. If you would like to speak, please feel free to call me anytime."

She took the card, glanced at it, and her eyes widened as she spun my business card in her hand.

In a low, almost inaudible voice, the young woman mumbled, "You are a bishop?"

"I am, but I much prefer the title of Pastor Paul. Please, I too know about pain. Being a pastor and serving as the bishop is just my job, in reality, I am, just a man."

She turned my card over and read the back of it where I printed my favorite Bible verse, The Gospel of John, Chapter 11 verse 35. In my opinion, that verse contained the two most powerful words in all of literature, and the two most important ones too. I used that Bible verse so many times in my career and in my own consolation that I always carried it with me both in print and in my heart.

Without speaking another word, she nodded, turned, and walked away. My heart sunk, my shoulders slumped, and I was tempted to run after her, but realized that I had this time given it my best shot. Experience told me that sometimes, whatever is going on in a person's life is unreachable, it is inconsolable, and for whatever reason, you have to heal on your own or, in fact, never heal. I had been there; I saw Harry reach that inconsolable place in his life when he lost his first wife, Sky Blu, and I had consoled countless persons during my career, who were there too. At least she had my card and contact information and if she wanted to speak and meet and wanted some assistance, then she could call. An answer to the prayers arrived, and I felt better knowing that I had not entirely blown this second chance. It was all that I could do for now.

On the other hand, was it?

I gave a glance in the young woman's direction as she disappeared into the maze of the city. The cold, Christmas wind blew down the city street, bringing with it some flakes of snow spitting out of the sky and I did not even feel its power, or even the slightest influence from it. My mind was elsewhere. I turned and gave a quick glance at the window and her palm imprint was there once again, in the same location. The jewelry in the same area on the other side of the glass seemed to be the same inventory as it had been for the last few days. I still had no way of knowing what it was that the young woman was seeking or feeling. Without further hesitation, I took a number of long strides, pushed open the front door, and for the first time, I entered "Clyde's Pawnshop."

I took a few steps inside the front entrance of the shop and a small bell tinkled above the door and rather happily announced my arrival. Once inside, I looked around. It was quite the display. Racks and racks of assorted items stood in a military formation in front of me. The racks seemed grouped into categories. There were electronics, house wares, some clothing, power tools and hand tools, musical instruments, even pottery, small furniture and small appliances. You name it and it was there, here, and everywhere. The expensive items, such as the jewelry, were under lock and key in glass display cases. What I presumed to be the most coveted pieces were in a glass display at the front counter. Multiple security cameras mounted all over the walls of the shop watched my every move and they all blinked at me with glowing red-colored pilot lights as they recorded every event within the confines. Behind the front counter was a large sign that read, "All transactions are recorded by video tape and all transactions, logged, and as required by law recorded and reported to the Newark, New Jersey Police Department on a daily basis. Two forms of identification are required for all items placed on pawn and all monetary transactions." I thought how interesting that there were such regulations, but it made sense. Stolen goods show up in pawnshops.

A music system with a "sixty-five" dollar cardboard sign hanging over the tuning knob of the radio softly played some Christmas music while it sat on a table next to the far-left-side of the front counter. Overall, it was certainly not fancy inside this shop, but it was not entirely unpleasant either.

The door behind the front counter opened and a short, thin-faced, balding man appeared from the rear of the store. He wore his glasses perched on the top of his head; he wore a heavy flannel shirt in a red plaid pattern and plain black pants. Venturing a guess, I would imagine he was in his early to mid-sixties in age and while he was thin, he was by no means weak in appearance. Quite the opposite. He walked with some stature and confidence. Indeed, this was the same man that I occasionally saw on the front stoop enjoying his cigar smoking.

He rather weakly smiled and to my surprise said, "Hello, there, Pastor Paul, or is it, Bishop Henson?"

"You know me? How?"

It was impossible for me to hide my surprise at the fact that he knew who I was.

He smiled widely and leaned in on the counter with his one elbow on the glass. The man put his head in his one hand and with his other hand; he touched the top of his head and made sure that his eyeglasses did not tumble off the top of his head. His face had a rather tired and somewhat rugged look to it. What little that remained of the hair on his head tended to stick out in multiple directions. His eyes, while they remained bright, had some elements of sadness in them, too.

While still leaning over the counter, but with his head no longer resting in his hand, the man said, "Oh, well, a better question would be how I would not know who you are? Let's see, now . . . long hair, a beard, a person would think you might be a leftover hippie from the late nineteen seventies rather than a Lutheran bishop. Very tall, actually you are quite imposing, a huge man with big muscles, handsome as all get-go because the women all swoon when you walk by and to top it off, you are a former professional ice hockey goaltender, who happened to be a legend in the New Jersey, New York, and Connecticut area. If that were not enough, you walked by the front of my shop most every morning and evening, for the past twenty-five years or so and other than a nod or an occasional word or two, you have never spoken with me within the context of a meaningful conversation, or stopped in until right now. How's that work?"

I nodded and felt just a hint of guilt for not being friendlier, but after some thought, I said, "That works. In retrospect, I guess that it was a rather stupid question."

"It was not stupid, Bishop Henson, but rather it is a verification of your reputation for being a very humble man. A man who tries very hard to blend and the world will not let him do so. I hold no ill feelings that you have never stopped by before this evening . . . Lutheran bishops ordinarily do not frequent pawnshops. For a variety of reasons."

"I think you are correct, but I do apologize. I could have stopped by, said hello, and been a bit more neighborly. Better yet, stop in and see if you need anything in the way of spiritual needs. I am at fault. It is no excuse, but often, I am lost in my own world. As I said, I have no excuse to offer for my behavior. A pawnshop or not—it might stop other clergy for whatever their reasons might be, but it should not have stopped me. I have no hesitation now about being here. Although, no one ever accused me of being conventional in anything that I have done over my careers. Both in hockey, my writing, and in service to our Lord. Despite my seemingly famous identity and reputation, please, let me formally introduce myself. I am Pastor Paul John Henson. I do not use the bishop title and never have been comfortable with it. Ever. I prefer Pastor Paul."

I walked over and reached out my hand to shake his hand and the man stood up and warmly grasped my hand and shook it. For a smallish man, he had a powerful grip.

"My pleasure to meet you, Pastor Paul. I am Clyde Peeples, owner, proprietor, and chief negotiator of this establishment. I will say to you, welcome to Clyde's Pawnshop. It will be thirty-two years next April. Can you imagine? Thirty-two years. We have been here for all of this time and it seems as if my life and times all passed in a flash. Oh, and by the way, my sincere condolences on the loss of your wife. Very sincere condolences on such a profound loss. As I said, everyone knows you."

I nodded and said, "Thank you, much appreciated. It has been difficult."

"I cannot even imagine."

Despite what I could tell was his sincerity at my loss, I deeply needed to change the subject, since my emotions ran high and bubbled over tonight, anyway. This man had such depth and intelligence. This conversation was taking so much longer than I expected it to take. On the surface, I thought this would be cut and dry. There was no way from simply observing only the smutty window display, in which I could have perceived the many layers of depth and emotion contained here.

"That is a long time for your shop to be here. Certainly, a very long time. A lifetime. It is my pleasure to meet you.

Grace and peace to you and happy Christmas, Mr. Peeples."

He stood back from the counter and for the first time, took his eyeglasses off his head and placed them over his eyes. It seemed as if he wanted to have a better look at me. On the other hand, that could have simply been a resounding assumption on my part. Honestly, I am not too sure of what Clyde focused upon with his eyeglasses over his eyes.

After a few seconds Clyde spoke. "Please, call me, Clyde. I too, prefer simple titles. I am not a religious man, Pastor Paul, but I appreciate your blessing. After a lifetime of wheeling and dealing and such, and as some people might say, holding people for ransom, I will need some major help to enter into the Pearly Gates of Heaven. If they do exist."

"Oh, they exist, Clyde. I can assure you that they exist."

Clyde did not comment, but I knew the face of a doubter. Over my career, I have gazed on those doubting faces many, many times. Even in the faces of professed believers, I have seen many, many doubters.

Once more, the eyeglasses went back on top of his head and he folded his arms across his chest in a slight display of defiance.

"Pastor Paul, I will not comment on the existence of Heaven, or even God or religion, but instead, cut to the actual reason your clerical collar and other parts of you decided to stop in here tonight. Sadly, despite any want, need or desire, I cannot release the name or information of the young woman who stops by here and gazes in the window. I am a pawnshop owner who abides by the law. Despite any preconceptions of what we do here, as required, I report all my transactions daily to the local law enforcement officials."

I allowed my eyes to wander to the sign behind the counter that stated the same facts, and Clyde nodded as he noted where my eyes wandered too.

Clyde continued to explain, "I guess that I can have my logbooks subpoenaed by the courts, but not by Lutheran bishops. My apologies in advance. I have managed to stay here for all of these years by always following the law to the exact letter. Not stereotyping, but being factual, especially so here in downtown Newark, New Jersey, where the temptation to bend some laws and rules, runs high. I know of your roots. Some patsy-ass you are not. Collar or not. Ice hockey made you a legend, but the streets of Paterson, New Jersey molded you years before hockey ever did so."

Clyde now wandered out from behind the front counter, took a spot on the side, and leaned upon the counter.

With his arms once again folded across his chest, Clyde said, "No, no, no," Clyde shook his head at the thought, "I cannot reveal private information for not even the famous, Pastor Paul."

"I understand, Clyde. I assure you that I would never want you to break any laws or reveal any information that would breech any privacy. I had no preconceptions of your business because I am not even exactly sure of how it works. I know that you provide loans based upon the value of goods, but besides that, I am not an expert. You are very observant to notice the young woman and our interactions. Surely, religious or not, I think you understand that I would be remiss if I did not try to help her. It was God's plan for us to meet and I was doing my best to follow it all up."

I gave a wave of my hands and summed it all up by saying, "That is really all there is to it. I gave her my business card and I sincerely hope that she calls me for assistance. I guess that is all that I can do."

Clyde nodded and put his head down and slowly walked across the sales floor and he returned to his post behind the counter.

Christmas Cocktails

It appeared as if I hit a dead end once again and I was preparing to lick my wounds and leave, when Clyde spoke once more. "Mine is a simple business, Pastor Paul. People in need of small loans come to me and they give me things. Pieces of their lives, some parts of their possessions and elements of their souls and they ask me, 'Clyde, how much will you loan me based upon the value of this item?' I look at the item and offer them a figure. Either they say no or they say yes. I do not ask any questions or sway them in any manner. Other than hitting up friends or family, where else can they get a small loan of a hundred dollars? Or fifty dollars? Or, what they need? A bank? I think not! Those car title loan joints only work if you have a car. They agree to the figure. I take their info and write a receipt for the goods. I tell them the terms, conditions and interest that I charge. If they pick up the item, pay the interest within the previously agreed-upon amount of time, plus the payback on the loan, well, then we are good. I give them back the item and all is well in their world and in mine. If I never see them again, then I put the item up for sale. I sell it, I recapture my loan, and sometimes, I even make a profit. Simple."

He put his left foot up on the edge of a stool that sat behind the counter, and he leaned in and with just the slightest hint of a smile on his face, Clyde said to me, "As I said, it is a simple business."

I froze in place. My eyes scanned the inside of the shop, and the many racks filled with parts and pieces of people's lives. The writer's side of my mind whirled with the stories behind all of these items and the motivation that forced a person to drop them here. Perhaps, some of the goods had no deep or actual meaning to the individual, while others not so much. It was difficult to tell.

At first, a question came to mind, and I needed to ask it so I did so.

"Interest? And what are the rates?"

"Honestly, Pastor Paul, they are high. Very high. At a week's end, if they pick up the goods, they can pay me thirty percent over what was initially provided to them. However, as I said, I give them the terms up front and I print them on the receipt too. Nothing is hidden."

With some long pondering, I stood in the same spot, just inside one of the last aisles before the front door to the shop. Clyde's eyes studied me and I felt him searching my mind and perhaps even his mind to gauge my response. Finally, the words arrived, and I did not sugarcoat them nor make them gentle. However, they were heartfelt and they were factual.

"So, where the banks fail, good old, Clyde steps in and saves the day. As long as they agree to the terms, and exorbitant interest rates, eh? Do you not wonder at their stories or, in some cases, their desperation? Do those thoughts ever cross your mind?"

"Everyone has a story, Pastor Paul. You do, I do, and they do. I cannot wrap my emotions or my money up in stories. Neither can I care why it is that people do what they do. I am a man of business."

With a nod, and just some little more emotions rising inside of me, I took a few steps back to the counter, stopped, and said, "I think the young woman has a story. A story that is painful, and difficult, and emotional." I pointed to various items around the store and explained my thoughts. "As does that trumpet on the shelf there and the clarinet next to it. I think the wedding rings in those cases have stories attached to them and so does that watch. Perhaps it is a Christmas present from years ago, perhaps it is a present to a loved one given by a secret and precious lover. Maybe. I for one—think there are an uncountable number of stories here inside of these walls and upon these shelves and money is the least important part of them. Money might be the motivator for them, and for you, but not the true root of their stories." I pointed at my heart and my chest and said, "This is where the stories lie. In the heart. Do you know the story of the moneychangers and how Jesus turned their tables over and dumped their money out, Clyde?"

Clyde's face showed some discomfort in my question, but he said, "I do. I have my issues with religion now, but I went to Sunday school a very long time ago, Pastor Paul, and I know the story. However, that was in the temple. The moneychangers and animal sellers were turning a profit on people who were in need in God's house."

I clapped my hands together so loudly and forcibly that Clyde must have jumped a foot in the air!

"Exactly! In addition, this is God's house, too! Where two or more are gathered. Everywhere is God's house, Clyde. Everywhere."

Clyde's facial expression changed, and I sensed that I had worn out my welcome.

I turned to walk out when Clyde said, "You are a powerful speaker, Pastor Paul. It is easy to see why you have such a stalwart reputation. However, you said that you had no previous preconceptions of my business and now that you know of how it works, you are judging my character based upon my business, Pastor Paul. I think that is unfair. I never force a person to give up their possessions. They come to me."

I turned around again and said, "I agree. I am judging you, and for that, I apologize. It is not Christian-like and wrong to judge you. Once more, I apologize, I really do. I also agree that you do not force them to give up their possessions. However, in my opinion you prey upon their situations and, in some cases, their desperation. True, they can always have, or more factually, buy them back. As long as they pay, back to you the rather exorbitant interest fee, plus the initial loan. Yes, indeed, a business is a business. Yet, sometimes in this life, when a person is down on their luck, and especially at Christmastime, you have to make other people's business your business. There comes a time when the business needs to take a backseat and money is not the real issue. Human hearts and souls are the issue and in reality, and in the big picture, money is only money. How much money is enough? Some people never seem to have enough and they go to every means available and stop at none to gain more and more. It is very sad." I looked at Clyde and carefully studied his face. My rant seemed to affect him and I asked rather bluntly, "Have you made a very good living here with your pawnshop? I imagine that you have since you have been here all of these years."

Clyde nodded and answered factually and from what I could determine, very honestly, too.

"Yes, I have, Pastor Paul. I have made quite a nice living here."

With a nod, I searched and found my final words and spoke from my heart, "Well, now, I guess the golden rule is really the most important rule. If you were desperate, Clyde, and down to your last nickel . . . I have to ask you . . . would you shoot your own heart full of holes and pay for your heart within a veil of desperation? The Herald Angels of Heaven first came to the lowly shepherds on the night of the birth of Christ, for a reason. Desperation always searches for hope. Even in the darkest of times, hope shines brightly in and amongst the desperation. Despite humankind's great attempts to screw that all up, hope always will shine brightly. Now and forever."

I paused and took one last look around the shop.

At the parts and pieces of people's lives.

"Good evening, Clyde. I am sorry to have taken so much of your time. If this was my shop, then I have to think that I would turn it into a thrift store. Yes, a thrift store and I would sell gently used goods at reasonable prices to persons in need. I think it would do an incredible business and the paperwork would be far less demanding too. So, would be the burdens on my heart. I would sleep so much better at night. Especially so at Christmastime and even more so on Christmas Eve. Yes, I would not have to keep one eye open waiting in fear of a visit from four ghosts. Besides, it would make for an easy cruise into retirement. Anyway, I do wish you a happy Christmas and blessings in the new year."

With those words, I turned and walked toward the door.

When my hand reached the door, and I pushed it open, I heard Clyde's voice yelling out to stop me, "WAIT! Pastor Paul, wait. Please."

I turned around and saw that Clyde was racing to catch up to me. He did so, put his hand on my back, and then gently held me by my shoulder to prevent me from leaving. Clyde motioned for me to close the door, and I did so. The exasperated storekeeper pointed in the front window of the store.

"There is a story. A very real story. A very sad story. The young woman pawned her wedding ring and engagement ring, too. I honestly do not recall which sets of the rings that were hers. However, there are two rings in there somewhere. I will need to make a careful study of the ring display, but if I recall, they were not an overly elaborate or expensive set of rings. Perhaps, three hundred dollars, or. . .."

Clyde's voice trailed off, and he searched my face. I think he already knew the gist of what my next words were going to be, but since I still was a pastor at heart, I preached them, anyway.

"That is the trouble with humankind. We think that we can put a price tag on everything and it makes the world right. We can put a price on a human's life, a child, an education, a memory, saving a person's life, even something as precious as love is." I shook my head, wiped the long hair out of my face, and continued, "It is one of our greatest sins and flaws. Covetousness of some of the most precious aspects of life that God granted us. It is very sad. Can you not see, Clyde, there actually is no monetary value to these rings? How can you place a value on holes in a person's heart?"

Clyde nodded, and his eyes rimmed with some tears as he said in a low whisper, "You cannot, Pastor Paul. You cannot. Her husband died of some type of horrible blood cancer this past summer. She pawned the rings, in order to buy some food for her children and to help to pay the rent. She lost her job, was down to her last dollar, and told me that she had little choice. Of course, she never returned for the rings."

I nodded and put my arm around his shoulders as I felt my own soul shudder and felt Clyde's pain at the shedding of the story and the reliving of the experience.

The young woman's words were so profound and exact when she said, "There is only pain on display here."

Recovering and wiping his tears away with his fingers, Clyde said, "I will need to pull the paperwork and check the numbers on the rings to find out which ones are hers. I will be right back." I gently held Clyde back as a thought raced through my head and despite the pain; I felt my heart fill with joy.

"No, no, no, I will not break any rules or laws or ask you to break them and violate any laws. Clyde, please, tell me how much money is all of this worth?" I waved my hands over the display in the window and said, "I mean to ask, how much are all of the goods on display in the window worth? Do you know who all the original owners of these goods are?"

Clyde looked at me rather strangely and after a pause for a moment or two, he answered me, "Well, yes, I can look up all the paperwork and track down the original owners. As far as the prices go, I dunno. That might take some time for me to figure out. I do not understand, Pastor Paul. These people cannot afford the goods. Otherwise, they would have picked them up long ago."

I nodded and said, "I understand and have a plan. Please, let's figure this all out. All that I need to know is the total price of all of the goods here. I need to know the prices, plus your profit, of course. I need you to recover your money."

Clyde shook his head again and said, "Okay. However, they cannot afford to pay me. Why would we do this? I thought we were focused on the young woman's rings?"

I put my arm around Clyde once again and I pulled him into me tightly.

"We are. As well as all the remaining hearts and souls, too. You see, there might be many stories here on display in front of us. There might be pain, there might be memories, and there might be desperation. Who knows? They cannot afford to pay you for them . . . but . . . I can."

He smiled widely, and I did, too.

"Clyde, do you like pizza? It is going to be a late night and we need to eat. Let's order from Joey's Pizza on the corner. Do you like his pie?"

Clyde smiled widely and while pulling his eyeglasses down over his eyes, Clyde said, "You kidding me? I love his pie. Best pie in Newark and I have tried 'em all. I have the phone number for Joey's Pizza jotted down on a note pinned next to the cash register. Eat a pie at least every other night. A half meatball and half-extra cheese pie is my favorite. I have a six-pack of beer in the refrigerator at the back of the store. We might need another six-pack of beer too. I heard that you Lutherans sure enjoy more than just a pint or two. I will order the pie if you run to the corner for another six-pack of beer. Is that a deal or what? I am a Big Boulder man myself."

I nodded, waved, and headed for the door.

While I went on my way, my words echoed in the doorway, hanging in the cold Christmas air, "Deal. Clyde, you are the man. I am a Big Boulder man too. Those

Dingleberry beers are too sweet. On the way. A half meatball and half-extra cheese pie, sounds good to me. In fact, it is perfect."

Once I hit the sidewalk, I breathed in very deeply. All the Christmas love that hung in the cold air filled my lungs, my heart, and mostly, it filled my entire soul.

I turned on my heels and headed left towards the package goods store and the pizza joint.

Christmas Cocktails

As was my usual practice, I took off from work for all of Christmas week and even stole a few days after New Year's Day, too. Martha was in and out of the office during the time, and Martha kept me up to date on what was happening. The Advent season and the Christmas season, and all of the associated over-hype of the seasons exhausted most pastors and churches. Therefore, the days after the big day were usually low key, anyway. Anything that required immediate attention, the amazing Martha could easily take care of for us. Martha was remarkable!

I checked my emails and such from my home office and spoke with Martha on the telephone, but mostly, I enjoyed the time with my friends and family. Over the holiday, Rose and I grew even closer. I felt as if God's plan for us was on our doorstep. Vance took a few days off from the hockey season and we had a glorious holiday. No frozen pizzas, only amazing home-cooked meals! Turkeys, hams, fine desserts, my traditional Christmas pudding, beer, wine and cocktails. Endless Christmas music played throughout the townhouse. We had glorious exchanges of gifts, and more importantly, love! Oh, my! What a grand time we all had! The food was great, and I gained a few pounds! Time to hit the gym and run a few miles too. For a few days, the townhouse filled with Christmas joy and I kept the ghosts at bay for a few days too.

All too soon, the Christmas season passes, and every year, we all wish and swear to keep Christmas in our heart all year long. I will do my best!

When I finally returned to work, I parked my car in the usual parking lot and made my way up Main Street; I have to admit that I stopped dead in my tracks at the sight in front of me. Until I turned the corner and directed some attention, I had my head down, my hands in my pockets and, honestly, I was thinking of Christmas cheer and the special moments that I shared with Rose, when I looked up and saw that the faded, old sign on the storefront of Clyde's shop was different.

Very different.

The sign was new; it was very bright and fabulous within its own grandeur. Now the sign proudly proclaimed, "Clyde's Second Chance Thrift Store" in a display of a grand illumination. Even in the daylight, I could see that all the letters lit up brightly. I smiled and stood in front of the store while admiring the new sign and the change in direction. The formerly smutty window was now bright and clean, the Christmas lights still hung in the window, and a Christmas tree still stood proudly in the corner of the window. The lights all lit up brightly. There were no unlit lights, and they were now neat and orderly instead of disorganized. On, display in the window were many types of assorted items. Housewares, some electronics, kitchen appliances, an electric guitar and a display of books. Many, many books were on display and a Holy Bible was on the end of the book display on a red cloth, with its cover propped up on a wooden mount to tilt the cover toward the street. The Bible seemed to be in near perfect condition.

I mumbled, "God's plan," I smiled and went to walk away, when the door to the store burst wide open and a voice called my name. I turned around to see who it was. It was with some shock and surprise that I saw that it was the young woman who dwelled by the window! I was ashamed to say that I didn't even know her name.

"Oh, Pastor Paul! Please, I have been hoping you would walk by! Please, I must speak with you!"

I stopped and smiled as the young woman ran up to me. She held her hands out and motioned for me to take them in her grasp. I did so and noticed that her ring finger had a wedding ring as well as an engagement ring upon them. I vaguely recognized them from the window display, or perhaps my heart convinced my mind that the rings were from the front window display.

She smiled widely as I said, "Well, now, it seems as if you take a few days off around here and things change rather quickly. Please, I don't even know your name. Please, tell me your name."

Her wide, doe-like eyes flickered and her gorgeous smile lit up an already bright morning.

"Melissa. I am, Melissa Davidson, and yes, this has been a magical Christmas." Her eyes danced at the rings on her outstretched finger and she smiled a million-dollar smile. "The rings are so symbolic to me. It might be foolish, but it means so much to me right now. I know you understand my feelings, because Clyde told me about your own loss. I am so sorry and I understand now when you said that evening that you know of the pain. When the rings were gone, it was so profound. I had nothing left. It was so empty. My husband is still gone, but at least, I have a part of our love to hold close to my heart and near to me. It nearly killed me to give them up. I had no choice at the time. I had been out of work for months and months and could only find part-time work. My unemployment was drying up. It was such a terrible time. There was no way that I could ever fill the immense holes in my heart. Yes, indeed, Pastor Paul, despite our terrible loss and the children missing their father and me missing my husband, it was a glorious Christmas."

Her eyes wandered around the city and the streets, and I admired the sparkle in them. Melissa was quite a pretty gal and with some hope planted in her heart, it chased away the sadness in her eyes. I watched while her eyes darted to the store window and a smile formed on her lips, along with a testimony.

"Pastor Paul, I learned that you have to put your head down and charge ahead. No matter what. I promised Mike that I would charge ahead. Mike is my late husband's name. You never get over the loss but you learn to cope and accept it in some sad sort of way. I have to tell you that when Clyde called and told me to pick up the rings and that I owed not even one penny on them, when I arrived here at the store, Clyde gave me some gifts and such for my children and for me too. It seems that some of the items, even when paid for, had no persons to claim them, so Clyde gave them to us! The toaster is awesome! Our old one gave up a month or so ago. It seems so silly to be thankful for such a small thing, but that is what our new store is all about here. My son now plays the keyboard and my daughter strums a guitar. Clyde also told me that after Christmas, he was changing his store into a thrift store and that if I was still looking for work, then I could have a job helping him run the new operation."

After telling me all of this, Melissa threw her hands up in the air, and her joy and happiness filled the entire world.

I swear that it did.

"Well, here I am! A decent and wonderful job! Finally!"

Her exuberance filled my heart with joy.

"Clyde will be in later. Please stop by. He is anxious to see you. He says, now that I am here, he is cruising to retirement. Someday, I might even own the store. I love this job and the store is doing very well. It is so glorious giving items and people second chances at life. That is what you gave all of us. I cannot ever thank you enough. You are a glorious man."

Melissa leaned in and motioned for me to bend over, and she hugged me and kissed me on the cheek.

"Merry Christmas, Pastor Paul," Melissa said as she wiped away some tears of joy.

"You are very welcome. Merry Christmas, Melissa." I said, while I stood back up and pointed at the window.

While I put my arm around her shoulders, pointed at the storefront window and pulled her in close, I asked, "What do you see in the window now?"

Without any hesitation, Melissa answered, "Hope. I only see hope."

I nodded and said, "Well, now . . . that's what I see too. I see hope too and I feel joy. I think that maybe, just maybe, I feel a little touch of Christmas love too. Yes, indeed, just a touch. Believe me when I tell you that Christmas love hangs in the air around here. Right here on this old city street. God's house is where we all gather. It is everywhere. Christmas love. It hangs in the air here on cold evenings. You can breathe it in and it fills your soul. In this life, I guess that you never know what you will see when you take the time to stop and look in the window. I dare say that, you might be very surprised at the results."

Her smile faded a bit while Melissa asked, "Will we both find love again in this life, Pastor Paul? I mean, not as we had with our spouses, not to replace them in our hearts, but actually, in order to honor them. Do you understand? Love?"

"Oh yes, I completely understand. My best advice as a pastor, as a man, and as a widower is to leave it all to God's plan, Melissa. Stay strong, keep your eyes wide open and your faith strong. Always pray and hope. God will open your heart to know if it is love or not. You will know, love. God will leave no doubt."

Melissa nodded, and she turned to the front window of the store, and with a wide smile, she placed the bare palm of her hand upon the surface of the glass of the window. With a nod of her head, she implied for me to join her and I happily did so. When I placed my palm on the window glass, Melissa gently reached over and placed her hand on top of the back of my hand. We stood there together for a few minutes, making imprints in the cold glass with our warm hands, but mostly with our joined hearts.

The window no longer had pain to absorb, this time it broadcasted joy and hope.

Melissa and I stood together watching the Christmas lights blink, glow, and broadcast their joyous signals.

We stood there in silence while absorbing it all into our hearts and souls.

THE END

Mr. Keating's Christmas

For lack of a better and more comprehensive description, Mr. Arthur Keating was a man known for his partaking in layers upon layers of jollification. Arthur was as tall as he was round; he wore a perpetual smile, his wide face embellished with rosy red cheeks, capped by a tuft of black hair that swirled as if it was the curls and twists of ice cream on top of a waffle cone. His blue eyes flickered with fun, his ears twitched in time to music and perked up with the slightest hints of a conversation and although, he tipped the scales at a few bobs, Arthur was light on his feet and quite nimble for such a large man. Arthur was quick with a joke, smart with well-timed wit, and his humor and happiness always remained contagious.

There was no doubt, whatsoever, that Arthur enjoyed more than his fair share of frosty mugs filled with a sudsy brew, but while he occasionally teetered and tottered, he never became obnoxious or nasty while under the influence of the drink. Luckily, in the small haven of Manchester Borough, on the outskirts of Paterson, New Jersey, Arthur lived within walking distance of more gin joints, pubs, taverns and other drinking establishments than any other locale in the United States. Therefore, with what amounted to merely a quick jaunt, a hop and skip, and Arthur arrived there, and while he owned a car, Arthur seldom drove the car, any more.

Mr. Keating married his high school sweetheart shortly after returning home to Paterson, New Jersey after serving his country gallantly in World War 2, while serving in the United States Navy as a cook upon an aircraft carrier. They saw their fair share of action, and Arthur always thanked God for surviving the horrors of war unscathed.

His ever-present jolliness was due in part to his thankfulness for returning home unscathed. He knew many of his friends and fellow Sailors and Marines were not so lucky.

As did many of his fellow servicemen and women, Arthur obtained a job with the United States Postal Service, which always accepted veterans for employment positions with open arms. There he stayed, for over thirty-five years, working a route as a postman and then a mail sorter. He bought a small home in the Manchester borough section of the city of Paterson, New Jersey, married the former Irene Clacksford and together, the Keatings, lived modestly and happily.

One more grand aspect about Mr. Arthur Keating was that he unabashedly loved Christmas! Totally, completely, and with all of his jolly heart. Christmas was what the entire rest of the year revolved around for Mr. Arthur Keating. Mr. Keating began decorating the exterior of his home around the first day of November. Lights lined the edges of the roof, chased along the length of the gutters, and then outlined the entire frame of the home. He had wreaths, a plastic Santa Claus and reindeer on his rooftop. Snowmen, elves, wreaths, sleighs, sat upon the front lawn and rows of candy canes lined the walkway from the driveway to the front door. You name the Christmas decoration, then categorize it and identify it and Mr. Keating decorated his home with it!

Mrs. Keating merrily went along with the entire holiday extravaganza. She held the ladder for her husband as his wide girth and "extra few pounds" as he liked to call his current weight, teetered and tottered on precarious ladder rungs while stringing lights or placing Santa and his multiple assistants on the rooftop. Together, they laughed and heartily enjoyed the entire process. Mrs. Irene Keating was just as round and just as jolly and happy as her husband was! Finally, after weeks of careful preparation and hours of work, the grand kickoff was at hand. The entire neighborhood gathered outside of the Keating's home for the countdown and in a glorious celebration, Mr. Keating flipped the switch. The electrical power generator at the Paterson Power Plant sighed and groaned, then gained R.P.M. and the needle on Mr. Keating's electrical meter took off spinning like the rotors of a helicopter. Cheers went up along with the traditional, "oohs and aahhhs." Children cheered and clapped and adults cheered and clapped too. It was a grand spectacle and every year the locals claimed that it was a better display than last year was. That might be a fact, because, every year, Mr. Keating added a few more pieces of Christmas decorations to his cornucopia of Christmastime delight. Bogart Street in Manchester Borough, New Jersey glowed as if it was a holiday beacon for miles and miles. Neighbors did not have to turn on their interior lights because the lights and glow from the Keating's Christmas display penetrated windows and illuminated their homes.

In half jest and in half seriousness, some people surmised that you could see it from Outer Space!

The night after the big kick-off was when the next phase of Christmas fun occurred. Mr. Keating cleaned out his garage (the decorations that were normally stored in the garage were now installed) and he rolled out a red carpet on the floor, placed a huge easy chair in the center, hung Christmas decorations all over inside the garage and then Mr. Keating dressed in one of the finest Santa Claus suits available. Yes, indeed, Santa Claus came to Bogart Street!

Mrs. Keating dressed as Mrs. Claus and together they held court for a seemingly endless parade of not only neighborhood kiddies, but kiddies and people came from miles and miles around to see the display and meet the famous, "Bogart Street Santa Claus." Mr. and Mrs. Santa Claus gave out candy and small inexpensive gifts to the children, Bogart Street became famous everywhere, and known as the street that Santa Claus lived on!

One Christmas, a change arrived on Bogart Street when an equally famous man moved into a house on the opposite side of the street and directly across from the Keating home. This famous man loved Christmas too! His own family was not unlike the Keatings and his family too held nothing back when it came to extravagant celebrations during the Christmastime of the year. Yes, indeed, it was a match made for the North Pole and Christmas fate was on the side of joy, when Mr. Harry M. Redmond Junior moved into the home on Bogart Street.

On the other hand, could it have been more than just Christmas fate that brought Harry to that home?

I for one would like to think so.

Christmas Cocktails

Harry M. Redmond Junior was my best friend. Actually, it was more as if he was my brother. We had been friends since we were around ten years of age or thereabouts, and we were as close as if we were two brothers. Harry tragically lost his first wife, Sky Blu, to cancer a few years earlier, and he fled New Jersey in grief and in an effort to find his lost heart and soul. We were out of touch during those few years for the first time in our lives together and his leaving left a huge hole in my life and in my heart. When Harry finally returned to our lives, we all enjoyed a glorious reunion of our lives and our love for each other. Many great things happened during our time apart. I married my love and partner, Binky Hobnobber Henson, and I retired from professional hockey and followed my calling to become a Lutheran pastor. In addition, well, Harry, during his time away, became a successful businessman, and he returned to New Jersey a very wealthy man. For two poor guys from the old neighborhood, we were doing quite well for ourselves!

Harry rented a small home a few miles away from our rented home, and Binky and I, as well as our mutual best friend, Rose, helped Harry settle into his new life. Harry resided in Manchester Borough, and Binky and I lived about six miles or so away from Harry in a town called Great Falls. I was in the last hurrahs of seminary and Binky and I loved our rented home, but we decided to wait and see what the future would bring to us after ordainment, to see where we would land before buying a home. Harry, too, was buying his time, feeling his way back into life and entertaining the possibility of rekindling his romance with our mutual best friend, Rose. Rose and Harry were an item many, many years ago and Binky and I both felt as if the sparks flew a little between them now, but time would tell.

God's plan and romance. They both required some patience to allow it to all unfold. For now, the four of us remained very close. Our lives were busy and still greatly intertwined, as they had been for so many years. Many things had changed, but Harry was still Harry. He remained bombastic, gregarious, overwhelming, and spontaneous in his actions and his plans, too. Oh yes, and telephone conversations with Harry lasted all of maybe twenty seconds or so, since he never allowed you to speak for very long and seldom, if ever, said goodbye. He was not rude, just always in a rush.

It was early in the morning on a Saturday in late November and I planned to catch up on some studies and to write one assignment paper for seminary. Binky was doing laundry and afterwards, we planned to have a date-night at a local tavern and relax. It had been a long week for both of us. Binky and I rode the train into the big city together, Binky worked in Manhattan and seminary was not too far from where my wife worked. Even though we spent time together sitting on the train during our common commute—it was always hectic and never quality time. The weekends were our time to catch up on household work and chores and spend some time together. Harry had mentioned something about catching up tomorrow and going out with Rose and the four of us would do something. But honestly, right for now, Binky and I were content to be alone and together.

No sooner than I picked up my pen, opened my books and settled in to write the paper, when the blessed telephone rang.

I heard Binky yell up to me from the basement, "Please, pick up that call, twenty-seven. Hands full of laundry down here and I cannot get to the extension down here!"

"I have it, Binky!"

I made my way to the telephone and picked it up on the third ring. Harry's loud voice and enthusiasm nearly blew my ears off.

"Hello."

"Twenty-seven! What are youse two guys doing?"

I knew even before answering that Harry would not allow me to speak or tell him what Binky and I were doing. Harry's voice was too excited. Something had the big guy on a mission, and I knew him rather well.

Regardless of the dabble in futility; I gave it a whirl. "Well, I have a paper to write and Binky is. . .."

"Okay, good. Get your asses over here. We have a priority mission to do. Rose is already on the way over. Tell, Bink-a-roo-ski to dress warmly. I know you will only wear a vest. This mission will be right up ya alley. It will appeal to the incurable Old Lady Syndrome floating in ya bloodstream. See ya in a few. If I ain't answering the door, come across the street to Mr. Keating's house."

"Well, ah, Harry, I really need to check with. . .."

"CLICK!"

Of course, the line went dead without so much of another word, let alone an actual, "Goodbye."

Binky magically appeared, and she stood in front of me holding a laundry basket filled with freshly laundered clothes as I slowly lowered the telephone handset in the cradle.

Binky set the laundry basket on the dining room table and as she picked out some clothes to fold, Binky said, "Let me guess, from the very short duration of the telephone call and the perplexed look upon your face that call was from, Harry. He must want us to come right over because I heard him cut you off when you tried to tell him that you needed to check with me."

Binky picked up what appeared to be very sexy and chic black lingerie and she held them in her hands while she smiled at me. Obviously, Binky wanted a conformation of her assumptions.

"Yes, right on, as usual, dear Binky. Something about running right over, for you to dress warmly, Rose is already on the way and this is a priority mission."

My wife shook the sexy lingerie out in the air, in order to neaten the material before folding, and while doing so, she smiled widely at her being proven correct. My eyes remained focused on the lingerie. It was difficult to recover because the visions of Binky wearing the lingerie seemed to have hijacked my thoughts.

Despite the distraction, the words arrived.

"Yes, he also said it would appeal to my Old Lady Syndrome affliction. Something about Mr. Keating across the street. I am not sure what he has concocted now, but I guess we better get ready and head over there."

Binky folded the black piece of allure and asked, "How long has Harry called you an old lady and according to Harry, how long have you been afflicted with this syndrome?"

"Since we were around ten years old."

"Remind me again. How long have you two been friends?"

"Since we were around ten years old."

"Oh, my, I see," Binky said as she smiled and placed the folded lingerie in the basket.

"I have to ask you, Binky," I said while pointing at the lingerie. "Are those new? I mean that . . . sexy lingerie."

Binky posed, fluffed her long blonde hair and draped it all over her shoulders and winked at me while saying, "Why yes, it is new, dear twenty-seven. So is the perfume that I bought this week and that I plan to wear for you. I thought an extra martini or two at dinner for me, combined with some Scotch for you, would provide just the ticket for lowering inhibitions. The lingerie was on sale. Sadly, the perfume was not. The lingerie, if I do say so myself, it fits me rather nicely. Especially so in and around my breasts. The perfume, the lingerie, and the extra drinks, were all parts of our evening plans for tonight. I guess our plans are going to run into a delay." Binky added another wink and a coy smile while lowering her voice into a sexy growl, "Luckily, your affliction is not exactly what your best friend thinks it is."

An hour or so later, Binky and I found Harry and Rose across the street in the garage of Mr. and Mrs. Keating's house. It was an overcast, nippy and cold day and Rose was dressed in a winter overcoat, a warm hat and a pair of black dungarees with boots on her feet. Rose, as usual, looked gorgeous. No matter what they wore, or what the situation was, Binky and Rose were both always looking gorgeous.

While the three of us all stood in the doorway opening of the garage and watched as Harry frantically rifled through numerous boxes and mounds of Christmas lights, plastic figurines and assorted decorations, I began to connect the dots on the mission. Harry had lived on Bogart Street for almost three years and each previous Christmas we all saw and enjoyed the remarkable Christmas extravaganza known as the home of the Bogart Street Santa. We also visited with Mr. and Mrs. Keating and watched as they opened their hearts and their home to the children as they enjoyed assisting Santa Claus in his mission of goodwill and peace on Earth. Today, there was something missing from the Keating home.

It was late November, a few weeks until Christmas, and the Keating's home was dark and silent. There were no Christmas lights lining the edges of the roof, nor did they chase down to the gutters and outline the entire frame of the home. No wreaths, no plastic Santa Claus and reindeer on the rooftop of the Keating's home. No snowmen, elves, wreaths, sleighs, or candy canes. Apparently, they were still in the mountains of boxes in front of us in the garage. The boxes that also had a Harry M. Redmond Junior within their midst.

"Ah, Harry, I am sure that this is a dumb question that only a person afflicted with the dreaded Old Lady Syndrome would ask, but do you have permission from Mr. and Mrs. Keating to go through all of their Christmas decorations and to be in their garage?"

Harry popped up from behind a huge cardboard box full of candy canes and he frowned at me while opening the box. He waved for us to come closer as he reached into the box and one-by-one handed us candy canes.

"Yup, always acting like an old lady, twenty-seven, but yes. I have permission. They ain't home."

Rose looked over at Binky and me, and she shrugged her shoulders. Even though Rose arrived before we did, apparently, Rose did not know much more than what we did.

While Harry pulled an armful of candy canes out of the box, Harry began to clarify his previous statement, "Well, I have permission to be in the house. . . ."

His voice drifted off as he worked on unpacking the blessed candy canes.

How many could there be in there?

I sensed a typical Harry twist and turn of the situation and background story. Now, please, do not misunderstand me. Harry did not lie; he just did not always give you all the details or background information on a situation. Harry set the box on end and he crawled inside of it and disappeared inside the huge box while he dug around inside. All we could see were legs and feet.

He stood up for air while holding even more candy canes and finished his explanation.

"I am watchin' the house while they are away. I am feeding and taking care of Dasher and Dancer. Well, I am doing the feeding. I was kind of hoping that Paul would clean out their litter boxes."

"I take it that Dasher and Dancer are the Keating's cats," I said as I felt the Harry vise of delegation closing in and around us.

"Yeah, they are. Can't tell ya which is which but yeah, they are cats. One is mean as hell and the other is nice. Anyway, c'mon, Paul, hold ya arms out. Ya gotta take piles of these, here, candy canes. We have to shake our doodles and get this done. Watchin' the house and caring for the cats is my mission, but this decorating part is a surprise."

Binky looked over at me and while holding an armful of candy canes, my wife shrugged her shoulders at the typically vague Harry-like statement. I had a feeling that the prospects of seeing Binky wearing that new set of sexy lingerie and inhaling amazing perfume tonight was falling by the wayside.

Harry waved in the air with his hands and spouted, "I ain't too interested in watchin' you shake ya ass, Paul, but Rose's doodle in those tight black dungarees and Binky's ass in those blue dungarees, both are mighty fine to my eye," Harry boldly spouted off and then the big guy, burst out laughing at his smug remark. After his laugh, Harry once more disappeared headfirst into the box while diving for more candy canes.

Rose shouted out as she watched Harry disappear into the box once more, "How many more of these blessed candy canes can there be, Harry? My goodness! They are endless."

Harry came up for air, handed Rose about four more candy canes and said, "These are it. C'mon, they go out here, along both sides of the sidewalk. From the driveway to the front steps. It is easy. Ya just push the stakes in the ground and make sure they are straight. That is why we gotta do this now. As in today. Snow is coming and the ground will freeze."

Harry darted out from behind the seemingly bottomless candy cane box and he ran to the front of the garage and out to the front yard.

Binky leaned in and said to Rose and me, "Do you notice how he is not carrying any candy canes?"

While Harry frantically pointed, showed us and demonstrated where, and how to install the candy canes, Binky asked the question that we all wanted to ask, but until now, we were too embroiled within the world of candy canes to do so.

"Harry, we love you with all of our hearts and souls and we understand that this is another mission and adventure for Harry, Paul, Rose, and Binky. I assure you that we are with you, but, please, exactly, why are we doing this? Can you please tell us why Mr. and Mrs. Keating are not at home, and why have they not decorated the house yet? What has happened?"

Harry paused from giving us candy cane instructions, and his face changed. I sensed the change in his demeanor, and so did Binky and Rose. Harry was on a mission for a reason. I knew that it was a very good reason, too.

"Mr. Keating had a stroke last week. A very serious stroke and it turned out that it was hit or miss for a few days if he would make it. Arthur ain't exactly a small guy and I guess his ticker is not too swift. He pulled through it but he has lost most of his mobility. His wife is with him now because they moved him to a rehabilitation center in south Jersey. Irene can stay with him there, cuz it is so far for her to travel. If all goes well, then he will be home in a few days."

Harry looked at each of our faces and he knew we were shocked and saddened at the bad news of the ill health of the jolly Mr. Keating, but I think he also felt the love and camaraderie that all of us shared. His usual loud and booming voice grew softer and Harry continued to explain with sincerity that I had experienced many, many times in our adventures and lives together. People who only knew the loud, bombastic, and overwhelming Harry M. Redmond Junior did not actually know the real Harry. Inside all the exterior, fluff and grandeur was an amazingly generous and caring man.

"Youse guys, at first, Arthur could not even speak and from what Irene told me he cannot speak too well. However, when he finally could speak and he saw his wife, his first words to Irene were, 'The house is not decorated for Christmas. Everyone will be so disappointed.' I sat here last night and watched through my front window as a parade of cars went up and down the street checking on the house. By now, most of the display is usually set up, the lights are up, and Christmas stuff is all over the house and the front yard. The usual grand opening flip of the switch is only a few days away. Neighbors come by and ask me questions. People passing by. They stop, and they ring my doorbell, and ask if the Christmas display will be up this year. We cannot let him down. Right now, he cannot walk and he cannot get out of a wheelchair, so I have my work crew coming out from my shop tomorrow to build a ramp here at the front door. I have another crew working in the bathroom. He needs a special toilet and a special bathtub too. We will knock it all out in a day or two."

Harry's eyes wandered and he waved his hands in the air while adding, "I love the snow around this time of the year, but I hope the snow holds off just a little."

After speaking, Harry kicked at the dirt with his boots and looked all around. He turned to the house and looked at it, then turned back to us.

The air was turning even colder and his warm breath made puffs into the air, while Harry spoke, "Growing up, Paul and I had very little. Our parents and my sisters, and our families were hard workers and honest and fair and they taught us what was right and what was wrong. They were the greatest. We were so fortunate to live the lives we lived with such amazing parents and families. We shared love. Now, we are in a much different position and we are very fortunate to have received such blessings in our lives. All the time, but especially, at the Christmastime of the year, you need to remember that sometimes, we all need love and someone to care and to help us when we are down on our luck. In thinking 'bout it, in our own lifetimes, we might have a million chances in our life to care for someone, to love someone, to listen when they need someone to listen, and for us to care. If everyone acted upon just 'bout half of those chances, then how wonderful would that be? This world will always need hope, and caring, and if we all take and never give, then the world becomes a very sad and desolate place."

Harry nodded his head in an agreement of his own remarks and he studied the three of us, but none of us said a word or moved. We did not want to interrupt his amazing speech.

Harry continued, "This morning, when the idea came to me, and when it came time to give, then I knew who to call for help. The three greatest people in the entire world. The people whom I love the most. The three people, who will always go along with me, support me, and help me, with these crazy and wacky ideas that I come up with and randomly enter my mind. No matter how crazy the idea, youse guys are here for me. Always and forever, we are together. Forever."

Rose's eyes filled with tears, and so did my beloved Binky's eyes. Honestly, I fought back a few tears, too. I looked at the house and realized that we had a helluva lot of work to do in a short amount of time. This job usually took Mr. Keating and his wife a few weeks to finish. However, with all due respect, we were not the Keatings! Harry, the weather, and Mr. Keating returning home made this a jam session of love.

I dropped my candy cane stash gently upon the ground, walked over to Harry, put my arm around the big guy, and pulled him into me very tightly.

While we embraced, I said, "Well now, yes indeed, I can certainly testify that you have had a number of crazy and wacky ideas over the years, but, Harry, I assure you that this is not one of them. Harry, I do believe you are correct. We do need to shake our doodles. Once we get these candy canes installed, what is next?"

Harry smiled at my words and without any hesitation, the big guy jumped into action.

"Okay, well, as I was sayin'. We have a ton of work to do here. We need to get busy and get this all done. For the candy canes, it is easy. The stakes push in the ground and then ya slide the plastic whoosie over the metal pin. . .."

While we decorated the house on that cold morning, the weather turned even colder, flashes of snow flurries spit out of the clouds, and the wind blew fiercely. However, a strange and fabulous thing happened. Neighbors wandered by and cars stopped and parked up and down Bogart Street. It seemed as all of Manchester Borough and beyond came by to see what was going on here.

People walked over and asked, "What is happening?" They asked, "Where is Mr. Keating? Is he going to be okay? When is he coming home?"

When we explained the situation, then these neighbors and random strangers all willingly pitched into help. Harry was in his glory because what had begun as a monumental task for the four of us to accomplish turned into a massive production of people from everywhere. People with no motivation other than that, they simply cared. Young and old, weak and strong. Everyone simply wanted to return some joy to the Bogart Street Santa Claus, and mostly, they wanted to return some of the love and Christmas happiness that he shared with them.

Harry quickly set up work teams, he directed the crews,

and before too long, we had a roof crew, a light crew and a ground crew. I harkened back to my days before hockey and seminary when I worked as an electrician and I led a makeshift electrical crew as we ran cords and wires all over the house, roof, and the front yard, in order to illuminate the massive display and make sure we had no fire hazards or circuit overloads.

Binky and Rose soon realized that with all of these people working, we needed food, drink and refreshments and they ran over to Harry's house and then to the food store to buy supplies and then prepare food, coffee, tea, and snacks.

Suddenly, the cold air and snow flurrying on that cold November day, meant very little because the warmth surrounding the Keating's home took on a very different meaning and feel. It was the warmth generated by caring and by love, and that type of warmth is very unlike any other kind. This kind of warmth—warms not only the body, but it warms the soul too.

When the ambulance pulled up in front of the Keating's home on Bogart Street in Manchester Borough, New Jersey, it was quite the scene. It seemed as if all of Manchester Borough and all the surrounding towns, in fact, maybe, the entire city of Paterson gathered there on the front lawn, on the sidewalk, and in the street. The Manchester Borough police blocked off the street and directed traffic and a patrol car, escorted the ambulance with Mr. and Mrs. Keating inside, right to their doorstep. Harry even tipped off the local press and the radio, television, and newspaper reporters all gathered there, too.

When the crew carried Mr. Keating out of the ambulance, they placed him in his wheelchair and then they rolled him to the base of his driveway; I flipped the switch on in order to light up the house and the decorations. I have to admit that I said a little prayer for the circuit breakers to hold and they did so. And the grand spectacle lit up in full grandeur as the huge crowd cheered and clapped as one. The crowd circled in and everyone extended a warm greeting to Mr. Keating, and welcomed the famous Bogart Street Santa Claus back to his home. Harry gave him a huge hug, and the flashbulbs flashed and recorded the moment. Tears of joy streamed down Mr. Keating's face as his eyes scanned the glorious Christmas display, the ramp that Harry's crews built, and the huge crowd gathered to show him love and to welcome him home. The stroke had left Mr. Keating with very little speech capabilities, but we listened carefully, as he waved his hands for us to gather in and listen, while he greatly struggled to speak.

With strength mustered up with some help from Heaven, Mr. Keating said, "Thank you. I love you all. Each one of you . . . I love you all and wish you all a very . . . merry Christmas."

The crowd cheered, and we all broke into a loud and spontaneous rendition of "We Wish You a Merry Christmas" and added Mr. Keating at the end of the verse.

It was a glorious moment that lives in all of our hearts forever.

Sadly, Mr. Keating passed away in July of the following year, but I have to think that Mr. Keating's Christmas of that particular year, filled not only his heart with joy and the hearts of many with the same joy, but that his amazing legacy lives on forever in and around Bogart Street in Manchester Borough, New Jersey.

Harry eventually bought the little house that he rented and lived in there, and he kept the house for many, many years as an investment property. He would never tell any of us, but Binky and I thought that he kept the house in order to retain some kind of presence on the famous street.

Still to this day, people identify the street by the legacy of Mr. Keating and his immense kindness and his love of Christmas, combined with his heartfelt joy. People in the know; always refer to Bogart Street as, "The street where the Santa Claus guy lived."

In New Jersey speak that is a testimony full of love!

To echo the wise words of the great, Harry M. Redmond Junior, "All the time, but especially, at the Christmastime of the year, you need to remember that sometimes, we all need love and someone to care and to help us when we are down on our luck. In thinking 'bout it, in our own lifetimes, we might have a million chances in our life to care for someone, to love someone, to listen when they need someone to listen, and for us to care. If everyone acted upon half of those chances, then how wonderful would that be?"

I have to think that it would be more than just wonderful.

I think that it would be glorious and because of wonderful people such as Mr. Arthur Keating, Irene Keating, and Harry M. Redmond Junior, the world has just a little bit more of a dose of hope, joy, and love.

At Christmastime, or any other time of the year, that sure sounds glorious to me.

THE END

The Magic Fox

A Christmas Fantasy Story
For Children of all Ages

As Told by the Character of Pastor Paul John Henson

The Magic Fox

"Please, Father, tell us a story before you tell all of us that we have to go to bed because it is so late," my daughter Heather Sarah walked up to me, while I sat in my easy chair, next to a roaring fire and with pleading eyes, she made her request.

"After we go to bed, then all the grownups will stay up late, drink beer and other booze and stuff that we can't have that makes everyone talk funny and laugh a lot and tell all those grown up, boring stories about all your olden days."

Heather Sarah took me by surprise, not by her honesty, (she was quite blunt, as her mother and grandfather were and she openly spoke what was on her young, but very sharp mind) but the nature of her sudden request took me by surprise.

We had been down these storytelling roads many times. I often told the children bedtime and family time stories, often utilizing my profession as a Lutheran pastor to spin Bible stories, but religion was not the only subject of our stories. I covered a wide variety of genres and subjects, including some famous Harry and Paul adventures. With those particular adventures, I remained a bit selective, since they often required a large amount of censorship. Now that I had returned to writing part time, I recorded some of those adventures on paper and I had little doubt that as the children grew older, they could read many of them on their own. I enjoyed telling stories. After all, I preached and wrote for a living, but Boxing Day was my day off to recover from the madness of being a pastor in a large church during the Advent and Christmas season. I very much looked forward to this day. It was early evening and my family and friends were once more having our traditional Boxing Day gathering at the parsonage of Reunion Lutheran Church. Our best friends, Harry M. Redmond Junior and his lovely wife, Rose and their daughter, Blue Cloud, were here. Also in attendance were my mother and father, my in-laws, Harry's sister Linda and her husband, Ronnie (the world famous Ronzo) and well, the whole gang was here. I was not actually in a storytelling mood; I had consumed quite a bit of food, a large helping of a Christmas pudding, and washed it all down with some copious amounts of beer.

Heather Sarah spilled some more inside information in her efforts to pry a story out of me.

"I don't think the beer helps you to tell any stories, dear Father, because Grandpa Henson let Paul William sneak a sip out of his beer glass, and my brother said it made his head a little funny and made his body warm."

Instantly, the entire room, led by my dear mum, and then my gracious wife, turned their eyes on my old man.

"Grandpa Henson!" Binky shouted.

Mum tapped my father gently on the shoulder and shouted, "Paul William Henson, the first! How could you? Your grandson is only thirteen!"

The old man at first shook his head in denial, but a quick gaze around the room told my father that he sealed his own fate and he rolled his eyes, waved his hand and mumbled, "Oh, what the hell! It will not hurt him. Look at his father, it made all his hair grow thick and long."

After some further reprimands from my wife, a few

laughs (and Ronzo agreeing with my father), the old man escaped further waves of wrath.

I dove in to divert attention from and save the old man, "A story? Why a story? You and your brother and Blue have all those new gifts that you received for Christmas and enjoying them sure seems to be more fun than listening to your father ramble on with a story. I thought you guys were all playing that new board game while you sat around under the Christmas tree. What brought this on? Are you sure that you want to hear a story?"

Heather Sarah, who now was eleven or so years of age, at first, stood and she carefully pondered my questions. I could envision the wheels spinning gently in her head. Our daughter then held one finger up to me as if to signal for me to wait a bit. Then she stopped and turned to Blue and her older brother. Even though Paul William was older, and Blue Cloud, a little younger than our children were, there remained little doubt that Heather Sarah was the leader of the group and the designated spokesperson. The group of children huddled up in front of me while in a serious conference, and all of us laughed as we strained to hear their muffled whispers. At first, I thought this was a diversionary tactic for all of them to stay up later, (or our son to sneak more sips of beer) they were growing a little old for stories, but in listening to the whispers in the huddle, I realized they really did want to hear a story.

My mother-in-law laughed aloud and commented, "Why, my goodness, this is all so serious. I wonder what the subject could be that they want to hear?"

When Heather Sarah broke the huddle with the verdict, she took the hands of her brother and Blue Cloud and the three of them marched up to me and our daughter declared the pronouncement.

"Yes, dear Father, we want to hear a story. We have all day tomorrow to finish our game and play some more new games. Anyway, I usually am the winner when we play these games, so Blue and Paul William are sick of me winning. Yes, before we have to go to bed, we want to hear a Christmas story. But not a Bible story. We are sick of them. Most of them are boring."

With that, the entire room full of adults burst into laughter and my father-in-law, who never missed a chance to needle me, jumped into the fray on the heels of his granddaughter's honest opinion. "We all are sick of them, too! Especially, after hearing your father babbling on for the last month with the same, old, boring, Christmas poppycock from the pulpit."

I squirmed a bit, but honestly, I was rather tired of them, too. Please, God, forgive me, but geez, there are only so many spins that you can put on the same old story. A manger, angels tending their flocks by night, high taxes and a long journey interrupted for the birth of a child. Oh yes, and we cannot forget the famous Three King Guys in the mix. The old man will never forgive me if I forget them.

"Well, I guess, but it is not exactly easy to whip up a story off the top of my. . .."

Heather Sarah interrupted me and once more spoke for the group. "And we want a snack too. We want home-baked Christmas sugar cookies and warm milk, while we listen."

"Since we are bunking here, then I want gallons of beer," Ronzo added.

Senator Hobnobber piggybacked Ronzo and proclaimed, "Good point, Ronzo! I need another double Scotch if I have to listen to my mind-numbing son-in-law ramble on some more within layers of boredom. At least, a Scotch induced haze will offset the pain of his drivel."

'My goodness,' I thought, 'such specific requirements to hear me tell a story.' I tried hard not to let it affect me too much.

Rose and my beloved wife, Binky, both stood up to head for the kitchen, as the floodgates opened on snack and drink requests.

The group now settled in for the long haul.

I guess my fate was sealed and since the story well was rather dry, I requested some additional liquid inspiration. "Please, I will have another beer, too."

Harry leaned over, took a gentle sip of his patented Wallcrawler cocktail and whispered to me, "Do you have a story in mind, Paul?"

I shook my head and told Harry in a whisper, "Nothing. Not a single thing. It is not so easy, just to make this stuff up, ya know. They always do this to me. Maybe you should give a story a whirl, number thirty-five. I think after all of these years that it might be your turn."

Harry immediately shook his head fervently and added a very valid point.

"Nah, Paul, c'mon now, ya know that my stories usually are not for children's ears and most adults too. Especially at Christmastime. We need ya old lady skills here to tell some sappy Christmas stuff. Make it sort of like them, there, cornball made for television Christmas movies on that old lady channel. You know the kind of movies where the plastic looking guy and the pretty gal with fancy hair constantly fight and don't like each other. Then the guy and the pretty gal end up kissing on Christmas Eve in the snow and then they end up gettin' engaged. Really corny. My stories ain't gonna make the Christmas cut."

"Well, you have a point. You are correct, but I can't come up with anything right now."

Harry nodded and whispered in return, "But it is our kiddlers. Ya gotta come through. Christmas, Boxing Day, ya know the drill. No Bible, stories. All of us want to hear something good too. No boring stuff. Pressure is on, buddy boy. What the hell are ya gonna do?"

"Dunno. Wing it, I guess."

Upon hearing my words, Harry shouted out to his wife as Rose approached our kitchen, "Better get twenty-seven a shot of high-test hooch. Make it a double there, baby. He is gonna need it. I am turning up the old lady dial on him right now to come up with sumthin' good."

Rose laughed and waved to acknowledge the request. One thing that I knew was that I could always count on Harry to support me. The drinks, snacks and other goodies arrived, Harry coaxed me into a nip of the hooch (usually, not my drink of choice) and as the warmth of the high-test liquid trickled down and floated around me, I felt just a bit numb and warmer too. My father jumped up, tossed another log into the fireplace, poked at it a bit and then settled into his chair next to dear Mum. The children settled in a semicircle on the floor in front of me, and all eyes focused upon number twenty-seven.

Just as Harry predicted, the pressure was now on me.

As the liquid courage worked some inner magic, I glanced outside and through the front window of the parsonage. I caught the drift of the snowfall that had begun falling an hour or so earlier. Snow, glowing fireplaces, fantastic Christmas lights on the tree, a family and friends gathered, Christmas, sappy stuff and my "old lady" knobs turned up to maximum by good ole number thirty-five.

Suddenly, I saw the story gates open within my mind and words began to tumble out of Heaven in front of me.

Another sip of the high-test, and with a hint of a smile and the trappings of a story in my heart, I began. . ..

In the winter majesty of the vastness of what the locals call upstate New York, far away from the influence of New York City, within rolling hills and low valleys, in the cold, icy creeks and streams and on the top of the snow-covered mountains, there is profound beauty. Within that beauty, there are elements of quiet mystery and within the vastness of the land; there are many stories and legends of old. At no time of the year are those stories told more often and the legends more pronounced than they are at Christmastime. When snow covers the land in layers of white beauty, when the moonlight of a cold, crisp winter evening reflects the diamonds hidden within their white magic while it flickers upon the freshly fallen snow, it is then that the magic of Christmas unfolds. While the residents, who call this land their home, huddle to celebrate the holiday within the warm and cozy comfort of their homes and the telltale smoke puffs from their chimneys tell of that warmth, the magical snow filters down and the wind whispers of the legends. One might need to have their eyes focused and wide open, and their ears finely tuned to hear the whispers in the wind, but it is all there.

You must first believe in the magic of the season, to be able to see it, to hear all the legends and most importantly, to allow them to enter your heart.

"As I have explained, the test results are rather conclusive, and they confirmed my earlier diagnosis. We will need to take immediate action to have the best chance at . . . ah, well . . . at treating this disease successfully. You will need to bring Becky to the best hospital available for this procedure and for further tests. If it proves to be that your daughter requires a bone marrow procedure, then a more advanced facility staffed with nurses, technicians and doctors specializing in this type of care, ah, well, obviously, they will be better equipped for such an intense procedure than we are here."

The doctor fiddled a bit with some papers on his desk and for just a few moments, he could not make direct eye contact with the heartsick parents of young Becky Helms. Even though he had been practicing medicine for over thirty-five years, these situations were never easy. Telling grief-stricken parents that if certain medical procedures are not highly successful, their seven-year-old child's life might be threatened, is not, and never will be, an easy thing to do. While Mr. and Mrs. Helms held hands as they sat side-by-side in the guest chairs in front of the doctor's desk, the good doctor continued to provide his best advice.

"The medical center in Albany is a wonderful facility with highly skilled doctors. Their facilities and equipment are all highly advanced, and even though it is a good distance south, it is the closest advanced facility that I can recommend for these types of situations. If you really want the best of the best, there are of course, downstate options in New York City, in New Jersey, or a ride into Boston. Regardless, I would check with your insurance provider to see what is covered, and where."

"We understand, Doctor Hudson. I will make some calls and we will make a decision right away. I know with Christmas only a few days away, it might make for a rather difficult season and some challenging travel, but I am on this. We want only the best for Becky and if that means traveling to the ends of the world, then that is what we will do." Becky's father explained, then let go of his wife's hand, stood up from the chair and extended his hand to Doctor Hudson. "Thank you for everything, Doctor Hudson. Mostly, thank you for your kindness to our beloved Becky and for your understanding."

As the two men shook hands, Mrs. Helms dabbed her eyes with a tissue and forced a smile and the good doctor said, "I wish all the blessings in Heaven and on Earth to Becky and you. I will pray for Christmas magic to be with you every step of the way and in your hearts, too. Please, let me know where the procedures will be, and what your final decision is. I will forward all the records and, of course, be available for any consultations or information that I may be able to provide. Please do keep me informed."

"We will, Doctor Hudson. We will. Much appreciated."

With that, Mrs. Helms slowly stood, forced a muffled, thank you, and the parents left the doctor's office to rejoin Becky, who was under the watchful eye of a few nurses.

"Hi, Mommy. Hi, Daddy!" Becky beamed when she saw her parents approaching. "Can we go home now? I want to send off my letter to the North Pole and finish decorating our tree!"

The bright-eyed, but somewhat tired, pigtailed, red-haired, little girl escaped the nurses with a few goodbye hugs and kisses; she then ran and then jumped into her father's arms. Mr. Helms picked her up as he mouthed a thank you to the nurses and forced back some tears as he held his daughter tightly in his arms.

"Yes, time to go home now. Let's go home, honey bunch. I will build a warm fire. You can finish your letter and we will finish decorating the tree. We can play some Christmas music and Mommy will bake some cookies. It will be a glorious night. Yes, indeed, a glorious night."

Despite the attempts at Christmas merriment, the evening was a disturbing one for the parents of little Becky Helms. They did their best to put on a strong front and maintain a happy face, yet it was not easy. At some point, they needed to tell Becky that she might be spending the Christmas season in a hospital bed, away from her home, away from her Christmas tree and far away, from where her heart wanted to be at this time of year.

Jeremy "Rusty" Helms was a hard worker. Rusty Helms did not mind the midnight on-calls for emergency repairs, or the wires that went down in the snowstorms and ice storms. He had a position employed as an electrical line worker for the local utility company, and while he did not earn a fortune in pay, he did receive union benefits that were outstanding. He was fortunate in this day and age to have outstanding medical coverage for reasonable fees, and he knew that right now, outstanding medical insurance was going to be very important. Jeremy also accumulated quite a bit of leave time because he seldom, if ever, called in for sick-days and rarely took vacation days; therefore, he had banked quite a few days of leave time. He knew that with these treatments for their daughter, time off from work was going to be very important. Rusty knew that an emergency call meant overtime wages, and right now, he was going to need to earn every penny that he could. Even with the outstanding medical insurance, Mr. Helms knew that if Dr. Hudson's predictions of intense medical procedures came into fruition, then the medical coverage at some point would run out and the out-of-the-pocket expenses could be overwhelming.

His friends and most of his family (except for his mother) all called him "Rusty" because of his flaming red hair, which he passed on to his lovely daughter. Rusty grew up here in upstate New York, he played ice hockey on frozen ponds as a youth and he was a rugged, loyal, and hard-working man. Cold ice and snow meant little to him. Except for the cold in his heart right now.

Mrs. Marilyn Helms worked in the cafeteria at the local high school for the county, and Mrs. Helms was a hard and diligent worker. Between the two of them, they lived well, not opulent or over their means, but they did what they could to provide all they could for their only child. The Helm's family lived in a small house, in a rural community far off the interstate, on a side road with other small houses. Mr. Helms drove an older model sedan, equipped with all-wheel-drive to propel them through the difficult winters. It was not pretty, but it was reliable and economical. Mrs. Helms drove a small, foreign-made, compact car, and she relied on her husband to bring her to work when the roads and weather were difficult. One good thing was that when the schools closed for work or weather, then Becky also was home. Babysitters were not so easy to find in these rural neighborhoods.

Mr. and Mrs. Helms were high school sweethearts, and they lived their entire lives in this area. They lived close to the Canadian border, where the air was clear, the winters harsh and the colors of autumn were picturesque beyond description. Both sets of Becky's grandparents lived in the community too, not too far away from the Helm's residence and while the rural aspects of living here presented some challenges, the Helms could never, and would never, want to consider living any place else. Rusty Helms was a fan of the outdoors, he hunted in the endless woods of upstate New York, and Rusty trout fished in the clear streams. It provided not only sport and recreation for him, but a little extra food on the table never hurt.

No, they were staying here in this glorious land.

Forever.

After all, the apple never falls very far from the base of the apple tree. It might shake loose, drop to the ground and roll, but it never rolls too far. Even when it eventually fades away and turns into dust, the roots of the tree absorb it once again and the cycle begins over again.

Rusty sat in his chair in front of the fire, in the living room. He was staring at the Christmas tree that the family had just enjoyed decorating. Becky was sound asleep in her bedroom, as was his wife. They both needed rest. The only company he had on this cold, crisp evening was the crackle of the logs and the gentle sound of the licking of the flames against the air. He sipped a hot cup of tea and took turns staring at the licks of the fire and the beauty of the glow of the many colors of lights on the tree. He knew that they needed to make some calls tomorrow, decide where to bring Becky for her medical care and then somehow, break the news to Becky of what lies ahead. Break the news. How? Gently, of course, but really and truly, how? The doctors had poked, prodded and put poor Becky through many levels of pain, and the little girl remained brave. She could not understand as to why, after all of those many procedures and countless doctors that she still did not feel well. Tomorrow, they needed to tell her of more tests and pain. Now it was going to get unbearable, both emotionally and physically. Then, he had his wife to support because, in some ways, Marilyn was a fragile soul, and this was all taking a toll on his beloved wife.

What began as headaches, listless and lethargic behavior and a lack of energy, up and down fevers and an initial diagnosis of the flu in the late summer, had now months later, turned into a life-threatening situation. Why? Rusty had no feasible or plausible explanations, they were not members of any specific church, nor were they big churchgoers; their attendance was mostly on Easter and Christmas Eve, but it was not as if he was a nonbeliever. Somewhere deep down in his heart and in his soul, Rusty believed in God. He just could not understand why a little, innocent girl had to suffer so. Rusty put his teacup aside on the end table and thought that he needed to pray for a miracle. It could not hurt, so that is what he did. He knelt down on his knees in front of the fire and the Christmas tree, and he prayed for a miracle. He also prayed for some of that Christmas magic that Doctor Hudson mentioned. It was what he wanted to do and what he felt in his heart that he needed to do. Moreover, prayer was free, and right now, prayer might be the only thing that they were not going to have to pay for.

The next few days, found Mr. and Mrs. Helms scrambling to discover information to make the best decision that they could for the welfare of their precious daughter. After many telephone calls, emails and consultations with the medical insurance provider and Dr. Hudson, they chose a specialty doctor practicing out of a world-renowned hospital in New York City. They felt, as did Dr. Hudson, that they were very lucky to have been able to schedule an appointment with such a highly regarded doctor, who was also a participant in their medical insurance plan.

Purchasing a round-trip airplane ticket for the entire family on such short notice, during the Christmas season, even with an emergency discount, would be very expensive and would still entail driving to Albany. From Albany, it was just over three more hours to the big city. In Rusty's mind, he wanted to save as much money as he could for the pending medical costs, and a three-hour drive was hardly worth flying or paying extra for train tickets. Even all the trains to downstate left out of Albany. Therefore, driving to the city made the most sense. It would require about an eight or nine-hour drive, a stay or two in expensive hotels in the big city, but they felt it was the best choice. The doctor's schedule was demanding, but since the holidays are not a popular time of the year to see doctors, it turned out that he had an opening right after Christmas Day. Their initial appointment for Becky to see the doctor was set for the first thing in the morning on the day after Christmas, or what other parts of the world call Boxing Day and with that in mind, the family decided to set out on Christmas Eve and check into a hotel close by the medical center. They felt they could have a limited type of Christmas celebration in the hotel room and make the most out of a difficult situation. Besides, if he could help it and plan it, Mr. Helms did not want to be wandering around confusing midtown Manhattan streets, rushing to make the appointment in time. All of this was pressure-packed enough and to risk losing a window of an appointment with this particular doctor was not what he wanted to do.

With kindness in their hearts and softness on their lips, Becky's parents broke the news to their daughter that she required another doctor's visit, this one will be far away and they have to set out on Christmas Eve to allow for some extra time to make the appointment. They promised Becky that they would celebrate Christmas as best that they could. Becky was very upset because the little girl felt as if she was missing Christmas!

The little girl had many protests and tears.

What about her tree that they spent so much time decorating? How will Santa Claus find her to deliver presents? She did not want to see any more doctors! Becky Helms wanted to stay home, in her house and sleep, in her own bed. It was heartbreaking, but her parents did the best they could to help her understand that this was to make her feel better once and for all.

"I promise that you will have Christmas, Becky. The tree will still be here when we return, and the presents, too. Santa Claus always finds you no matter where you travel too. We can buy a little tree and have some Christmas fun in the hotel room too." Mr. Helms did his best to assure Becky that Christmas was not going anywhere.

Early in the morning on Christmas Eve, the Helms family loaded up their sedan with their luggage and some supplies and headed out on their long journey. It was at least an hour and one-half ride for them to make it to the New York State Thruway; therefore, Rusty Helms was anxious to get an early start. Just to add to the anxiety the overcast skies looked ominous, and the winter air had that heavy smell to it, which all residents of snowy lands know to mean that snow was in the air. Between Christmas music playing on the sedan's radio, the weather broadcast rather joyfully announced that there was to be a white Christmas this year, and the prediction was for a rather heavy and blinding snowstorm to move in, dump great amounts of snow and then move out of the area by Christmas morning. Ordinarily, if the family were in their home, all snug, warm, and readying for the holiday, then such a forecast would be glorious. Not today, no, no, no, not today. This heavy snowstorm was not the type of weather that a family ventured out in for a long journey, and Rusty Helms hoped and prayed that he could outrun the storm and they could make it to the highway. There, he could follow the huge snowplows and their hope was that, downstate, the storm would not be as fierce. The prayers and the hope proved fruitless and about forty-five minutes into the drive, what had once been a snowfall of fine flakes of snow turned into a heavier, driving snowfall.

Why could they not even catch one small break of luck here?

Mr. Helms knew the main roads quite well, however, some of these roads farther south of their county; he was not as familiar with these days.

"I think this road takes you over, Silver Fox Mountain. I think that it is a shortcut to the New York State Thruway," Rusty explained to Marilyn and Becky.

Not wanting to doubt her husband, yet knowing that he was nervous about making it to the Thruway, Marilyn gently touched her husband's arm and asked, "Silver Fox Mountain? Do you think you should just stick to the roads that you know, honey?"

"I am not sure, but I think, in order to outrun this snow, we have to make it to the Thruway quickly. Going over the mountain, cuts miles off the trip. Once we are on the Thruway, we will be fine. We can follow the plows . . . if we can only make it there. I am positive that we will have clear driving."

Mrs. Helms did not say anything else; she knew to trust her husband's judgment. Especially now, when they all had to stick together. Rusty turned off the main drag and drove onto a road, which was a shortcut to the Thruway. It entailed going over Silver Fox Mountain, which was a steep, very high, and right now, a slightly ominous mountain. In good weather, it was a place of grandeur and beauty. There was even a very famous ski resort with lodging near the top of the mountain. Within the pending grip of a heavy and blinding snowstorm, the mountain was an unforgiving monster looming in front of them. Mr. Helms felt that his all-wheel-drive vehicle could handle it. Besides, the snow was not too deep yet.

Jeremy "Rusty" Helms was upset, nervous, and while doing his best to make wise decisions, this shortcut route might not have been his wisest decision. When they passed by the Silver Fox Ski Resort and Lodge, which sat near the very top of the mountain and the family ran into flashing blue and yellow lights, Rusty knew that he had not outrun the storm at all. In fact, the family had run smack into the very thick of it. Just to add more layers of wretchedness to this situation, Mrs. Helms reported that Becky's fever was spiking and her head now was throbbing with pain.

A New York State Trooper and a group of road maintenance workers met the sedan, and they informed Mr. Helms that the maintenance workers now closed the road on the other side of the mountain due to treacherous conditions. Even worse, turning around and returning down now on the other side might not be a wise choice, all-wheel-drive or not.

"But, sir, we are trying to get to the New York State Thruway, our daughter is very sick and we have to get downstate to see a special doctor on the day after Christmas."

The trooper was kind and sympathetic, but he shook his head and reported, "I cannot allow you to risk it. Perhaps, if you had a large four-wheel-drive truck, but not in this sedan. Even the maintenance workers are standing by, waiting for the storm to pass. Right now, it is very intense." The trooper then suggested, "Why don't you turn around and head for the ski lodge and resort. It is only a half-mile or so down the road. The last I heard, they had no more rooms in the main lodge and hotel, but the out cabins near the slopes had vacancies. This storm is going to pass quickly. By Christmas morning, maintenance will have cleared the road and you can safely be on your way. Let's all be safe now. I know you are anxious, but this is your best choice. Besides, it will be quite a nice Christmas setting, for the little one to enjoy. Even if she is not feeling well. I do wish you and your family all the best."

The head maintenance worker leaned in and told them that he would jump in a plow and carve a path for them to make it to the lodge. "This is a flat stretch. It is not much of a risk of becoming stuck in the snow or sliding off the roadway from here to the ski resort road and it is only a short distance. I am not supposed to do this, but after all, it is Christmas and your little girl is not feeling well. I will plow ahead of you to clear that road."

Despite the interruption in their plans and their anxiousness to be on their way, the trooper's advice and the maintenance worker's decision to close the road were sound. Since Becky's mother wanted to administer aspirin and some care, she advised her husband to do as the trooper suggested and to head for the resort and lodge. Rusty agreed, and he thanked the workers for their help.

He also thanked the trooper for his advice, for his assistance, and then wished him a merry Christmas. Rusty turned the vehicle around and he carefully followed the snowplow.

Before you knew it, they were in the warm and gaily decorated lobby of the resort. Finally, a stroke of luck! The trooper was correct. The main lodge and hotel had no vacancies. It was booked solid with skiers rejoicing for the fresh powder, but there were two or three cabins still left vacant. Apparently, with the storm bearing down harder and harder, no one else could make it up the mountain to rent them. The Helm's family checked into the resort and booked one of the small cabins to ride out the storm. This storm at Christmas time was a skier's dream but a traveler's nightmare. They had to pay top price for the cabin, but they would have had to do the same downstate. The main restaurant for the lodge had meals and snacks and the lounge served drinks, wine, and beer.

"A beer or two will help you to relax," Marilyn coaxed her anxious husband. The front desk clerk explained that the cabin had a fireplace and they could build a nice, cozy fire with firewood they supplied, but the fire damper required an adjustment. A maintenance man had the call with him, and he would be there in short order once he completed a call that he was working on right now. Once the damper repair was complete, then they could use the fireplace.

The lobby desk clerk told them that the cabin had a small kitchenette with a cooktop and some pots, pans, and tableware. Upon hearing about the kitchenette, Mrs. Helms purchased some canned soup, instant coffee, tea, some hot chocolate and other sundries and supplies from the small store that was located in the lobby of the resort's hotel. Marilyn was happy to be able to prepare some small meals and snacks in the cabin, especially if Becky did not feel well enough to sit in the restaurant. Mrs. Helms reassured her husband that while this was not part of the initial plan, it worked out rather well. Becky could rest, take some medication and the trooper was indeed correct. Despite the situation, it did feel a little like Christmas here. Certainly, to the Helms, more so than a big-city hotel in the middle of New York City would. If the weather cleared, as predicted, they still had plenty of time to make it to the hospital in the morning. Marilyn made a phone call to the hotel downstate and explained the delay in their arrival due to the weather. The family made their way up a small roadway that the resort maintenance workers cleared of snow, and they checked into their cozy and warm cabin at the base of the ski slopes.

Once they settled in a bit, even Rusty had to admit that this was a good plan and the cabin and the snow, and the situation, rather, did have a Christmas air to it. Now, he found himself wishing that they had a Christmas tree and a few presents for Becky to soften the blow of this trip, the situation, and the disappointment that Becky was feeling for missing her beloved Christmas celebration.

Christmas Cocktails

The cabin was gloriously warm and cozy. There was a delightful fireplace with stacks of wood for the fire, and a large glass picture window allowed for a breathtaking view of the ski slopes and the adjoining woods. There was a bathroom on the first floor, as well as one bedroom. The fireplace was the main feature of the living room, which sprawled into an open floor plan with a kitchenette and the cooktop and a small refrigerator being the anchors in the far corner of the living space. The cabin had a large front porch and a smaller rear deck, which overlooked gentle fields of snow and wooded paths. It was a warm and inviting log cabin set at the top of this mountain and under different circumstances; this would have been quite the holiday setting for the Helm's family.

The snowfall, which was once an enemy, was now gentle and picturesque. Jeremy had to admit that they were safe and secure, and that was the main objective right now. Be safe, warm, and secure. Finally, Jeremy felt some relaxation creeping into his soul. He had been so tense driving in the snow, and his death grip on the steering wheel caused his overall demeanor to be nervous and anxious. He kept telling himself to stay optimistic. After all, they were almost two hours south of their home and they were that much closer to their final destination.

His wife stopped him when he pulled a road map out of one of his bags in order to double check their route. This time, he listened as her gentle touch on his arm, and the touch of her warm lips on his cheek, while she gently kissed him, reassured him that it was time to relax and that all will be well.

"Please, relax, Jeremy. This is fine. We are safe, the storm will pass and we can be on our way in the morning. Please, honey, sometimes, things work out for a reason. Look, how Becky is all snug in that chair. The aspirin relieved her fever and her headache is so much better. This is a gorgeous place. Please, my love, let's relax a little before our journey. Here, we can have some type of Christmas celebration. I will make some hot soup for us. Once the maintenance man comes and repairs the damper, why don't you build a fire? And look, there is a radio too. Later on, maybe we can buy a bottle of wine from the lounge and we can listen to some Christmas music around the fire. It will be so pleasant."

Her husband looked over at Becky, who was warmly snuggled in a chair in front of the television. She was watching and enjoying a Christmas cartoon on the television, and Jeremy smiled.

"Yes, soup and wine would be nice. You are right. I will make a fire once the maintenance man arrives and, I promise, honey, that I will do my best to enjoy this and try to relax." With those words, he put the road map back in the case and gently kissed his wife once more. Jeremy deeply loved his wife and often, she was the one who grounded him and made him face reality with a clear mind and a reasonable vision.

"I wonder when the maintenance man is coming? The desk clerk said he would be here right after his other repair. If they do not come soon, I will give the front desk a call. Now, I am very much looking forward to a warm fire. Not only for the warmth but for the ambiance too."

No sooner than he had finished speaking the words when there was a gentle knock on the door of the cabin.

He shrugged his shoulders and commented, "How is

that for talking them up?"

Jeremy walked over to the door, unlocked the deadbolt, turned the knob, and opened it. Standing on the front porch of the cabin was a short and stout, older gentleman, with rosy and ruddy cheeks from the cold weather and the snow. He had silver hair, a longish silver-white beard, and a smile a mile wide on his face. He was dressed in a black woolen button-up overcoat with a matching black knit cap on his head. In his hand, he held a cloth tool bag. On his feet were black work boots. They were leather high-top boots and you could see that he had tucked the legs of his pants into the boots to prevent snow from entering them.

"I am sorry to disturb you folks," the maintenance man said. "I was trying to make it back here before anyone rented the cabin, but they sent me in a different direction. I am Barney Barnstead. Actually," he explained with a continuous smile and a warm laugh, "McHale is my real name. I am not sure what my parents might have been thinking on that one, something about a great uncle's last name or something like that. However, gradually, everyone began to call me, Barney. Therefore, please call me, Barney."

Rusty smiled, as did his wife, and immediately, they felt relaxed around the jolly and happy maintenance man. Barney had a calming influence on them.

Barney continued to explain as he stomped his boots on the doormat to knock off some snow and ice.

"I go through life and I fix things here and there. It makes me happy to do so, and it sure seems these days as if things need fixing more and more. Right now, my mission is clear. First, I need to make a quick adjustment to the damper on the fireplace there."

He finished his explanation, pointed at the fireplace, and smiled. Jeremy waved him in and some ice and snow came in, along with a whip or two of cold air.

"Please, yes, come in, please. The front desk clerk told us

that you would be here. You have perfect timing because we were just thinking about how nice it will be to have a fire on such a winter's night."

"Sorry for the delay. I actually reported the damper to the front desk. I noticed a while ago that it wiggles too much and that it was a little loose. Meant to fix it sooner, but you know how it is when things are busy and are getting all kinds of jammed up."

Jeremy closed the door behind Barney and nodded as he said, "I do understand about being busy. I fix things too. I am an electrical utility worker."

"Is that so? Nice way to make a living. Fixing things gives you a feeling of satisfaction. It is very important to fix things. All kinds of things in this world require fixing," Barney commented as he scurried over to the fireplace, set his tools upon the hearth and removed his woolen cap. Barney smiled at Marilyn and said, "Good afternoon." Then he looked over to Becky and smiled even wider and spoke a little louder, "And hello to you, very pretty, little gal. I love the red curls and pigtails. You are quite the pretty one. Take after your momma." Becky bashfully smiled at the compliment, looked over to her mother, who mouthed that she should thank Barney for his compliment.

"Thank you, sir," Becky squeaked.

"Sir? No, please, call me, Barney." He bent down to pull a wrench out of his bag and knelt down on the side of the fireplace to work on the handle of the fire damper, while explaining, "You know . . . it seems as if these days, I have a few different names." He laughed once again and said, "I guess that I have multiple identities. Let's see now," Barney said while studying the repair, "McHale is my real name, Barney is my nickname, and now that I am older and my hair and beard are silver, some folks they call me, the Silver Fox. I guess because of my hair or because of the mountain. Some folks say, I am named after the mountain, or in fact, now that I am so old, maybe the mountain is named after me." Barney stopped speaking, he studied the damper mechanism and it appeared as if for a few seconds that he searched for some more words to say.

A few more twists and turns of his wrench, then he smiled and pointed over to Jeremy while commenting, "Looking at your daddy here, I know where you got all that pretty, red hair from. Bet they call him, Rusty."

Jeremy laughed and said, "They do! How did you know that?"

"I know some things, but mostly, it was a lucky guess," Barney said with a sly smile and a twist of his wrench. Jeremy smiled, walked over to Barney, and extended his hand. Barney was such a gregarious man that you could not help but to like him.

"Hi, I am, Jeremy Helms. You can call me, Rusty." Jeremy then turned and pointed to his family. With a wave of his arm, he introduced his family, "My gorgeous wife, Marilyn and our daughter, Rebecca, or as she prefers, Becky Helms."

Barney stood up, tossed his wrench into his tool bag, and genuinely and forcibly shook Rusty's hand.

"My pleasure. Indeed, you are a lucky man. Fine family. You can call me anything that you would like, McHale, Barney, or the Silver Fox. Just please, do not call me late for Christmas dinner." Barney laughed at his own remark. He turned and rechecked the damper and asked, "I do not see any skis? You folks here for the holiday? This is working fine now. Please hand me the wood there, Rusty, and I will be glad to start a fire here."

"Oh no, Barney, you are too kind, I can do it."

"No, it will be my pleasure, besides—I need to double-check the draft, now that I have the damper working. Part of the work order. A full-safety check. You have to be careful. Safety first."

Rusty nodded, reached for the wood and handed pieces of the wood off to Barney, who stacked it in the firebox, along with some kindling, and while Barney struck a match and fanned the flames, Jeremy explained, "No. No, holiday celebration and no skiing for us. We are on our way downstate to New York City. Becky here is not feeling up to snuff, and she has to see a very special doctor after Christmas at the big medical center in the city. We were trying to make the New York State Thruway and beat the storm, but Silver Fox Mountain was a little too much for us. At the advice of a wise, New York State Trooper we pulled back and were very lucky to find this cabin to rent for the night."

The flames began to overtake the logs, and Barney studied them carefully to make sure the smoke was rising up the chimney. You could see the flames flickering in his clear blue eyes. He might be older, but he was very spry and sharp.

Satisfied at the fire's progress, he turned back to the family and commented, "Yes, a very wise choice. The mountain is beautiful, but in these types of storms, it can be unforgiving. Things happen for a reason." Barney looked at Becky and he said, "Not feeling up to snuff, huh? I see. Well, hunker down here and you will be fine. We cannot have beautiful little girls not feeling up to snuff now. Not feeling well is not what we can have! Especially, at Christmas time."

"Becky also is very sad about missing Christmas. She wanted to stay home and be next to her tree and sleep in her own bed tonight," Marilyn added. "We are doing our best at trying to cheer her up."

Becky piped up and immediately told Barney, "Santa will never find me here. I am going to miss Christmas."

Upon hearing those words, Barney seemed to pause, his rosy face turned a bit redder, and he reached down, tossed the box of matches and the rest of his tools in his tool bag, tucked the halves of his tool bag closed, picked it up and carried it over to where Becky was sitting. He smiled widely. In a few strides, he walked over to where Becky sat, and he knelt down next to her chair.

While setting the tool bag next to him, Barney began to speak, "You will not miss Christmas, Becky. No matter where you are. I assure you that Santa and the magic of Christmas, will always find you. As long as your heart is wide open, then you will never miss Christmas. Above all, you must concentrate on feeling better, and know and feel, deep within your heart, that you will be better. You must always believe."

Barney's voice grew more intense, and while he knelt next to Becky, his eyes widened and he waved his arms in the air. It seemed as if he wanted to pull the entire world into his arms.

With the intensity of his voice growing and growing, and his arms waving, Barney explained, "Let me tell you that, you are in a special place. This mountain has many stories to tell, many legends to hide, and very few to reveal. However, with the touch of just the right magic, then you never know what can happen. The snow that delayed you tonight is a very special snow. It is a Christmas snow, and magic is contained in every snowflake. Believe me, I know of these things. I have lived here forever and a little longer. A Christmas Eve snowfall on this mountain brings miracles and magic, and on nights such as tonight, is when they happen."

Barney's eyes closed, then opened and his voice lowered. With one finger pointed to the large picture window and towards the landscape lying beyond it, Barney continued to speak, "Living here, deep in the forests of the mountain, is a special, silver fox. The mountain holds his name and now, I guess, I share the name too. No one can ever capture him. No trappers can ever outsmart him and he has lived here forever. He is a Magic Fox. I have only seen him once. He crossed my path a long time ago, on a snowy Christmas Eve, such as this is, and my life was never the same. For they say, if you are lucky enough to see him on this magical night, when the moon lights up the fresh snow like diamonds and the spirit of God is alive, and if you wish as hard as you can for anything that you need or your heart desires, then the Magic Fox will grant you that one special wish. As I say it and as surely as I kneel here, then believe me when I tell you that, I saw him in the glowing moonlight of a Christmas Eve a long time ago. He is much larger than other foxes and his silver fur glows in the night. His tail has rims of golden fur and his eyes glow like beacons of gold in the night."

Becky was wide-eyed at his words and the little girl sat up in the chair and asked Barney, "How did the Magic Fox change your life? What did you ask for, Barney?"

The old man smiled and lowered his voice as he answered, "I simply asked the Magic Fox to show me what to do with my life and to give me a purpose. From then on, I had a mission."

"Like a job?"

"Yes, Becky, like a job. However, I think it is more of a mission than a job. Now, I fix things. My job is to fix things. Everything from fireplaces, to love, to broken hearts."

The old man once again waved his hands in the air as if to demonstrate what happened to him. His magical tale captivated Becky and her parents. Barney shifted his knees and leaned in even closer.

"Believe in your heart that the magic is alive, and on this holiest of nights, miracles do happen. Believe in it and a Christmas tree will grow right here in this living room. If it is not a tree that you can reach out, to touch, to feel, and to smell, then it will be a tree that exists in your heart. Please, believe me that Santa Claus, as well as the magic and the love of Christmas, will find you no matter where you are. They both will find you in your own heart."

Barney smiled; he gently reached out, took Becky's

hand, patted it, and squeezed it. He then let go, picked his tool bag up and stood up.

"Well, let me get to the next stop. So many more to make this afternoon and tonight. So many things to fix here within our little world on this mountain. I have taken up enough of your time. Thank you for your patience and I do wish you all the best. This storm will be out of here by midnight. The moon will be out and the stars will shine. It will be a special night. A holy night. The fire will feel so safe and warm tonight. You will have safe travels tomorrow. A long ride, but it will be a safe one. I can tell. Old Barney . . . well, I know things."

"I will let you out. Thank you, Barney. Merry Christmas to you." Rusty let Barney out into the cold as the old man donned his hat and coat once more. With a wave, Barney said goodnight and wished them a merry Christmas and Becky and her mother waved and bid Barney the same. The two men stepped out onto the porch and into the cold and the snow.

"Thank you, for being so kind to our precious, Becky. I know that she enjoyed your Christmas fantasy tale and the words of hope that you gave to all of us were very kind. It is not a good situation. The disease is very powerful, it is a blood cancer, and it is very serious. Life threatening, in fact. We are going to see one of the best doctors that we could find, who specializes in treatment of this disease. However, we know the facts. If the treatments are not successful," Rusty's words choked off before he managed to say, "then Becky might not see another Christmas Day. Oh how, I wish that we could give her the Christmas of her dreams, presents, a fantastic tree, Magic Foxes, Santa Claus, and of course, a miracle."

The old man set his tool bag down on the porch; he reached into his coat pocket and pulled out a pair of gloves.

As he slipped them on his hands, Barney said, "I see. I am so sorry. Then you will do it. Bring Becky all of those things and more. I know that Becky faces a formidable foe, but you too, need to believe, my young friend. What I told you in there was not a Christmas fantasy tale. It was hope. It was the truth. Now, you too must believe."

"Believe? In what? Santa Claus and Magic Foxes that creep across snow-covered hills to grant wishes and provide miracles. I do not think that will help us too much. Not right now, at least. I have prayed so hard for her to heal. In fact, just last night, I got down on my knees and prayed for a miracle of healing."

"Yes, you must cling to hope, just as a child does. Magic Foxes, and all. That is the trouble with us when we grow older. We lose our childlike ability to believe in the unseen, to have faith despite adversity, to dream and to hope. Believe in miracles and magic and believe in all that is good and is kind. Believe that you arrived here tonight, for a reason. Believe it with all of your heart and all of your soul. Praying hard, well, that is very, very good. We need to pray often. Always, always, pray. Both in good times and in bad times. Prayer is free, and it is powerful, and so is the power of hope. There are many things that we will never understand, but one thing that my long life has taught me, is always to have hope."

Barney very gently touched Jeremy Helms on the shoulder and it might have been Jeremy's imagination, but his touch sent a ray of warmth throughout his body, even though they stood in the cold and in the snow.

"You had better go back inside. It is so cold and you have no jacket on. Are you going to dinner? The main lodge restaurant food is very good. It will be packed to the rafters, but it will be worth it."

"Yes, yes, Barney. We will. Maybe after five or so in the afternoon."

"Oh, good. Do you mind if I slip back in here to recheck that draft and the damper while you are at dinner? I have a master key card. Always have to be careful where safety is involved. The fire should be hot by then and the draft should be strong. I feel better when I triple-check on these sorts of repairs."

"Please do. We really do appreciate the diligent service. Thank you for the dinner suggestion, your kindness, and the amazing words. All we have had all day are some snacks and such. Some solid food will be very special. Thank you again, Barney. You are a kind and special man. Please, let me give you a few dollars for being so kind. . .."

Jeremy reached for his wallet in his back pocket, and Barney held his hand on his arm to stop him.

"No, please, I would never take it. I do not need money. What does money mean in the light of this evening? Nothing. Not a thing. This is why I am here. To fix things. Please, love your family with all your heart and soul and believe in the magic of tonight. Please, never doubt again. Becky will be well soon. Your faith in that fact is all the payment that I need."

Jeremy nodded, put his wallet back in his pocket, and said, "Thank you. I do not know what to say other than, yes, you have my promise that I will do that. How many more stops do you have to make today? You said you were very busy. I guess all the skiers packed the resort for the holidays."

Barney did not answer Jeremy. He only smiled and waved as he turned and walked down the steps and into what was now a darkening late afternoon. Jeremy stood and watched him walk up the snowy path until he lost all sight of him in the falling snow and the fading light.

Becky was ecstatic after the visit by Barney and his sharing the words of hope and his tales of folklore and magic. If nothing else, Barney inspired the little girl to dream of Christmas magic and to believe that she will get better. Her parents did not try to dampen her joy, they only tried to teach her and emphasize how Barney was trying to make her feel better by asking her to dream and envision Christmas in her mind, but not to lose any focus on the main goal, which was to feel better.

Marilyn and Jeremy both had to admit to each other that they, too, felt inspired by Barney's words and his positive attitude. As far as the magical tale of the folklore of Silver Fox Mountain, well, they chalked it up to an old man's imagination and his attempts at spreading some joy at a desperate time.

Marilyn warmed and prepared the soup. They switched on the radio, tuned in some Christmas music for background ambiance, they sipped the hot soup, and the family relaxed in front of the warm fire. The afternoon waned, and the night closed in. After some relaxing, some more discussions, and a recheck on Becky's fever, Jeremy called the resort restaurant and checked on the availability of a table for three to dine. They were in luck. There was an opening and since Becky was feeling a little better, they bundled her up, jumped in the car and made the short drive down to the main building to eat dinner. The resort's maintenance crew was hard at work plowing the roads and keeping the flow of skiers and guests coming and going. The snow was still coming down, but it seemed to have eased up just a little. And with nightfall approaching, Jeremy hoped and prayed that all the predictions were correct, and that the snow would end before midnight. That would allow enough time for the road crews to clear the mountain roads and they could be on their way downstate. There was at least a foot of snow on the ground now and the last weather report they heard on the radio predicted another three to six inches of snow to fall before the storm ended.

They had an enjoyable meal, and both Marilyn and Jeremy were thrilled that Becky actually ate a good amount of food, and she even asked for a dessert. In fact, she picked her plate clean! It provided her parents with great joy to see Becky eat so well. As of late, all Becky would do was to weakly pick at her food here and there, and it was a struggle to get her to eat more than just a few bites. One disturbing aspect of the illness that Becky suffered from was a large loss of appetite; therefore, her eating an entire dinner was very encouraging. Marilyn chalked it up to a very long day and the fact that other than the soup and some snacks, they really had not eaten much of anything all day. Jeremy had a few glasses of beer, Marilyn enjoyed a few glasses of wine, and the family enjoyed a relaxing and joyful time. The family had to admit that maybe Barney was correct. This was a wonderful place to be, and perhaps things do happen for a reason. Jeremy purchased a bottle of wine to take back to the cabin, and the plan was to relax some more and celebrate a quiet Christmas Eve together in front of the fire.

Upon returning to the cabin, all of the Helms were quite anxious to escape the snow and cold, and with full bellies, the plan was to sit and relax, before going to sleep and for all of them to enjoy a good night's rest. On the surface, it was a good plan, but upon entering the cabin, this

Christmas Eve took a very different turn.

A swing of the door, a warm fire greeted them, but so did a surprise in the corner of the cabin's living room.

"Santa Claus came while we ate our dinner! Look! Look! Barney was right! I knew that Santa would come! I wished for it with all of my wishes from my heart!" Becky called out in joy at the sight of a fresh-cut Christmas tree standing in the corner of the living room. "He brought a tree and presents!" Becky shouted as she collapsed on the floor of the cabin, picked each present up, and studied them in glee.

It was a glorious tree, about six feet high, its trunk propped up by a wooden stand. The tree had decorations consisting of a small smattering of different color miniature lights, a string of threaded popcorn, and its girth was dressed from top to bottom with a multicolored chain of a paper garland. On the very top of the tree sat a handmade star, fashioned out of sticks of hand carved tree limbs. Telltale puddles of water lying underneath the tree, matching the width of the crown of the limbs, told the story of the snow that melted off the tips of the tree and from within its branches. Just the aroma alone of fresh-cut pine filled the room with a glorious fragrance of healing joy. Under the tree sat ten or so gaily wrapped gifts. While Becky laughed and shouted in joy, Jeremy held onto his wife, and he tried very hard not to drop the bottle of wine.

"Well, I can't imagine," was all that Jeremy could manage to mumble. Marilyn leaned in, grabbed her husband, pulled him down to her level, and kissed him on the cheek.

"Barney," she whispered to her husband, "what a glorious man. How did he ever do this? A tree and presents too?"

Jeremy recovered from his swoon and whispered back, "He sure is. He told me he was coming back to recheck on the fire damper while we went to dinner. He told me that he had a master key card and I told him to please come in and recheck it. I never expected this."

"Mommy! Daddy! Please, can I open the presents now? Can we have our Christmas now? It *is* Christmas Eve!"

Becky shouted while she ran up to her parents, pleading to open the presents now rather than waiting for the arrival of Christmas Day in the morning. It was quite amazing how this very ill little girl, who just a few hours ago, had a fever, a headache, was upset, lethargic and listless, and had little to no appetite, now had seemingly boundless energy, she just ate a huge meal and right now, she seemed quite normal.

Ever since the visit from Barney and listening to his poignant words, everything seemed quite different.

Jeremy smiled at their daughter's Christmas joy and after a head nod from his wife, he leaned in and told Becky, "Of course, you can open the presents now. We will need to hit the road early tomorrow, so go ahead and please open them now." Marilyn took the bottle of wine from her husband and headed for the kitchenette.

"There is a corkscrew in the drawer. I saw it before when I made the soup. I will open this, pour our glasses and watch while Becky begins to open the gifts from Santa."

Becky ran to the tree and enthusiastically dove into her presents. Jeremy sat on the sofa in front of the tree, and Marilyn joined him with the glasses of wine. First, there was a beautiful doll, then a puzzle or two, followed by a popular board game. The board game was the exact game that Becky had been asking for since the end of the summer! Each gift that was opened brought another cry of joy and laughter from Becky and a swoon from her parents, because it was difficult to believe that all of this came together so quickly by the efforts of one, little, old man with a heart of gold and a spirit filled with Christmas joy.

It was magical.

Marilyn leaned in and whispered, "How did Barney know that was the game she wanted? Now, she has two of them. One here and one at home."

Jeremy almost laughed aloud, but he caught his laugh, as not to give their secrets away.

He patted his wife gently on the leg, held his wine glass in a toast and smiled while whispering to his wife, "Well, now, my dear wife. Santa always knows. Seems as if Barney has more than just a touch or two of magic in his tool bag too." There were more presents, with a fantastic stuffed teddy bear, a few coloring books and crayons, and the crown jewel of the presents, a stuffed fox. This was not just an ordinary stuffed fox, this stuffed fox was covered in thick silver fur with a flowing tail filled with rims of golden fur, and the eyes of the stuffed toy were golden glass marbles. It was the most gorgeous stuffed animal that they had ever seen.

"The Magic Fox! Mommy and Daddy! It is the Magic Fox! Just like Barney told us about. I am going to wish that I feel better forever and never have to go back to the doctor or a hospital."

Becky held the fox in the air and danced around the room, and their mutual joy filled the entire cabin. Jeremy and his wife were stunned. Marilyn unsuccessfully fought back tears and Jeremy did his best not to cry tears of joy, too. At first, they celebrated with their daughter and then, as best as they could, they tried not to allow the situation to overwhelm them. It was quite difficult to do with all that was happening before their eyes.

"Will you play the game with me? Please, Mommy and Daddy. Please, play the game with me. Why are you crying, Mommy?" Little Becky asked as she held the stuffed fox tightly in her hand and she studied her mother, while Marilyn tried hard to wipe the tears away. "We are all so happy. Please do not cry, Mommy. This is the best Christmas ever!"

Marilyn wiped the tears away once again and smiled at her daughter while saying, "I am very happy. These are tears of joy. Yes, I agree. And so, does, Daddy. This is the best Christmas ever. Sure, Becky, we will play it together. We can open it and play it here. Go ahead and get the game and we will set it all up and play. First let, Daddy and Mommy refill our wine glasses."

Becky nodded, and then she happily scooted off to pick up the game. Marilyn and Jeremy went to refill their wine glasses. Actually, the refills of the drinks were diversions to allow them to talk and recover from all that was occurring. In a soft whisper, out of an earshot from Becky, they spoke.

"I can't believe all of this. It is beyond amazing, Jeremy."

"It is. After Becky goes to sleep, I need to call the front desk and have them get in touch with Barney. We have to talk, offer to pay for all of this and thank him. . .."

Marilyn's gentle touch upon her husband's arm stopped him from speaking.

While she poured the wine, she softly told Jeremy, "I heartily agree with you that we must speak with him and thank him for all of this. We must pay him back for all of this. The toys, the tree. Everything. However, Jeremy, my love, please, do not call until tomorrow. In fact, we can explain in person at the front desk when we check out. Barney has most likely gone off his shift, and even if he is still working, then do not disturb him. Not now. He wants this time to be ours. I feel that in my heart."

Jeremy nodded, smiled and in a whisper said, "Yes, Marilyn, I agree and I know that you are correct." He then picked up the glass and called out to Becky, with joy in his voice, "Okay, our precious little girl. Here we come!"

They played the game while sitting in front of the fire, they laughed the rest of the night away, and when the laughter from little Becky turned to yawns; they all knew that it was time to go to bed. Becky washed up, dressed for bed, and they tucked their precious little girl into the bed in the first-floor bedroom of the cabin. She held her precious silver fox in her little arms and the teddy bear sat happily upon her pillow. After a few goodnight kisses, Becky Helms was off to dreamland, or better yet, Christmas dreamland, within a few short seconds of her head hitting the pillow. The excitement of Christmas joy and the activities of the day caught up with Becky.

Jeremy and Marilyn sat in the front of the fireplace, the radio softly played Christmas music in the background, and they sipped the rest of the wine and basked in the day and their love. When it came time for them to retire, Jeremy suggested that Marilyn sleep with Becky to keep an eye on her, and he would sleep in the bed in the loft.

With a few hugs and goodnight kisses, they parted. Jeremy sat in front of the fire for a while longer. He had his share of wine floating around in his veins, but his soul filled with Christmas joy and it also filled with something else. It filled with what Barney asked him to fill it with earlier this evening.

His soul filled with belief and faith.

Jeremy added a few more logs to the fire; he emptied his glass of the rest of the wine and sat in the easy chair in front of the fireplace. Before he could even ready himself for bed, he drifted off to sleep in front of the fire as the magic and peace of Christmas took over his soul.

Christmas Cocktails

Midnight came, midnight went, and Christmas Eve turned into early morning on Christmas Day. Jeremy "Rusty" Helms never moved from the chair in the living room of the cabin. In fact, he hardly stirred at all or even moved a muscle. The fire grew lower and lower, but the magical Christmas tree happily glowed and broadcasted warmth into every corner of the cabin. The radio played Christmas music softly in the background, struggling to overcome the snores of Jeremy. Perhaps it was the wine, food, and drink or it was just the emotions and activities of the day, but he was exhausted and his sound sleep reflected that fact.

Around three in the morning, or thereabouts, Jeremy abruptly awoke from his sound sleep. He slowly and somewhat reluctantly opened his eyes, took a few moments to find his bearings, and he gazed at some glowing embers remaining in the fireplace. It was then that Jeremy realized that he had fallen asleep in the chair and not moved a muscle for many hours. A glance at his watch told him that it was just past three. What had awoken him from such a tight slumber? The fire was no longer broadcasting warmth, the embers glowed faintly, but the majority of the wood was gone now. Thankfully, even with the dying fire, the cabin was still warm because the furnace inside of the cabin provided warmth. Deep in his slumber, he thought that he had heard a noise. Deep, deep in the confines of sleep, his senses alerted him to a sound. He was sure of it, and slowly he stood up. The wine still floated around a bit inside his system. He could still slightly feel the influences.

Jeremy never even changed into different clothes; he fell asleep in the chair with a sweater on and still wearing his boots on his feet. Once upright, he looked around and carefully observed, as well as listened. There were some soft pops and crackles from what remained of the logs in the fireplace and Jeremy thought how he would add one or two in a minute in order to bring the fire back to size, but right now, he needed to follow his senses.

'Perhaps, I was only dreaming,' Jeremy thought as he made his way to the bedroom where Becky and Marilyn were sleeping. He gently opened the bedroom door and peered into the darkness. They were safe and secure, both sleeping tightly, Becky still clutching her silver fox. Maybe a snowplow rolled by the front of the cabin? Suddenly, his thoughts turned to the day's mission and the resumption of their long journey, as his thoughts raced with wonder to check to see if the snow stopped falling and the storm passed away. A careful gaze out the front window of the cabin revealed that there was nothing out of place, nor were there any snowplows. Only the Helm's family car sat in the small driveway in front of the cabin. The snow had stopped, and it appeared as if the sky was bright and clear. From his position inside of the window, Jeremy could see moonlight reflecting and dancing through the tall pines in front of the cabin from the brightly shining moon that was high in the sky behind the cabin.

While he tested the front door lock on the cabin, Jeremy mumbled aloud, "The door is locked. Must be nothing. Just a dream. Yet, I swear that I heard a noise."

Jeremy stood in the front of the window, he listened for noises inside the cabin, and his eyes studied the darkness. The radio still softly played music, the wood in the fireplace popped here and there, and the rest of the cabin was still and quiet.

Another thought came into his mind, 'What if, the noise came from the rear deck?'

Maybe snow slid off the cabin roof, tumbled down upon the wooden deck in the rear of the cabin, and woke him from his slumber.

With that assumption in mind, Jeremy made his way to the rear door of the cabin, just past the counter of the kitchenette, and he opened the door and stepped out onto the deck. There was a small overhang where the floor of the deck received protection from the snowfall, but mountains of snow now piled high on the deck. Sure enough, off to the left side corner of the deck, the snow was deep, and it layered in uneven piles of snow. The moonlight allowed him to see that indeed, the roof of the cabin was bare in that spot and the snow slide had caused the noise and disturbance of his rest. It seemed unusual that on such a cold night and early morning, the snow already tumbled off the cabin roof, but so it did. Usually, snow cover tends to glide and slide, in the heat of the sun, rather than tumble off in great waves and piles on such a cold night. Furthermore, the cabin roof was not too steep, but the evidence was there in front of him.

Regardless, the snow had slid down and landed hard on the rear deck.

Satisfied that he had found the source of the noise that woke him from his deep slumber, Jeremy turned to return inside when he paused. Despite the cold of the early morning and the fact that he wore only a sweater, Jeremy Helms could not move his feet. Something told him to stay and admire this moment. The scene was captivating, and Jeremy paused to appreciate it. Waves of gentle snow glistened as if they were mountains of diamonds settled upon the land. The mild curves of the snow-covered land seemed as if they rode up and down, or more so, as if they were gentle rolling waves of the ocean rolling into the shore on a calm and placid day. Dotted between the waves of snow there were rows upon rows of majestic pine trees, and hardwood trees, all of them holding snow on their branches as if God had reached down from Heaven and painted the white on their branches. It was magnificent, and the silver moonlight illuminated the snow and the entire scene in a glorious and heavenly light. Even with his wood fire dying now, Jeremy could still smell some lingering odor from his burning logs floating in the air. The smells were grand, and they capped the scene with a taste for one more of his senses.

Jeremy stood for a few minutes and enjoyed the Christmas scene. There was no breeze or wind at all. All that remained was simply a quiet calm and a peacefulness, which invaded his soul. Out of the corner of his eye, a few feet off the edge of the deck, Jeremy spotted some movement in the tree line. At first, he thought that it was dancing moonlight in the trees or that suddenly, a breeze had stirred, and then he realized that it was not either of those causes. Someone or something moved out there and the first thought that Jeremy had was that some deer were making their way through the snow, foraging for food and adventure in the deep snow. Not too much else would be stirring at this time of the morning and the cross-country ski trails did not pass along these edges of the cabin lines, so it could not be any skiers out early in the morning enjoying the fresh snow on their trails. Perhaps it was a small moose. Occasionally, a moose or two roamed around their neighborhood at home and even if they were farther south from their home, the moose still roamed these parts too. Jeremy's eyes followed the noises, and he carefully watched the movements as they grew more hurried and closer to the cabin.

When suddenly, through the trees and into the open fields of snow, a gray fox appeared, Jeremy's heart stilled. On the other hand, was the fur of the fox gray? Or was the fur of the fox actually a deep silver in color? While his heart raced and the words of the fantasy tale told by Barney flooded his mind, Jeremy carefully plowed through the deep snow of the deck and made his way to the edge of the deck. There in the bright moonlight, the fox dashed and danced through the deep snow, making great leaps and dives as the fox tried hard not to slip under the waves of powder. Jeremy grew intense. He put his hands on the rail of the deck to steady his body and while ignoring the pounding of his heart; he glued his eyes on the animal in front of him. After one great leap, the fox stood on a mound of snow that supported the body weight of the fox and the animal rested for a moment. It was then that Jeremy swooned and his knees grew weak at the sight in front of him. He gripped the wooden rail even tighter to test to make sure this was all real and not a dream.

The blood flowing in his fingers and his heart pounding in his chest told Jeremy that this was real.

Very real.

Too real.

In the glowing illumination of the moonlight, he could clearly see the fox. The fox was much larger than a normal fox was, and the animal had a long, flowing tail, in which the moonlight highlighted the rim of golden colors in the fur of the tail.

Barney's testimony ran ramshackle through Jeremy's mind.

"Living here, deep in the forests of the mountain is a special, silver fox. The mountain holds his name and now, I guess, I share the name too. No one can ever capture him. No trappers can ever outsmart him and he has lived here forever. He is a Magic Fox. I have only seen him once. He crossed my path a long time ago, on a snowy Christmas Eve, such as this is, and my life was never the same. For they say, if you are lucky enough to see him on this magical night, when the moon lights up the fresh snow like diamonds and the spirit of God is alive, and if you wish as hard as you can for anything that you need or your heart desires, then the Magic Fox will grant you that one special wish. As I say it and as surely as I kneel here, then believe me when I tell you that, I saw him in the glowing moonlight of a Christmas Eve a long time ago. He is much larger than other foxes and his silver fur glows in the night. His tail has rims of golden fur and his eyes glow like beacons of gold in the night."

The fox spotted Jeremy on the deck, and the animal turned and stared at the man staring at him. Jeremy's heart might have stopped when the moonlight illuminated the golden eyes of the fox, but Jeremy recovered enough to recall the reciting of the legend from Barney.

The Magic Fox, despite the usual wariness of a fox, did not run or escape. Instead, the fox continued to stare back at Jeremy while the words softly escaped his lips.

"I humbly ask for a miracle cure for our beloved daughter, Becky. I ask that this wretched disease leave her, never to return, and she is happy, healthy, and gentle in her spirit all the days of her life. I promise that I will never doubt again, not in prayer, in hope, or in faith. Never, ever, will I doubt again."

When the words ended, the fox turned and continued on the way. Leaping and diving through the deep snow, the fox plowed through the snow, guided by the moonlight. Jeremy carefully watched with a smile on his face and peace in his heart until he lost sight of the Magic Fox in and amongst the trees and in the dancing moonlight. The cold air crept into his bones, and he realized that he needed to return to the warmth of the cabin. When Jeremy did so, he recalled the words of Barney when he told them all what he asked the Magic Fox for during their fateful meeting of long ago.

"I simply asked that he show me what to do with my life, give me a purpose. From then on, I had a mission."

"Like a job?"

"Yes, Becky, like a job. However, I think it is more of a mission than a job. Now, I fix things. My job is to fix things. Everything from fireplaces, to love, to broken hearts."

Jeremy whispered, "You sure do, Barney. Whoever you are. You fix things."

Jeremy returned to the inside of the cabin, and despite the magical experience, he remained calm. This was all so believable to him now. There remained no elements of doubt in his mind.

Closing the door to the deck behind him, his eyes noticed a piece of paper on the floor. He was sure it was not there before. Perhaps, the opening of the door caused it to drift from somewhere on the counter of the kitchenette. He stooped down and picked it up. In the dim light of the Christmas tree, and what embers remained in the fire, Jeremy perused the paper. It was a work order request. The paper was from the maintenance department for the resort, and it detailed a repair order for the fireplace damper that Barney had repaired. Jeremy was going to dismiss it when the time of work order completion and signature line caught his eye.

He read it aloud, "Tightened damper lever mechanism. Checked operation. Completed 3:20 P.M. December 24, 2016. Christmas Eve. Signed, Kevin Marks."

Now Jeremy swooned some more. He rushed to where his luggage remained stacked in the corner of the living room and pulled out the paper that the hotel desk clerk gave to them upon check-in yesterday. The time stamp of their check-in was 3: 15 P.M.!

Jeremy recalled the desk clerk's words when he said, "There is a work order for a repair on the fireplace damper lever in that cabin. I will call on the radio and have a maintenance technician scoot right over there. For sure, you will want to use the fireplace tonight. There is plenty of wood on hand there in the cabin."

With a smile frozen on his face, Jeremy neatly folded the

work order receipt and tucked it into the pocket of his shirt. Why did he want to keep it? As to the answer to that question—he could not be entirely sure.

A keepsake, he thought. A keepsake because he no longer required evidence, just verification that this entire episode, in fact, the last twenty-four hours or so, was not a dream.

Could the entire experience on the deck with the snow rolling off the cabin and the appearance of the Magic Fox all be a byproduct of the consumption of too much wine and drink?

No, after careful consideration, Jeremy "Rusty" Helms did not think so. Instead, while he walked over to the wood cradle on the hearth on the fireplace, picked out a few select logs and placed them on the fire, he knew it was all true. His heart now had hope instilled deep within it. Unshakeable, unbroken, and never doubted or disregarded, hope. A special hope that would remain there forever more. While Jeremy knelt, and watched the embers of the fire turn to flames, his soul glowed as if it were a beacon in the now growing early morning Christmas light. And unlike the fire's flames, this glow would never diminish.

Christmas Cocktails

Christmas morning was here! Jeremy did not return to sleep, instead he sat in the chair enjoying the fire, pondering this incredible experience and enjoying the glow of the Christmas tree, until it was time to wake his wife and daughter. The family rose, greeted each other with a hearty amount of love and a merry Christmas, and prepared to pack up and head out on their long journey downstate. Becky bounced off the walls of the cabin; she played with her toys and pleaded with her parents for breakfast.

"I am so hungry! I feel great. I am not sick today." The little girl told them.

Marilyn checked Becky's forehead with a gentle touch of a mother's hand. A hand that God had built special elements of love within when he created all mothers.

"Hmmm . . . no fever. In fact, you are perfectly cool. My goodness, this new appetite is so good to see. We will pack up, put all your toys in the car, along with our luggage, and then we can check out. We can have breakfast in the restaurant in the main lodge and then be on our way. Does that plan work for Daddy too?"

Jeremy nodded and smiled. He chose for now not to share his experiences of a few hours ago. He also chose not to reveal what he found with the work order or any other elements of this magical story with Marilyn. He would wait for the right time. He had one more question for the hotel clerk at the main desk and then the final piece of the puzzle will be in place. Jeremy already knew what the answer was going to be. However, he just wanted to wait for the entire magic to take over and fill their lives before telling his wife the truth.

"Did you have a pleasant stay, Mr. Helms?" The same desk clerk who was working the front desk yesterday afternoon asked. Therefore, he was aware of the circumstances that led them to the resort.

The desk clerk explained, "The road crew and police reports are that the mountain road is clear and is now safe and wide open, the sun is coming out, and it will be a glorious Christmas Day. I hope your stay was enjoyable. Please come back and stay with us during better circumstances. Merry Christmas to you and your family, the best of everything and please, safe travels."

"Yes, it was glorious. Thank you, for everything. For sure, we will be back here. Maybe, next Christmas. It is a very special place."

The clerk nodded his head in agreement and processed the payment with Jeremy's credit card.

While they waited for the machine to spit out the receipt, Jeremy told the clerk, "Oh, sorry, I almost forgot to mention this, but we have a Christmas tree set up in the living room of the cabin. We left it in place there because it is so perfect and beautiful. I thought whoever rents the cabin next might enjoy it. It seems to have a bit of Christmas magic to it and we did not want to throw it away unceremoniously on Christmas Day. If there is an extra charge for that, please charge me the amount."

"Oh, no trouble. We will leave it there. Sounds as if it will be something that the next guests might enjoy. I will make a special note on that cabin's information sheet. Thank you." The clerk handed the receipt to Jeremy, along with Jeremy's credit card and a pen. While Jeremy signed the receipt, and Becky and Mrs. Helms hustled off to the car, he knew it was time to ask the key question—a question of which he already knew the answer, but he still needed to ask.

"Say, does Barney Barnstead still work here? Actually, his first name is McHale but he goes by Barney. I think I stopped here a long time ago and met him. I wonder if he is still around these days?"

The clerk mumbled, "Thank you," while Jeremy handed the receipt and the pen back to him. He then pondered the questions and answered, "Barney Barnstead. Barney, huh? No, I do not think he still works here. At least not that I know of or have ever heard of. What department did he work in?"

"Property and facility maintenance. He fixes things. Everything. He is quite a handyman, to say the least."

"No, I am sorry. I know that he is not currently working on the maintenance crew. Honestly and frankly, I have never heard of him. I can ask if you would like me to do so."

"No, no, no, it is fine. I was just wondering. I am sure that I will run into him somewhere, sometime. Just curious. Thank you and merry Christmas."

The two men shook hands, and Jeremy turned and walked away. Jeremy's heart, mind and soul had no doubt inside of it at all.

None.

Yes, indeed, that was exactly the answer that he knew it would be! Once Becky fades off to sleep and he is sure that she will not overhear the conversation, he would tell Marilyn the details, and once Marilyn realizes his sincerity and he assures her that he was, and still is sober, he was sure his wife would be as full of the same amount of hope and spirit as he was. Now, it was time for the doctor's visit and for the next answer and to hear the glorious news that this amazing experience will bring to them all.

An answer and news that he already knew ahead of time what they would be.

The answer arrived, and it arrived, within the glory of hope, and peace, and joy.

Even though, due to the amazing events of the past few days, Jeremy felt in his heart that he knew what the news was going to be, he could hardly contain his joy and the words flowed upon layers of profound elation, "You mean all the tests are negative, Doctor Breckinridge? There is no sign of any blood cancer or any disorder? This is truly beyond fantastic! It is a miracle!"

While Mr. and Mrs. Helms held hands as they sat side-by-side in the guest chairs in front of the doctor's desk, the good doctor continued to provide his best answer. "Yes, it is beyond remarkable! Over the last few days as a prelude to our appointment, I poured over Doctor Hudson's notes and his test reports. There is little doubt that Becky was seriously ill. None whatsoever. Yet now, she is in the clear. I had the lab rerun the test three times for confirmation. Almost like a miracle, I must say. Especially so, at the Christmastime of the year. I must say that my initial examination hinted at what the results might be. During my examination, Becky seemed so well, no fever, no runny eyes, no signs of infections. I only recorded healthy vital readings and observations. She is so alert, so full of spirit and health. Yet, those were only my visual and initial observations. The tests, however, provided the evidence we required. All the blood work is conclusive. I cannot explain it. When the test results came in, I confessed to running into my office and doing another careful reread of Dr. Hudson's reports and to review the lab results from the upstate hospital, one more time. Maybe it was the tenth time . . . I cannot say for sure. The results are all here in front of me. I have no explanation. Nothing more to chalk this up to other than a miracle. It is magical. Right for now, I recommend no further action. Please follow up with Dr. Hudson religiously for continued tests to make sure there is no recurrence. Right now, Becky is cancer-free."

When he finished speaking, Jeremy thought, 'Yes, indeed, that was exactly what I knew the doctor would say!'

Doctor Breckinridge shuffled the papers together, took his glasses off, and wiped his eyes of a tear or two. Jeremy and Becky wiped some tears away, too.

The good doctor replaced his glasses and smiled as he said, "Forgive me. It is just so often . . . much too often . . . that I have bad news that I have to give to wonderful people such as you both are. When I have joyous news, it tends to wring the emotions out of your soul. It gives you hope, joy and such glorious peace."

Jeremy stood up, held his hand out and shook the doctor's hand while profusely thanking him.

Marilyn, who now knew the entire story, because Jeremy had shared his experiences and testimony with her, stood up too and she walked around the desk and hugged Doctor Breckinridge and said, "Thank you for you and for all that you do, and yes, it does give you hope. Profound and glorious hope. We understand and assure you that we all share the same feelings."

In the winter majesty of the vastness of what the locals call upstate New York, far away from the influence of New York City, within rolling hills and low valleys, in the cold, icy creeks and streams and on the top of the snow-covered mountains, there is profound beauty. Within that beauty, there are elements of quiet mystery and within the vastness of the land; there are many stories and legends of old. At no time of the year are those stories told more often and the legends more pronounced than they are at Christmas time. When snow covers the land in layers of white beauty, when the moonlight of a cold, crisp winter evening reflects the diamonds hidden within their white magic while it flickers upon the freshly fallen snow, it is then that the magic of Christmas unfolds. While the residents, who call this land their home, huddle to celebrate the holiday within the warm and cozy comfort of their homes and the telltale smoke puffs from their chimneys tell of that warmth, the magical snow filters down and the wind whistles of the legends. One might need to have their eyes focused and wide open, and their ears finely tuned to hear the whispers in the wind, but it is all there.

You must first believe in the magic of the season, to be able to see it, to hear all the legends and most importantly, to allow them to enter your heart and for them to rest upon your soul forever.

"Becky Helms grew up to be a strong, beautiful, woman. She married and had a family of her own and gave to her firstborn, as a special Christmas gift, an old, yet carefully preserved, stuffed silver fox toy. The Helm's family did return to the Silver Fox Mountain Resort and celebrated several Christmas Days there, but they did not have any additional encounters with Barney Barnstead or the Magic Fox. There was no need to. They all now had hope instilled in their hearts and souls, and in the end, that is all that we really ever need."

I stopped speaking, and I realized that I had rambled for quite a long amount of time, and for a moment or two, I did not know what to say.

Since everyone was waiting and staring, I finally said, "I guess, well, that is the end of the story."

I finished my story, looked up at my family and friends to gauge their reactions to my long tale, but it was difficult to tell if I bombed or not. I shrugged my shoulders, and then smiled at all of them, and they smiled in return. But no one said a word.

I looked over to Harry, and he grabbed my empty beer mug off the table next to me.

The big guy shouted out to his wife and to my wife, "Binky! My dear, Rose! Ya had better get Paul a'nudder beer. He is gonna need it, in order to stay up all night and type up this story. Better yet, forget the beer and make it strong coffee!"

The gang then rushed over to me. The children jumped

in my lap and hugged me, thanked me and kissed my cheeks.

"Thank you. It needs some work, but I might consider writing it."

The old man looked at me and asked, "Work? I thought it was pretty good the way it is. Leave it alone. I could picture it all in my mind. However, it was just a Christmas fantasy . . . right?"

"Yes, Dad. All fantasies. Christmas fantasy."

Even my Gloomy Gus, father-in-law, extended his hand out, while I did the same with mine.

We shook hands while the good senator said, "A remarkable tale, Paul. I have to say that it is quite remarkable for you to be able to form such a story within your eccentric and warped mind like that and to tell the tale in such a captivating manner. I have to say, you should write it all down. Soon. Despite your wacky and weird tendencies, you are quite the storytelling talent. Thank you for sharing that story and the day, it has been quite an enjoyable Boxing Day celebration, capped off by a glorious session of storytelling. A far better experience than suffering through another one of your boring and incorrigible sermons."

I took all that as a supreme compliment coming from the eternally acrimonious Senator William T. Hobnobber.

As my old man always said, "Consider the source."

Binky walked over, took the empty beer mug from Harry, leaned over, hugged me around my neck, and kissed me.

"Thank you, Paul. I agree it was a glorious story. One of your best. Are you going to write it down?"

The children who were all now crowded around me in a group all immediately shouted and pleaded with me to do so. Heather Sarah forced her way onto my lap, and then they all asked a million questions about elements of the story.

I answered them the best that I could, and when the fervor died down, I answered Binky's question. "I guess that I will, when the time feels right. Yes, I do think that I will write it someday. Perhaps, on some Christmas Eve, when the snow covers the land in layers of white beauty, when the moonlight of a cold, crisp winter evening, reflects the diamonds hidden within their white magic while it flickers upon the freshly fallen snow. It is then that the magic of Christmas unfolds. Yes, that is when I will write it all down. Until then, we must always believe and allow the magic of Christmas, and in fact, the magic of every day, unfold in our hearts."

THE END

Paul John Hausleben

On Christmas Day

The feelings arrive every day
They are as if they are the ticks on a silent clock
Every day, they arrive
When the sun rises and the sun eventually sets
The feelings are always the same
No days are different, nor do the days vary
I miss you
Your face, your voice, your smile, the lick in your eyes
Yet, of all the days of the year, I miss you most of all
On Christmas Day

When I stare at my Christmas tree and the colors softly
glow and fill my heart with awe
I miss you
When I walk the floors alone and I try my best to recall the
moments of love and joy
I miss you
Every day,
Yet, of all the days of the year, I miss you most of all
On Christmas Day

When I eat my Christmas dinner,
Alone
When I pray for hope for the weary world
Alone
When I feel the pangs of Christmas joy trying to spring
forth from my soul
When the memories of Christmas Days of the past
Dance in my mind
That is when I know that I miss you most of all
On Christmas Day

Christmas Cocktails

I turn, look, and swear that I felt your touch upon my arm.
I swear that I heard your voice in my ear
Are you there?
No, it is just a ghost of the past
The ghosts never leave me alone
They float above my head and follow me everywhere
They never allow me ever to forget you
Or to miss you more than I do right now
On Christmas Day

I miss you
Oh, how I miss you
The worst time of all is when Christmas evening arrives
When the calm settles in and the day draws to a close
Another Christmas Day begins to end
It makes my heart ache
It makes my soul melt away
Because I miss you so much
I miss you every day
But I miss you most of all,
On Christmas Day

I sit alone in my chair
The song on the radio sings to me of a sad story, of wanting
to be home for Christmas
I try hard to convince my heart that I am home
Am I really home?
No, I am not home
Because you are not here
On Christmas Day

Outside, the sky has turned purple and dark
The lights on the Christmas tree glow and twinkle in
glorious colors of joy
The peace settles in

Paul John Hausleben

The day fades to a quiet memory
My heart begins to ache once more
Tears fill my eyes and I cannot stop them
Because I miss you
Every day, I miss you
Yet, of all the days of the year, I think that I miss you most
of all
On Christmas Day

Epilogue

A gentle calm settled in over the town of Wayne, New Jersey, on this Christmas Eve. There was no snow falling, but it was very cold and the calm signaled peace. Indeed, it was a quiet, gentle calm and in the home of Fred and Marlene Kelleher, there was some Christmas magic settling in too.

The home was a typical suburban New Jersey home found in a quiet suburban town. A modest, split-level home with a nice backyard, located on a quiet street tucked in off a main drag. A home filled with glorious memories and glorious love, too.

Fred had not earned a fortune in his career as an accountant, but he earned enough to raise a family, provide college educations for their children and to give to Marlene the life that he promised to her. While the home might be too large now for just Marlene and Fred, it was a home that had too many memories attached to it to sell it and move away. The Kelleher's raised two children here, and it was a home that had seen too many Christmases, Thanksgivings, birthdays, anniversaries, and other celebrations, to count them all.

Remember them, yes; however, to count them all was impossible.

Tonight, on this quiet Christmas Eve, there was to be one more celebration. Fred planned it all out very carefully and he lovingly banned his wife from the dining room of their home while he prepared for the celebration. Fred slowly and gingerly shuffled back and forth from the kitchen to the dining room. His back was not too good these days and arthritis crept into his legs and ankles. Yet

Fred kept moving. First, the red tablecloth, then the candles with the holly and berry Christmas centerpiece. Then, some quiet Christmas music for the backdrop and as Fred checked his suit jacket pocket a few times or so on this Christmas Eve, he felt no nervousness.

Only joy.

After all, sixty years ago on this very night, the love of his life accepted his proposal and while there were ups and downs, some good times, and some bad times, and Fred was quite sure that Marlene wanted to wring his neck a few times along the way, their love remained strong and powerful.

Fred put his eyeglasses on. First, he checked on the roast beef in the oven. The meat was cooked, and it was just on a warming setting now. Perfect mashed potatoes (right out of the packet) as well as perfectly cooked turnips along with a helping of hearty green beans. Slices of chocolate cake waited for dessert, but first Fred needed the prelude.

The all-important prelude.

The magic.

Fred stared into the pages of the "Bartender's Guide to Amazing Cocktails" and while he certainly was not Hal, the amazing and gloriously skilled bartender, Fred Kelleher remained determined to give it his best shot. Earlier in the day, he had picked up all the ingredients for the Christmas cocktails at the corner liquor store, and now it was time for the mixing magic to occur. With crossed fingers and perhaps some toes too, Fred carefully selected the glasses and mixed the drinks. First, a bourbon Manhattan in a cocktail glass with ice and then a rye whiskey sour. Fred studied them and he had to say that they looked perfect to his old eyes. He slowly shuffled off and delivered the drinks, set them at their places at the table, and lit the candle. The candle flame flickered and danced, and combined with their small tabletop Christmas tree, along with the music, Fred felt as if he created a perfect Christmas Eve setting.

Satisfied, Fred checked his suit jacket pocket once more to make sure it was still there.

It was.

Fred pulled at the lapel of his jacket and mumbled, "Not too bad for an old coot. No lumps in those potatoes, either. I love those premixed packets. Fred Kelleher, you are indeed, a very lucky man." He then turned and called for his wife. "Okay, Marlene! Honey, you can come down now! Dinner is ready. Along with some Christmas cocktails."

Fred heard the door close to their bedroom, and he stood at the base of the stairs and watched as his wife appeared. Fred was a little wobbly in his knees from old age, but his wife's beauty just about knocked him over. Marlene wore a black dress and those same amazing white pearl earrings and that glorious white pearl necklace from so long ago. Fred swore that she was more beautiful tonight than she ever was before in their sixty years of marriage.

Stunning!

Marlene floated on Christmas magic. Fred met her at the base of the stairs, held his hand out, and she took it as the old couple teetered and tottered their way to the dining room table.

"You are the most beautiful woman in the world, Marlene," Fred said while Marlene smiled. He held the chair out for his wife and Marlene sat at the table and admired the amazing setting.

"Oh my, Fred, this is so glorious! You are a remarkable man. The meal smells heavenly!"

Fred smiled as he too sat at the table and said, "It is not our quiet nook at our favorite restaurant, with a view of the city and the snow falling down . . . but I guess it will do."

Marlene smiled and said, "It is even better."

"Please, let's try the Christmas cocktails. I bought a silly recipe book and I would like to think that I did my best. A toast," Fred said as he lifted the glass and Marlene did the same. "Merry Christmas, my love, and thank you for sixty glorious years."

"Thank you, Fred. My darling, Fred."

They each took a sip and Fred had to think that he did a pretty good job on mixing the cocktails.

"Oh, Fred, this is delicious! Thank you. Honestly, this is the best sour that I have ever had. There is just something magical about Christmas cocktails! I have to say that Hal would be very proud of you, my dear. Perhaps, you will get me tipsy and take advantage of me later tonight," Marlene said with a coy wink and a smile.

"That's part of my covert plan, my dear. Besides, I put some magic in that Christmas cocktail, and now, I have just a touch more." Fred reached in his suit jacket pocket and pulled out the box. "I am too old and too stiff to get down on one knee for too long. Therefore, I will stand up and hand it to you. Here, Marlene. Merry Christmas and I will love you forever and just a little more too."

Fred stood up, walked over to Marlene, slowly opened the lid to the box, and then handed it to his wife. Marlene gasped at the diamond necklace inside, and she burst into tears as Fred gently took the box and removed the necklace. As he motioned for his wife to stand up and Marlene tried hard in order to gather her emotions, Fred gently removed the pearls and replaced them with the diamond necklace.

"Oh, Fred, it is gorgeous. Thank you for the gift and for this wonderful and remarkable evening. I will love you forever, Fred Kelleher. Merry Christmas."

They kissed, and as they did so, a gentle snow began to fall outside. The snowfall began very slowly, and the flakes drifted silently to the ground. The peace and the calm remained; it simply received a coating of white.

Yes, indeed, there was some extra magic in those Christmas cocktails.

Christmas Cocktails

It was a glorious Christmas Eve and a peaceful evening. The snow covered the land in layers of white beauty and the moonlight of the cold, crisp winter evening reflected the diamonds hidden within their white magic while it flickered upon the freshly fallen snow. On this peaceful night, the magic of Christmas slowly unfolded.

We must always believe and allow the magic of Christmas, and in fact, the magic of every day, unfolds in our hearts.

Along with the peace and the calm and the love.

ABOUT THE AUTHOR

If you ask Paul John Hausleben, he will tell you that he is not an author, he is just a storyteller. His mission is to continue to write and tell stories to warm your heart, make you laugh, and sometimes make you cry, just a little. Most of all, he deals in memories, and helps you to remember the good times of your own life, and the special people who touched you along the way. Paul was born and raised in Paterson, and then nearby Haledon, New Jersey, and began writing at an early age. He revisited a writing career later in his life, and he now is the author of a number of novels, compilations, short stories and audio and video works. Most of his work, touches upon nostalgic remembrances of simpler times, and tells the stories of heartfelt, humorous, and special human relationships. Other than writing, among many careers both paid and unpaid, he is a former semi-professional hockey goaltender, a music fan and music reviewer, an avid sports fan, photographer and amateur radio operator. He now resides in Somewhere, U.S.A., but his heart always remains along Belmont Avenue in good old Paterson, and Haledon, New Jersey.

Other Work by Mr. Paul John Hausleben

The Time Bomb in The Cupboard and Other Adventures of
Harry and Paul

The Night Always Comes, Another story from the
Adventures of Harry and Paul

Reunion, A sequel to the Night Always Comes and
Another story from the Adventures of Harry and Paul

The Autumn Collection

The Christmas Tree and Other Christmas Stories.
Tales for a Christmas Evening

Crows on a High Wire

The Miracle Tree, Another story from the Adventures of
Harry and Paul

The Summer Collection

Reflections. The Christmas Collection

Tales of the Quiet Stranger in the Black Hat

Geyer Street Gardens
Beneath the Mask of a Hockey Goaltender
Another story from the Adventures of Harry and Paul

And a few others too!

Paul John Hausleben

You may write to the author at ctte27@gmail.com

Follow Paul John Hausleben on Facebook and enjoy samples of his photography, receive updates on new releases, and enjoy his general meanderings

Published by God Bless the Keg Publishing
Somewhere, U.S.A.

You may write to the publisher at
Godblessthekegpublishing@gmail.com

"Life's simple pleasures are so often the best ones!"

Christmas Cocktails

Printed in Great Britain
by Amazon